EVE

Miles wondered whether frustration and bewilderment were to be his lot in Singapore. He could normally understand the Chinese – at least part of the time. But he was now having extraordinary difficulty in understanding anyone, Chinese or otherwise. His talk with Turner Lee had only deepened his perplexity. The old connoisseur remained an enigma cocooned in a myriad tissue-paper-thin hints regarding his attitude towards Peking and his mission for Peking. Miles concluded that he was not any closer to penetrating the puzzle posed by Humphrey's bold talk and murky death. If anything, he was further from his goal than he had been when he started.

ROBERT ELEGANT

THE EVERLASTING SORROW

Mandarin

A Mandarin Paperback
THE EVERLASTING SORROW

First published in Great Britain 1994
by Mandarin Paperbacks
an imprint of Reed Consumer Books Ltd
Michelin House, 81 Fulham Road, London SW3 6RB
and Auckland, Melbourne, Singapore and Toronto

Reprinted 1994

A CIP catalogue record for this title
is available from the British Library
ISBN 0 7493 1796 5

Printed and bound in Great Britain by
BPC Paperbacks Ltd
A member of
The British Printing Company Ltd

PRELUDE

CANTON, 17 APRIL 1974

Elbowed painfully again, Miles Corrigan whirled round, his right hand cocked high in threat. Two stocky Japanese pressed closer, their faces masks of bland unconcern. While they diverted the red-haired American, three Japanese in baggy grey suits swept around them. Cut off from the glowing ranks of porcelain vases, Corrigan stepped back frowning.

A tall Chinese in a blue tunic scurried towards the angry men. The wares were fragile – and scuffling for position could explode into fights, often among the Japanese themselves. Although his scarlet badge read *Reception-ist*, he was a 'cadre' of the People's Republic of China and a salesman. But a sales pitch was hardly necessary. The dealers, particularly the Japanese, would buy anything.

A little sheepish, Miles Corrigan mastered his anger. He leisurely replaced the ox-blood Ching Dynasty vase he had been examining and flicked a speck of dust from his shimmering Thai-silk sleeve. For the third time in an hour Japanese had jostled him away from the display shelves. And the last time – for a while at least. Turning his back on the vases, he overheard an exchange in staccato Japanese.

(1)

'Buy! They're medium quality, if that. But they'll go for five times as much in Tokyo. Buy!'

Surrounded like a Mafia *capo* by beefy henchmen who were both advisers and bodyguards, the grey-haired senior Japanese barked at the relieved cadre: 'Fourteen pieces, right? I'll take them all. Precisely twenty-five million yen. Right?'

When the cadre nodded agreement, the Japanese charged towards the next display. The Spring Trade Fair had just opened in the metropolis of Canton, ninety miles from British Hong Kong, a single step across the inhospitable threshold of Communist China. Twice a year, the People's Republic cracked its gates ajar for a few hundred merchants from the outside world – after culling thousands of applications. Most hoped to sell their own goods in the vast market they saw in China's 800 million people, but they invariably bought more from the hard-headed Chinese than they sold themselves.

Miles Corrigan decided he was through looking for the morning. In the mêlée the Japanese had created, his fading skill in unarmed combat was as essential as his knowledge of Oriental art. The mediocre vases had brought 100,000 American dollars, by his estimate seven times their worth. Why compete with the swarms of Japanese who even checked each other with body-blocks? The *objets d'art* were second-rate, not for his cultivated clientele. Anyway, profit came from selling to the Japanese, not from bidding against them.

The new-rich of Tokyo and Osaka would buy anything from a polished rock or an undistinguished carved cinnabar box to a dubious Rembrandt or an even more dubious Shang Dynasty bronze tripod at two to three times the world market price. Japanese dealers bought as if all currencies, including their own overvalued yen, would be worthless tomorrow. Their new divinity was Mammon, the rapacious God of Wealth – and they ritually sacrificed billions of yen to propitiate Mammon.

Each year, Corrigan reflected, the Japanese made it harder to like them. His green eyes still smouldering, he strolled towards the partition in a corner of the hall. The red stain of anger had receded from his cheeks, but his lips were clenched above his stubborn chin. A fraction short of six feet and almost disproportionately powerful in shoulders and chest, he overtopped the thrusting Japanese, as well as most of the willowy Italians and the rotund Germans.

Most Westerners came to the Canton Fair to peddle merchandise like computers, grain, and fertilisers or to buy such prosaic goods as textiles, menthol, and pigs' bristles. The Americans and British who had once dominated the Oriental art market were now hard-pressed, and few were buying. Miles, too, was a seller this morning. With luck, he would relieve the People's Republic of considerably more than it had just taken from the Japanese. He knew that the Communist panjandrums in Peking badly wanted the piece he was offering. Automatically smoothing his unruly hair, he knocked on the plywood door of the makeshift office.

'Ah, Mr Corrigan, welcome!' The elderly Chinese behind the cheap deal desk was effusively polite. 'Good of you to be punctual. But perhaps you've already seen some interesting objects?'

'Very interesting, Comrade Wong,' Miles replied drily. 'At least, the Japanese find them so.'

'Ah, the Japanese!'

Comrade Wong laid his immaculate palms on the unvarnished desktop, the gesture at once resigned and contemptuous. Corrigan knew the slender Chinese only in his public personality as a 'responsible cadre in the field of fine art'. His personal history was veiled, as were his personal opinions. But Comrade Wong clearly knew his trade – not only the intrinsic worth of his wares, but their prices in a market gone mad.

Miles sipped astringent Iron Goddess tea from painted thimble-cups that might have come from a Chinese doll's house. In the New China of Communist Commissars, as in the Old China of Imperial Mandarins, tea before business was not merely a courtesy, but a necessity. The pale fluid lubricated the wheels of trade just as alcohol did in the West.

'I'll walk around later,' Miles said. 'But I'm afraid there won't be much left.'

'A few objects might interest you. A fine Wei Dynasty funerary village. I can guarantee its authenticity. Also some amusing, ostensibly Tang figures of barbarians . . . ah . . . foreigners.'

'Ostensibly?' Miles asked. 'Would you sell them otherwise?'

Smiling deprecatingly, Comrade Wong replied: 'It's true we're eager to buy back our historic treasures. Not sell, but reclaim our national heritage . . . I hear you've got an object that may interest me.'

Miles took the cue after that clear signal that, courtesies having been observed, business should begin: 'It will interest you greatly.'

'We have seen the photographs. But, of course . . .'

'Naturally, I haven't brought the original. It might've embarrassed your Customs.'

'You are, perhaps, too cautious, Mr Corrigan. The People's Customs Service is not easily embarrassed. And I cannot, of course, discuss the matter seriously until I've seen the original.'

'Naturally. Your people can see the original anywhere you choose.'

'But without embarrassing our Customs by bringing it to China, Mr Corrigan? *So* thoughtful of you!'

'Of course I have perfect confidence. But I could hardly move the piece until we had begun to discuss price and terms.'

'*After* we've seen the original.'

The verbal rapier-play was stimulating after the frontal attacks of the Japanese, but Corrigan would not risk his treasures being summarily seized – as it might well be if he brought it into China.

'Shall we,' he asked, 'say Hong Kong?'

'Quite agreeable, Mr Corrigan. When?'

'In two weeks' time. I do have other commitments . . .'

The slight Chinese drained the last thimble-cup, signalling that the negotiations were suspended. But, as Miles rose, he spoke again. 'One more thing, Mr Corrigan. I must ask how the object came into your hands.'

'Why?' Miles demanded. 'Why, once you're satisfied as to its authenticity?'

'I see no need to explain, Mr Corrigan. I will not press you now. But before we buy . . .'

'Shall we say two weeks from tomorrow? Tuesday the 25th, at the Mandarin Hotel?'

'Mr Corrigan, we must know *exactly* how the object came into your hands.'

Miles drew the door closed behind him. He had not expected to encounter insistence on the object's precise origins before the People's Republic would purchase a masterpiece it considered its own property. After all, the Chinese really knew more about the work than he did.

His battered Hillman taxi honked imperiously through throngs of bicycles towards Canton's railway station.

Their well tailored suits rumpled, European executives jostled slovenly Chinese cadres. Comrade Wong's parting question reverberated in Miles's mind as the train crawled through green-and-silver paddy fields towards the wooden bridge to British Hong Kong.

The object, as Comrade Wong called it, had come into his hands in another era. Only two decades ago the Japanese had still been ostentatiously humble, seeking their grand purposes with apparent humility. The Chinese had been assertive and arrogant, trumpeting their determination to remake the world in their own image. Both Japanese and Chinese had since changed radically – at least on the surface.

Corrigan reviewed the train of events that had led to his guarded conversation with Comrade Wong. Some of the pictures that flashed on the screen of his mind were ugly, indeed repulsive. Others were poignant or tragic. And some were overwhelmingly beautiful.

I

Veins writhed like worms under the black silk socks covering the high-arched feet, which were encased in scuffed opera pumps. Those feet were tantalisingly familiar, but they were not quite identifiable.

The feet were all Miles could see of the passenger in the seat a row ahead of him and across the aisle, as the airliner trundled down the runway of Tokyo's Haneda Airport. The engines' whine became a high-pitched scream when the DC-7 clawed its way into the sky, thrusting him into the sponge-rubber under the blue upholstery. The airliner banked sharply, dipping its wing in a last salute to the web of light that was Tokyo at night. The engines settled down to a throaty murmur as the pilot pointed the nose towards Hong Kong, two thousand miles to the southeast.

The naggingly familiar feet tapped restlessly when the *No Smoking* sign flicked off. A stubby finger pushed the call button, and number 2A on the call-board pinked on and off repeatedly.

Corrigan fumbled a pasteboard packet of ten Peace cigarettes from his pocket. He reminded himself to buy a packet of American cigarettes from the stewardess as soon as she was free. Meanwhile, he savoured the after-taste of brandy on his tongue as he looked down and said yet another farewell to the irrepressible city that both exhilarated and frightened him.

It had been a good party, he recalled, a fitting end to his successful round of purchases from hard-pressed aristocrats who were letting go their Chinese and Japanese treasures piece by piece. Everyone had imposed the same condition in virtually the same words: 'This piece *must* be taken out of Japan. No one is to know I'm selling off my collection.'

Miles was flattered not only by their trust in his promise to sell elsewhere, but by their assumption that he would offer a fair price. There had been no haggling. It was not necessarily his command of Japanese, always a mixed blessing, that led the proud old men to receive him. '*Corrigan-san* is a gentleman, not a merchant', he had overheard an aged count tell his even more ancient steward.

He had, perhaps, been meant to overhear. Corrigan the connoisseur basked in such approval, but Corrigan the businessman wondered if he had not paid the count too much for a Tang Dynasty camel that was probably booty from 'the China incident', Japan's invasion of her enormous neighbour. Buying had been hard work, despite the astringent charm mustered for the American who was keeping dispossessed noble families from poverty, even if temporarily, and, equally importantly, was keeping the families' noble names untarnished.

The rowdy party at the geisha house called Raku-Raku, appropriately enough meaning Joy-Joy, had been all pleasure, although some of his guests were astonished at finding themselves in the company of the others. Gentle little Mr Ohno of Yamato Arts, owner of the finest collection of Edo Period armour in the world, had blinked at lifting his sake cup to the sumo wrestler Futoshinobu. The bright boys from the Foreign Office had concealed both their fascination and their consternation at meeting Goro Matsumoto, the most subtle – and most successful – agent on either side during the War in the Pacific.

Amid the farewells at the airport, Corrigan had hardly noticed his fellow passengers. Aquiline Goro Matsumoto wore an understated dinner jacket, but one instinctively looked for the *samurai*'s ceremonial swords at his side. The young men from the Foreign Office, red-faced and boisterous after so much beer and sake, strove for professional coolness. They, too, were intensely involved in life.

Asia would always move him, Miles mused, because her people lived so close to the bone. They were truly more joyful – or truly more desperate – than the smooth young men and the earnest young women who came to cocktail parties at his duplex on Fifth Avenue. The Americans sprawled on the carpeted stairs as they paraded problems, psychological and intellectual, they largely created for themselves. Despite their formal manners and the bitter neuroses bred by their rigid society, the Japanese lived closer to elemental reality. They were, therefore, more truly alive.

A blue skirt and a pair of self-indulgent ankles, plump within nylon casings, flicked by as the stewardess's ballet-slippers hurried towards seat 2A, where the opera-pumps were becoming frantic, flexing on their toes as if to dash down the aisle. Just as she should, the stewardess looked like the eternally youthful blondes in Coca-Cola advertisements – with a touch of the knowing naïveté best caught by Norman Rockwell.

'You call yourself an *international* airline?' a deep voice demanded. 'Yet there is no Pernod on an *international* airline? An outrage! You may bring me a double whisky: Dimple or Black Label. No soda, no ice, no water – just a double whisky.'

Miles's mind flitted back to Nanking in the late 1940s. He had been a very young lieutenant junior grade of the US Navy when the Chinese Nationalists were making their last stand against the Communists. He gestured to the stewardess, who was trotting back to the galley to fill the indignant passenger's order. Her blond hair, escaping from the black band that held it back, fell over her eyes when she bent over.

'Can you tell me,' he asked, 'the name of the eager customer across the way?'

'I'll have to check, Mr Corrigan.' She dimpled. 'I know you, of course. You're on our VIP list. But I haven't looked at the passenger manifest yet. Can I get you anything?'

'Some American cigarettes, non-filter, when you have a moment. Tell me, what does he look like?'

'Well!' She paused. 'Sort of like a nineteenth-century Shakespearean actor I'd say.'

'. . . a big pot-belly, a large red nose, and a monocle on a metal chain strong enough to anchor a small ship?'

'That's right. A friend of yours?'

'Let's say an old acquaintance.'

The stewardess hurried off to return, balancing an old fashioned glass full of Scotch on a small tray.

'Enwright.' She leaned over and whispered. 'Humphrey Enwright is his name.'

'Would you mind slipping him a note?'

The nylon ankles tensed as she handed Humphrey Enwright the glass. The opera-pumps cocked back appreciatively as he took a long sip. Her ballet-slippers waited poised while his deep voice boomed: 'Better than nothing! Bring me another double now.'

As the ballet-slippers retreated, the opera-pumps leaned back, relaxed. Abruptly they planted themselves on the blue carpet. Humphrey Enwright was upon Miles Corrigan, right hand extended.

'Miles, my dear boy!' Humphrey Enwright sank into the adjoining seat. 'So good to see you.'

'Hello, Humphrey,' Miles said. 'Sorry about the Pernod. But after all the mao-tai you drank in China, I'd think your palate could take anything.'

'Better times, my boy, better times,' Humphrey boomed. 'Things have been going rather well for one lately. Not like that . . . that unfortunate incident in Nanking. Too much, of course, to expect a stuffy ambassador to distinguish between conservation and . . . ah . . . appropriation. However, one has become accustomed to better things – first-class travel, as you see. We must drink to this happy meeting.'

Enwright punched the call-button enthusiastically.

Miles wanted marc, the pungent thrice-distilled brandy Pan American sometimes stocked. But, after Humphrey's exhibition over Pernod, he contented himself with cognac and the packet of Pall Mall the stewardess had finally brought him.

Two sleeves lay side by side on the central armrests. Miles Corrigan's was well cut beige Thai silk; Humphrey Enwright's was slightly frayed, slightly green like his grey worsted jacket, which clashed with his rusty tan trousers. Humphrey might be flying first-class this once, but the better times he boasted of were not otherwise apparent. And the sing-song intonation of his Levantine background still crept into his pseudo-Cambridge accent.

Outwardly, little had changed since Ambassador Sir

Archibald Courtwright, who had misunderstood much, including political change in China, had thoroughly understood Humphrey's manipulation of eighteenth-century jade figurines for his own profit. Humphrey had left Nanking on twenty-four hours' notice, angrily protesting his 'victimisation' – and the British Council had decided not to appoint another Cultural Consultant.

The British Embassy had reluctantly asked the advice of a very junior American naval officer on an embarrassing internal matter because the American had some knowledge of Chinese art. And Miles had confirmed that Sir Archibald was making no mistake regarding Humphrey's culpability. Automatically filtering the chaff from Humphrey's outpouring, Miles wondered idly who was currently sufficiently attracted by Humphrey's tarnished expertise and unabashed opportunism to pay for this flight.

'Where're you off to?' he asked.

'Hong Kong . . . a little matter of business. It could turn out super . . . sensational.'

Humphrey's predatory red beak hovered over his third double Scotch. He downed the drink swiftly, sighed appreciatively and hiccuped gently.

'Beastly food in Tokyo, too,' he complained. 'It'll be good to get some decent British food, roast beef well done and Yorkshire pudding at the Peninsula . . . For the nonce another drink would not be amiss.'

A small gong chimed in Miles's mind, counselling caution, but he disregarded the warning, since he was drinking only one brandy to two double Scotches. Besides, Humphrey rarely had anything to say that merited close attention. His grubby intrigues were normally of interest only to himself and his victims – and, of course, to those who had to clean up the mess.

'What are you doing with yourself nowadays, my boy?'

Humphrey asked. 'Out of the Navy, I assume. Have you also given up spooking . . . hung up your cloak-and-dagger?'

'After my uncle died . . .'

'My dear boy, I'm so sorry . . .'

'. . . I took over his gallery. After all, Uncle Ben made me take almost every art history course Columbia had to offer, particularly Oriental art. He practically forced me into specialising in Asia, languages and all.'

Miles felt he was talking too much. But he was revealing nothing new and, after all, it was only old Humphrey.

'The Navy rubbed its hands over my smattering of Chinese and Japanese. Then it made me really learn the damned languages. Afterwards . . . unavoidably . . . the art business. When I was a kid, I wanted to be a lawyer, just like Dad. Some adolescent notion of carrying on after he was killed by a crazy Red Indian client with a six-shooter – and left me penniless. But Uncle Ben was picking up the tab, paying the tuition and everything else. So he called the tune.'

'I never knew,' Humphrey said, 'you dreamed of being a Titan at the bar.'

'I was for a while . . . the wrong kind of bar. But I outgrew beer guzzling. It's not a bad life now, selling things they don't need, but do appreciate, to old ladies with inflated incomes. After the Navy, I couldn't imagine running an ad offering the services of a Chinese and Japanese linguist, with passable German and French plus some old spook tricks. I still do karate and judo to keep in shape. That training was so rough I can never forget it.'

'Cultured connoisseur with iron fist, eh? And what brings you out East this time – the *objets* or the popsies? Talking of popsies, that little girl without the Pernod seems interested.'

'She might,' Miles mused, 'be interesting herself.'

'On more weighty matters, my boy, if you're buying, we could do business. Maybe even now . . .'

'What do you have in mind?'

'That's it. Merely something in mind, not in hand yet. But maybe something in hand very soon. But let's not natter about money. Too crass. Let's talk about the wonderful new Jap woodcuts. Are the moderns copying, improving, or debasing the old masters?'

Humphrey ordered his fourth double Scotch, and Miles settled down for a lecture. For once, the old charlatan was not talking about himself or boasting of imaginary triumphs. He was now discoursing on the masterworks the Japanese cherished, officially designating them as national treasures.

'. . . the Horyu-ji, that splendid shrine ten centuries old. Just burned to the ground. Glorious . . . priceless . . . murals lost forever because a carpenter wanted to warm his hands. The Chinese're more sensible. They're making quite decent reproductions of their old Buddhist cave-paintings. You've seen them, of course?'

Miles nodded.

'Other hand, the Communists're even touchier about national treasures than the Nationalists were. They won't let anything over eighty years old out of the country. But it's not impossible. As usual, things can be arranged – if you know the right people. It makes my mouth water. Just imagine something easily portable, completely unique, and incredibly beautiful. Also infinitely valuable and easily negotiable.'

'Of course you know the right people?'

'Ah, you cloak-and-dagger boys, always probing,' Humphrey said with alcoholic guile. 'Well, you'll not winkle anything out of me. You know it costs a packet, a flight like this. I'm not paying for it, not me. Some people value my expert opinion – about men as well as *objets* . . . Come, my boy, let's have another drink and forget such crass matters!'

Just another of Humphrey's pipe dreams, Miles decided. He was always hot on the trail of the pot of gold at the end of the rainbow – and it always ended in ludicrous failure. Still, someone had paid for the first-class ticket.

The blonde stewardess responded to the call bell with a tall bottle of Johnnie Walker Black Label in one hand and a squat bottle of Courvoisier VSOP in the other. Her broad smile revealed dimples and leached her words of any possible offence.

'You're both big boys,' she said. 'So I can trust you with the bottles – and give myself some time to look after the other passengers.'

Miles grinned in appreciation and thanked her elaborately for her confidence in their discretion. As she turned away, he asked Humphrey: 'Is a customer called P. T. Barnum treating you to this trip?'

'Barnum? Don't believe I know the chap.'

'It's not important. He was an American showman with an interesting theory on over-population and credulity.'

'You are mixed up with some queer types,' Humphrey observed. 'To tell the truth, I'm not certain myself who's treating me. But it's nothing to do with show business.'

'That's reassuring,' Miles replied drily, annoyed at himself. Humphrey had brought out an aspect of his character he disliked: the eternal sophomore always cracking wise. It was foolish twitting the pathetic China Coast drifter about P. T. Barnum's remark: 'There's a sucker born every minute!'

Such behaviour marred Miles's image – the image he wished the world to see: the suave, yet sensitive aesthete with an encyclopedic appreciation of art. The connoisseur of other good things in life: fast Porsches, fine food, splendid wine, great brandy, and, of course, the ladies.

That was the sophisticated image he deliberately, even self-consciously, cultivated – only in part because it was right for the trade he had somewhat reluctantly entered. American dowagers, as well as Japanese aristocrats, admired the dashing, but always honourable and sensible Miles de Sola Corrigan.

Yet the smart-aleck sophomore kept popping out from behind that painstakingly constructed façade. Deep within himself, Miles knew, lay a prickly core of discontent, a generalised dissatisfaction with life and with himself he could never quite either suppress or define. He could only assuage that constant unease temporarily with danger deliberately sought, or with sexual adventures that normally left him further disgusted with himself.

Brooding, Miles again lost the thread of Humphrey's monologue. The grifter had referred to 'something unique and incredibly beautiful – infinitely valuable and easily negotiable, truly a national treasure'. Humphrey did not enlarge on those meanderings. He offered no facts. He did not even hint at the age or the character of the object over which he rhapsodised.

Sensing Miles's withdrawal, Humphrey rose and stretched elaborately. Scuffed opera-pumps straddle-footed on the blue carpet, he cradled his bottle of Black Label.

'I'll just catch a few winks before we land. If we miss each other at the airport, I'll be at the Peninsula for a few days.'

It was not Miles's night for sleep. When the opera-pumps had taken themselves off, the ballet-slippers appeared at his side.

'Oh, Mr Corrigan.' The hostess settled herself on the armrest. 'I was hoping you were *the* Mr Corrigan when I saw the manifest. Jane Simpson's told me about you. You were supposed to come to a party at our apartment. We were so disappointed when you didn't show up.'

The call bell of seat 2A tinkled impatiently.

'Oh, darn that thing.' The stewardness pouted. 'I've got to run. My name is Sally Hutchins. Jane said I was to ask you to show me Hong Kong. This is my first trip out here.'

Miles's interest quickened. But, at the moment, he needed sleep more than stimulation.

'You'll be at the Peninsula?' he asked.

'Oh yes, all the crews stay there.'

'Shall we say 7.30 tomorrow night, then?'

'That would be lovely.'

Sally moved across the aisle to seat 2A. Miles closed his eyes, hearing Humphrey boom: 'May I have some ice this time, my dear? Mustn't drink too much. Just enough to help me drop off.'

When Sally Hutchins came down the aisle again, Miles was ostentatiously asleep.

II

In that small capsule of luxury, the first-class cabin at the front of the airliner, Miles pursued elusive sleep. The brandy acted as a stimulant, rather than a soporific, but the protective curtain of his eyelids remained lowered. Tomorrow night was time enough to explore whatever diversions Sally might offer. Tonight he found her exuberance a little wearing.

Even such fitful relaxation, Miles knew, was impossible in the tourist class compartment at the rear of the aircraft. 'Steerage', as the crew called it, was an utterly different world from the hushed comfort of the forward cabin. Babies cried, toddlers raced up and down the aisles, and old ladies screamed over strangers' heads in clacking Cantonese. Though the air was calm, two young women vomited into air-sickness bags, their retching audible above the general din. Their example was infectious. A middle-aged Japanese engineer clutched an air-sickness bag and spewed out his supper. His wife followed his example within thirty seconds, daintily careful not to stain her brocade kimono.

In a dimness feebly illuminated by night-lights, the tourist class passengers lay in contorted positions, legs and arms twisted unnaturally. Their hand baggage crammed all the space beneath their seats, above their seats, and on their seats. Harried passenger agents at Haneda Airport had given up trying to enforce restrictions on the luggage passengers could take into the cabin, leaving the stewardesses to struggle with stowage. Unofficially the word had come down: 'You can't fight it. If they can lift it, let them carry it into the cabin – even if it's a baby elephant.'

Baskets full of prickly fruit nudged cartons containing massive stereo tape-players and speakers. Folded babies' buggies with sharp metal frames skidded against unwary ankles. Unwieldy packages done up in colourful bandannas teetered in the overhead luggage racks, threatening unprotected heads with their hard corners. It would have taken a Brueghel reborn into the modern age to depict the little corner of hell the passengers had created for themselves in all its grotesque misery.

Aloof from the voluble suffering of the other passengers, two stocky men of indeterminate age sat stiffly self-contained at opposite ends of the tourist compartment. Their round, pale faces offered no clear indication of their origins; they could have been Japanese or Thais, Koreans or Chinese. They were dressed alike in nondescript grey suits. Nestling beneath their feet lay identical green-canvas carry-alls.

If Sally and her fellow stewardesses had not been preoccupied with their passengers' demands, they might have wondered at the immobile self-possession of the two men – and their striking resemblance to each other. But Sally herself was holding a baby under her left arm and a rubber-nippled bottle in her right, while an iron-bound suitcase threatened to crash down on her head. Besides, it was her first trip to Asia, and her roommate Jane had advised her never to be surprised at anything that might happen on an airplane anywhere west of Honolulu.

Precisely an hour and fifty-five minutes before the airliner's scheduled landing at Hong Kong's Kaitak Airport, the two grey men rose simultaneously. They glanced at each other, their eyes meeting down the long tunnel of the rear compartment.

The first then pushed aside the blue curtain that cut off the first-class cabin and strode towards the forward lavatory. Disturbed by the creaking of the lavatory door, Miles's eyelids lifted momentarily. But he was not concerned about a tourist passenger using the first-class facilities; Pan American could enforce its own rules. He closed his eyes again.

An instant later, at the rear of the airplane, the second man in grey skirted a puddle of slime on the rubber mat. A disgusted stewardess was cleaning up the evidence of a retching teenager's failure to reach the lavatory in time. His movements precise, almost delicate despite his bulk, he vanished into the lavatory and shot the latch closed. The *Occupied* sign flashed on just ten seconds after the *Occupied* sign of the forward lavatory.

Ignoring the stench from a toilet blocked with nappies and hand-towels, Number Two blinked in the blue glare of the fluorescent light. His movements were unhurried. He had more than time enough if he worked efficiently – and he had been chosen because he was constitutionally incapable of inefficiency. He was one of the finest all-round mechanics in Asia, his inborn ability sharpened by long experience. And he had rehearsed meticulously for this mission.

Number Two unzipped his carry-all and extracted a torch, a tool-kit rolled in canvas, two tapered rubber plugs, and a grey metal cylinder shaped like a champagne bottle capped by two threaded brass nozzles. He pried loose the inspection panel behind the toilet and directed the torch's beam onto the maze of cables and tubes that lay along the airliner's skin like metal tendons and arteries.

Drawing in his breath in satisfaction, he loosened the short pipe-joint that connected two sections of the largest tube. Just six turns clockwise, precisely six turns with an aluminium spanner, and he stopped. Clasping his hand gently over the joint, he nodded in self-approbation and laid the spanner on the washbasin. The joint remained reasonably air-tight, and the most delicate task awaited his sensitive fingers.

Number Two edged the metal cylinder into the opening, letting it hang from a loop of wire around his left wrist. With a single quick twist of his right hand, the pipe-joint came away and fell tinkling into the abdomen of the big metal organism that was the airliner. Both hands moving simultaneously, he jammed the tapered rubber plugs into the open ends of the tubes.

He could not pause to wipe the sweat from his forehead. Instead he snapped the twin nozzles on the cylinder into readiness, and the next instant, he extracted the rubber plug from the right-hand tube. The matching nozzle, threaded to rotate like a garden-hose connection, clicked onto the open tube and was tightened with a flick of his fingers. After attaching the left-hand nozzle, he wiped his forehead with the back of his hand and glanced at his watch. This crucial phase of the operation had taken forty-five seconds. Since the tubes had been open to the air for no more than ten seconds each, there should have been no loss of pressure.

Number Two checked the joints and repacked his tool kit before extracting another metal cylinder slightly larger than the first from the carry-all. A flexible rubber tube connected it to a brightly coloured mask.

He checked his watch again before strapping the cylinder to his belt and slipping the mask loosely over his head. Still unhurried, he zipped up the carry-all. His eyes on the second hand of his watch, he reached through the open panel to flick a switch on the shiny metal cylinder he had fitted into the aircraft's pressure and ventilation system. After snugging the mask to his face, he watched the second hand make two revolutions and opened the door of the lavatory.

A strange silence had fallen over the noisy tourist class compartment. The childrens' treble voices were fading; all the retching had ceased; and even the old ladies were no longer clacking in Cantonese. The passengers were drowsy, on the edge of sleep. Number Two nodded in satisfaction and walked slowly up the aisle, swinging the canvas carry-all. His gaudy mask did not draw as much as a curious glance from the somnolent passengers and stewardesses.

Number One's initial assignment was less demanding. After strapping on the parachute from his carry-all, he waited in the first-class lavatory, peering at his watch. At the exact moment when Number Two flicked the valve on the metal cylinder, he pulled his own mask over his face. He would wait precisely two and a half minutes before stepping into the cabin, which the gas would by then have permeated.

The pilots in the cockpit should be protected by their separate pressure system, but he could pilot the aircraft if necessary. It would not, in any event, be for long.

Both men had been meticulously trained; their equipment was tailored to the mission; and the mock-up on which they had rehearsed was a precise replica of a factory-fresh installation. But the airliner was old, and the joints of its tubing were slightly worn. As Number One waited and Number Two walked up the aisle, the right-hand nozzle of the gas cylinder slipped minutely on an irregular ridge in the thread of the tube.

The drop in pressure was negligible. Even so, a red warning light glowed before the captain's eyes after ten seconds. Though it signalled no more than possible danger of a loss of pressure, the captain's well-drilled response was instantaneous. He punched a button, snatched up his oxygen mask, and moved the control yoke forward. The co-pilot and the flight engineer donned their masks as the *Fasten Seat Belts* sign flicked on and off in the passenger cabins accompanied by shrill chimes. The airliner was diving to avoid even the threat of partial decompression.

Alarmed, Number One threw open the lavatory door and stepped through the adjoining door into the cockpit without breaking stride. The compact Uzi sub-machine gun in his hands commanded instant respect from the flight crew.

Miles's eyes flicked open when the lavatory door slammed, and he just saw Number One's broad back disappearing into the cockpit. A parachute made the man look hunch-backed, and an oxygen cylinder swung awkwardly from his belt.

Catching a faint onion odour, Miles reflexively unhooked the portable oxygen-cylinder clipped into the open overhead luggage rack. The drill from many flights over mountains in unpressurised DC-3s came back to him automatically. He pulled the black rubber mask over his nose and opened the valve to release the flow of oxygen. His perception heightened by the rush of adrenalin through his veins, he assessed his predicament coolly.

Forewarned by the slammed door, his reflex reaction

had saved him from the gas that was overcoming his fellow passengers. With a conscious effort, he mastered his body's instinctive demand for immediate action. With the danger ill-defined, unconsidered action could be disastrous.

Crouching low in his seat, he heard a metallic scraping. The rings of the curtain that isolated the first-class compartment were sliding on their rod. Miles pulled a blanket over his head to conceal the oxygen mask – and peered warily through its folds.

Number Two stalked into the first-class cabin, nodded in satisfaction at the sleeping forms, and stooped to unzip his carry-all. When he straightened up an Uzi dangled loosely by its sling from his right hand. His eyes swept the cabin again, lingering on Humphrey Enwright's snoring form. His gaze passed quickly over the other sleepers and ignored the blanket that covered Miles.

Behind the closed and bolted door of the cockpit, Number One played the scene he had so often rehearsed. Bracing himself against the bulkhead to resist the pressure of the dive, he tossed a 1-to-100,000-scale aircraft chart to the captain.

A red cross marked a point in the ocean ten miles east of the Tachen Islands, which had been surrendered to the Communists by the Nationalists a few months earlier. A typewritten note clipped to the chart read: *You will proceed to the marked point, descend to 3,000 feet and circle. The man behind you is an expert navigator and pilot. Do not attempt deception. It will be vain. Resistance can only end in death for your passengers and yourself.*

Number One jerked the muzzle of his sub-machine gun upwards to command the captain to level out. In response to that emphatic message, the captain pulled back the control yoke. Everything had happened so fast that the co-pilot was still trying to raise Hong Kong to advise of a possible loss of pressure. Contemptuously, Number One reached up and turned a switch, shutting down the radio.

At Kaitak Airport, a sleepy radioman in the control tower heard only the static-broken words: 'Pan American 002 call . . .'

After repeated efforts to raise the aircraft, the radioman concluded, reasonably enough, that he had overheard a fragment of a message intended for another station. Since there was no unidentified blip on his green radar-screen, the plane had to be out of range. Radio waves played strange tricks.

The radioman in Hong Kong was conscientious, but it was late evening. He assumed that the Pan American flight would call again if it wanted him. He opened his eyes wide – and willed himself not to sleep.

Taipei's Sung Shan Airport expected no Pan American flight, though it was routinely monitoring the dark green blip which represented the Pan American airliner on its long-range radar screen. Taipei was constantly on the alert for any deviation from normal flight patterns, since a deviation could be the first warning of a Communist attack. But neither the civilian control tower at Sung Shan nor the string of radar-domes manned by the Nationalist Air Force around the island was initially alarmed.

Taipei Tower also concluded that the broken message had been intended for another station, probably Hong Kong. The radioman at Sung Shan assumed that the Pan American flight had switched to another frequency.

Regardless of the complacent reactions in Hong Kong and Taipei, the airliner was beyond all aid from the ground. No assistance could be rendered by anyone outside the self-contained metal world hurtling through the air at 400 miles an hour. Even if fighters were scrambled they could only hover ineffectually. Any action they might take would be more dangerous to the passengers and crew than the hijackers themselves. Pan American Flight 002 was on its own, totally isolated from outside intervention.

Within the aircraft so abruptly cut off from the earth, Miles watched Number Two stoop to pull two bulky cloth objects from the canvas carry-all. The American saw with amazement, through the folds of the blanket, that a butterfly was painted on the mask that concealed the hijacker's features. The colourful pattern stirred a vague memory, but Miles could hardly pursue that tantalising thought down the corridors of his mind. He had to move while the grotesque figure was preoccupied with the carry-all and the Uzi hung loose from its sling.

Miles lifted a corner of his oxygen-mask, the blanket concealing the slight movement, and sniffed cautiously before letting it snap back. No ill effects! He sniffed again, but detected no odour. He then peeled the rubber mask from his face. The other passengers slept on, but the soporific gas had obviously been dissipated by the ventilating system.

Apparently just two men were involved. If he could take out one, even create a diversion, the crew might deal with the other. Chances of success were slim, but he had to make an effort. That was better than being delivered like a trussed pig to the hijackers' destination.

When Miles moved, Number Two was struggling into the parachute that would earlier have impeded his progess through the cabin. Hefting the brandy bottle Sally had pressed on him, Miles slammed it against the back of Number Two's head. The glass shattered, and the hijacker was stunned. Ignoring a gout of blood, he shook his head, and snatched up his sub-machine gun. But he was hampered by both his breathing apparatus and by the parachute that dangled half-on and half-off. Despite the danger to the aircraft, he had to use his weapon.

As Number Two's finger slid towards the trigger, Miles desperately levered the muzzle away from his chest. The Uzi was pointing upwards when it fired a quick burst, filling the enclosed space with cordite fumes. Miles exerted all his strength to push the barrel down.

The next burst slammed into Number Two's chest. Moving up with the recoil, bullets stitched a row of holes through the gaudy butterfly mask. Number Two's face dissolved into a mass of raw red flesh, yellow teeth, and white bone.

The deadly little Israeli weapon fired another ten shots in the seconds before Miles wrenched the dead finger off the trigger. Already shaking in shock, he lifted the Uzi and lunged towards the cockpit door.

Hearing the shots outside, the captain had ignored the threatening hijacker and thrown the airliner into a steep dive. Though not certain, violent decompression was possible if the plane's skin were badly punctured. He had to descend quickly.

Having turned automatically at the first shots, Number One was no longer braced against the bulkhead. The sudden dive threw him completely off balance, his feet sliding on the floorboards. The co-pilot and the flight-engineer hurled themselves at the falling figure as Number One reflexively fired a burst that passed between the pilots' seats, smashing the windshield.

In the grasp of the crewmen when Miles hurtled through the door, Number One looked into the smoking muzzle of Miles's Uzi and dropped his own.

The captain eased back the control yoke, gradually slowing the rate of descent. Levelling off at 900 feet, he turned to check the cockpit.

A snow storm of papers had flown out of the shattered windshield, followed by every moveable object. The air-pressure was now abruptly reversed. The wind stormed into the cockpit and slammed the door shut. Co-pilot, flight-engineer, Miles, and the hijacker were pinned against the bulkhead by the pressure.

'Well, the wings stayed on!' the captain exulted. 'Always wondered if they would.'

He tested the controls, waggling the wings and swayed the tail.

'Flight-engineer,' he commanded with odd formality, 'you will remain with me. First Officer, you and the gentleman with the machine-pistol will see to the passengers. But, first, get that thug out of here. I'll descend to let you get out, then climb a little to slow us down.'

The co-pilot and Miles bundled the hijacker out of the door. His body limp, Number One offered no resistance.

The aircraft levelled off, then raised its nose slightly, and the cockpit door slammed shut. In a cabin strewn with luggage, pillows, bottles, and cutlery, Miles and the co-pilot lashed the hijacker's hands with his own tie. When they pulled off the butterlfy mask, the pale, round face was placid.

'This man is dead!' Miles shouted over the creaking of the airframe and the roar of the wind. 'Can't you smell almonds?'

Prussic acid had been routinely issued to American intelligence agents who might be tortured. Tucked into a hollow tooth, it could be broken by biting hard, even by a man otherwise immobilised.

His hands trembling in reaction to the violence, Miles wanted a brandy. He glanced around the cabin and smiled ruefully when he smelled the wasted brandy amid the lingering cordite. And the irrepressible Sally was fully occupied reassuring passengers.

Miles realised that a third parachute lay on the floorboards, the green pack incongruously utilitarian against the plush carpet. Did the two hijackers, he wondered, have a confederate aboard or had they planned to take a hostage?

III

A wounded eagle, the great airliner dipped low over the turbulent Taiwan Straits. The small Stars-and-Stripes painted on its tailplane glowed fitfully between the scudding clouds. In the cockpit, captain and flight-engineer crouched low in their seats to avoid the full blast of the gale-force wind funnelled through the shattered windshield.

The high instrument panel offered only partial shelter, and their faces were tortured into clownish grimaces by the gusts. Cheeks puffed out like chidren's balloons, then pressed inward to expose grinning teeth in skull-like faces. Hair was swept back, then rose straight up in a caricature of fright.

Given a modicum of essential luck, their trained reactions could prove the salvation of the DC-7 and its human cargo. Among the objects sucked out of the cockpit when the windshield shattered was the 'book', the bulky manual that laid down procedures to meet every misfortune men could imagine afflicting the great machine they had conceived. Nevertheless after thirty-six thousand hours aloft, the book was inscribed on the captain's brain. He was still flying by the book.

The airliner gradually climbed to 4,000 feet to gain a margin of safety, without imposing discomfort on the shocked passengers. The greater the distance from earth, the more time the crew would have to respond if a vital part of the complex fabric should give way because of damage inflicted by the Uzi's salvoes or the violent manoeuvres. Every additional foot of altitude offered the captain further options, above all a wider choice of places to touch down.

The book counselled him to request an emergency landing at the 'nearest airport', which was, in this case, on the nearby Chinese mainland. Only in desperation, however, would he deliver his passengers and his aircraft into the hands of the vehemently anti-American government that ruled the mainland. Sung Shan Airport on the island of Taiwan, which was ruled by a nominally friendly government, was the logical alternative. But the radio reported Sung Shan totally obscured by fog, and he knew that its Ground Controlled Approach guidance system was, at best, erratic.

Throttling back to his lowest practical cruising speed of 200 miles an hour, the captain nursed the stricken craft towards Hong Kong, 515 miles away. By choosing the longer distance he was accepting a grave risk.

True, the damage to the airplane appeared superficial. Yet, the book warned him not to gamble his passengers' lives on the hope that damage would not worsen during a protracted flight. The captain was, however, on the edge of the razor, the psychological point of no return where the book could only offer guidance. Human judgement had to take the ultimate decision – and accept the responsibility for 105 lives and $5 million worth of intricately worked metal.

The co-pilot's first hasty survey had, however, revealed

no significant damage beyond the shattered windshield and the pattern of bullet holes in the overhead of the first-class compartment. Shortly thereafter, when the plane was in level flight, the captain had sent the flight-engineer to conduct as thorough an examination as was possible while in the air. The engineer reported the same conclusion, and the controls were answering normally as the DC-7 droned through the night.

To the crews of the air-sea rescue amphibians that were due to rendezvous within half an hour the big airliner would appear perfectly normal, except for its reduced speed. The red navigation light on the left wing tip and the green light on the right wing tip shone normally, as did the white tail-light and the flashing red beacons above and below the fuselage.

But within the airliner all was chaos. Miles was later to remember the two-and-a-half hour flight as a seemingly interminable purgatory. After his cool response to the threat, his emotions were in turmoil. To him, the suffering of the innocent was always the most harrowing aftermath of any violence.

Any male of his generation who had not skulked at home during the Second World War could have seen much violence. But Miles felt he had seen more than his share because his life was set in Asia, where violence was endemic. From the suicidal defiance of the Japanese on Okinawa to the vicious barbarity of the Chinese Civil War, he had witnessed a Devil's Carnival of maiming, pillage, torture, and sudden death — as well as the bureaucratic murders the self-righteous called execution.

Nor had the 1950s lessened those blows. The war in Korea was as brutal as any ever seen, while the atrocities perpetrated by terrorists in Malaya almost made him despair of humanity — at least Asian humanity. And the

Philippines, where almost every male over fifteen carried a gun, celebrated elections and resolved business disputes with massacres.

Nor had the Chinese Civil War ended yet. Even in 1955, skirmishes were still fought between the Nationalists on Taiwan and the Communists, who controlled the vast mainland of China. Had he, Miles wondered, just seen such a clash?

Some men gloried in daring violence and brushing against death. In particular the pilots who had dealt out death antiseptically, although terrified of cremation themselves. A warplane could become a flaming coffin in an instant. Some men, Miles knew, were still flying clandestine missions, for the Nationalists, the Central Intelligence Agency, or even shadier sponsors, not merely drunk on their own bravado, but addicted to mortal danger.

Miles himself found it increasingly harrowing each time he encountered violence. He sipped brandy, afraid too much would exacerbate his reaction, but the alcohol hardly helped. His hands were trembling, and the queasiness he always felt after action was intense, almost nauseating. Yet this had been a relatively minor incident, its consequences no more than two anonymous hijackers dead and a few dozen passengers badly shaken.

Fortunately, most had heeded the captain's routine advice to keep their safety-belts buckled loosely. But their hand baggage had cascaded through the fuselage, smashing at soft flesh and hard metal with impartial ferocity.

A mother still bleeding from a torn forehead cradled her stricken five-year-old son on her lap. The child was playing in the aisle when the gas seeped into the cabin, and his limp body had been tossed about by the plane's gyrations.

(33)

The middle-aged Japanese engineer who had vomited on take off was half-conscious, his face red with blood from a scalp wound. Careless of her brocaded kimono, his groggy wife was trying to staunch the flow.

A baby's buggy had wrapped itself around the metal frame of one row of seats, imprisoning three teenage girls. All were miraculously unhurt. Bright coloured bandannas, torn loose from the packages they wrapped, fluttered like carnival flags.

Miles looked for Sally, the stewardess he had met only two hours earlier. He found her small rounded shape crumpled beside the rear exit, nylon-sheathed thighs exposed pathetically. Her face was unmarked, though her stockings, her skirt, and her blouse were torn.

Sally was groping towards consciousness. Somehow she had slid the length of the cabin without injury. She had suffered the full effect of the gas because she had been standing, her head level with the ventilation outlets above the seated passengers. The tightly packed rubber life-raft beside the rear exit had evidently cushioned her body when the airliner gyrated, tossing cutlery, plates, baggage, and human beings about like a gargantuan cement-mixer.

'Nothing broken, I think.' Sally clung to his arm. 'But I must look a mess.'

Automatically, she tucked the shreds of her white blouse into the waistband of her torn blue skirt. Her hands rose to adjust the black band that restrained her blond hair, and her hair miraculously fell into order.

'I'm better now.' She smiled tremulously. 'Must look after the passengers.'

For the next hour and a half, Sally and Miles worked beside the four other stewardesses and the five young Chinese men and women who had quietly offered their assistance. Some injured passengers they could at best make a little more comfortable. Others were soothed, and minor wounds were bandaged. The cabin gradually began to look less like the aftermath of an earthquake and more like a casualty station.

The plane droned steadily through the clouds, the air-sea rescue amphibians hovering protectively on either side. And so they arrived at Hong Kong.

The metal eagle dipped slowly towards the bright lights outlining the runway, broad wing-flaps fully extended, engines labouring. Three green lights on the instrument panel assured the captain that the landing-gear was down and locked. But the fragile metal organism shuddered when its wheels touched the concrete runway. The airliner bounced high into the air, settled, and bounced again, while the captain fought the control yoke.

At last he felt the spinning wheels settle and remain in firm contact with the runway. He thrust hard left rudder against the strong cross-wind, gingerly applied the brakes, and threw the propellers into reverse.

Then the captain could only pray, his lips moving in silent supplication as the DC-7 hurtled towards the choppy water at the end of the runway. Despite his expectation of disaster, the undercarriage did not collapse. On the verge of the water, the headlong rush slowed, and the crippled eagle settled to earth.

After taxiing to the parking bay, the captain slumped exhausted in his seat. Under the glare of floodlights a fleet of ground vehicles converged on the airliner – ambulances, police vans, firetrucks, buses and tractors. Pan American Flight 002 had landed safely, and many hands were raised to succour its battered human cargo.

IV

Sally Hutchins, Miles Corrigan, and Humphrey Enwright slept exhausted in three high-ceilinged, briskly air-conditioned rooms on three different floors of the Peninsula Hotel.

Nude beneath the light blanket, Miles tossed uneasily. He gritted his teeth and clenched his fists. Visions of Sally and himself falling through a barrage of butterfly-masks chased across his mind.

Having kicked off her blanket, Sally was covered by a gauzy black night-dress. She was curled on her side, but her body jerked spasmodically from time to time. The night-dress had worked up to uncover her thighs and the angry red abrasion on her right leg. One soft vulnerable breast had escaped from her low-cut bodice.

Clad in soiled undershorts, Humphrey Enwright lay on his back and snored stertorously. He hardly stirred. Insulated by Scotch and by his own insensitivity, he was virtually untouched by the shocks of the night.

Waking first, Miles automatically checked his watch and flicked on the bedside radio. After six minutes of hard rock introduced by inane chatter in a mock American accent, the hourly news bulletin reported the airliner's mishap in mellifluous pseudo-Oxford tones.

'A Pan American aircraft landed this morning at Kaitak Airport several hours late after experiencing difficulties in flight.

'First reports indicate an attempted hijacking. The landing was uneventful. But several passengers suffered injuries due to turbulence in flight. Police are investigating, and we hope to have further details soon.'

Miles flicked off the radio and smiled. The broadcasting station was controlled by the British Colonial Government, which was ever wary of political complications. Loath to offend its enormous neighbour, the People's Republic of China, Radio Hong Kong would not even intimate that Peking might have been involved in the incident. At four in the afternoon, twelve hours after the hairsbreadth landing, the police were still 'investigating.'

Miles called room-service to order a breakfast steak before asking the operator to connect him with Miss Hutchins. Humphrey could wait – if there were indeed any point in seeing him aside from nostalgia. The old rogue might come up with an interesting object once in a blue moon, but the moon wasn't blue this month.

Waking to the trilling of the telephone, Sally stretched lazily. She primly pulled down her night-dress before lifting the receiver.

'This is Miles Corrigan. Do you remember me?'

With drowsy narcissism, she admired her exposed breast. But she tucked it into her bodice before speaking.

'Umm . . . yes, Miles! How could I forget? . . . You didn't ask, but you did wake me. And I don't mind.'

'How are you? Still feeling shaken?'

'A bit sore, but no lasting damage.'

'Do you still want to see Hong Kong tonight?'

'Umm . . . I suppose so,' she answered slowly. 'Yes, I'd love to . . . with you.'

'We'll dine later. Meet me in an hour in the lobby?'

'Make it two hours,' she said. 'I need time for running repairs.'

Sally finally entered the baroque lobby of the Peninsula at half past six. Miles happily watched her approach, her hips swaying genteelly, just enough to make her point. She was also, he reflected with amusement, just late enough to emphasise her independence. He smiled in appreciation when she pirouetted coquettishly.

The long skirt of her white silk-jersey dress swirled around her ankles, but was snug across hips, revealing the minute swell of her belly. The gold-trimmed bodice was cut low to expose the inner curves of her breasts. A skein of gold chains hung around her throat, and gold earrings heavy with cornelians clasped her ear-lobes.

Her light-blond hair, released from the confining Alice band she wore on duty, hung in a pageboy that brushed her shoulders. The rippling curtain framed features that would have been too regular, too conventionally perfect, were it not for the quizzical glint in her wide-set corn-flower-blue eyes and a smile that was a bit crooked. Her nose was small, straight, and slightly *retroussé*; her eyebrows, shaped but not plucked, were a shade darker than her hair. Her round face could almost have been insipid in its symmetry, but prominent cheekbones, the gift, perhaps, of some Slavic ancestor, gave her an enigmatic air.

Those dark eyebrows, Miles reflected, could mean either that both brows and hair were natural or, alternatively, they could mean that neither was natural. Her manner was, however, completely natural. She had put off the breathlessness, the eager ingenuousness that could so easily cloy, with her sky-blue uniform. The schoolgirl naïveté had also vanished, and she was obviously measuring him as he measured her.

'All right?' she draped her cream Kashmiri shawl over the back of the chair. 'Do I pass inspection?'

'With high marks! The dress is a great improvement on Pan Am's uniform. What'll you drink?' Miles turned to the hovering waiter: 'A Martini on the rocks, twenty-five to one, stirred gently with a twist of lemon peel.' When Sally nodded, he added: 'Make that two, please.'

Relaxed and silent, while waiting for their Martinis, Sally gazed around the spendid lobby she was seeing for the first time. The massive cut-crystal chandelier that was the management's pride glittered beneath the ornate gold-and-red moulding of the ceiling. Small teak tables surrounded by armchairs were oases on the deep-piled crimson carpets. White-coated 'boys', most of them elderly, scurried among the tables bearing drinks and snacks.

'The international acculturation and guzzling hour', a frivolous sociologist from Hong Kong University had once called this moment. Ceremonial high tea on the right, the English side of the mosaic floored lobby, and the ritual cocktail hour on the left, the American side. From the stairway that curved in an inverted Y at the rear of the lobby, a central aisle led to banks of glass doors attended by teenage boys wearing pill-box hats, red-trimmed monkey jackets, and white trousers with red stripes. Their sole duty was to open the doors for arriving or departing guests. On a red-carpeted dais set in the aisle, a Filipino band thumped out a medley from *The Merry Widow*.

The music and the drinking would continue until the indeterminable moment that the facetious academic called the 'invisible blending hour'. When the lights finally dimmed late in the evening, both British and Americans always seemed to melt into the chairs in which they had sat for hours.

Tragically, the splendid lobby was scheduled for 'modernisation'. The frenetic new breed of Hong Kong residents – whether Americans, British, or Chinese – was impatient with such leisurely ritual. Tourists could not spare time from spending their money on bargains, while residents were compulsively occupied in amassing money.

'This must be the real old Hong Kong,' Sally remarked. 'It sure looks like it.'

'A sight that's passing,' Miles said. 'Enjoy it while you can.'

'Not at all like last night,' she ventured. 'You were wonderful. The captain told me.'

'Any red-blooded American boy would've done the same!' He laughed. 'I couldn't let them get away with it, even if I am a little long in the tooth for such heroics.'

'Hardly!' She smiled. 'Miles, what did they want?'

'We'll never know now. I could guess, but . . .'

'Why not guess?'

'I do *not* think they wanted to deliver us all to jolly old Uncle Mao Tse-tung.'

'What then?'

'You know they ordered the captain to circle near a Communist-held island. And both had parachutes – plus a spare. So . . .'

'So what? Come on, Miles.'

'Maybe they wanted to take a hostage . . . bail out with him. Crazy as it sounds.'

'It does sound crazy. Who ever heard of parachuting a hostage from an airplane? Maybe the chutes were just in case.'

'Why haul around a cumbersome spare? When the Police Special Branch check the manifest they might find somebody . . . maybe a political enemy . . . the Communists're anxious to get their hands on.'

'That *is* far-fetched, Miles.'

'I know.' He grinned. 'But can you think of a better explanation?'

'Maybe just to capture the plane . . . hold us for ransom.'

'Pretty elaborate planning just for . . .'

'Maybe there was somebody very rich aboard. I hear Chinese gangs're always kidnapping millionaires.'

'Gangsters, not commissars. Anyway . . .'

'Whatever it was, you were great.'

'Thanks again,' he replied. 'Now what would you like to do tonight?'

'I want some excitement.' She smiled at her own words. 'Not excitement like last night, but fun excitement. Show me the real Hong Kong.'

'One place you might like: the Peking Nights Club. Interesting, even if it is halfway respectable.'

'Let's, Miles.'

Miles was not quite sure what she meant by 'the real Hong Kong'. But tawdry, sensual, commercial, violent Wanchai by night was a bit too ripe for her. The red-light district frequented by merchant seamen, US Navy sailors, and British other ranks was not only rowdy and raunchy, but often dangerous.

He had, therefore, chosen Peking Nights, which was less gamey, though it, too, could be a little raw. Sally was burnished white-and-gold against the vermilion-and-gold pillars in the crimson-shadowed dimness that reeked of incense. Her composure was, however, untouched by the suggestive atmosphere. She moved closer to him on the silk divan while they chatted desultorily over *deem sum*, Cantonese tid-bits. She talked of the Asia she was eager to discover, and he carefully avoided sounding as if he knew it all. They both speculated idly on the hijackers' motives.

Later, Sally moulded herself to Miles on the minute dance-floor while hostesses in high-slit cheongsams muttered angrily about amateur competition. Sally smiled. The meaning of their complaints was quite clear, although they were uttered in cacophonous Cantonese. When she smiled, her mouth quirked slightly lopsided, and she looked conspiratorially into his eyes.

What, Sally wondered, was she planning to do with this unquestionably glamorous man whom her roommate frankly coveted? Jane would sigh, recalling wistfully that she had slept with Miles once, only once, and it had been wonderful. But she couldn't get him into bed again, much less get any farther. Did she, Sarah Jane Hutchins, think she could succeed where her roommate had failed? Not just to sleep with Miles, which she was, she realised with some surprise, already contemplating but to bring him to some kind of emotional commitment.

That was all, of course. He was undeniably dashing, and he was no more than five or six years older than her own twenty-six. But he was not a man one could even consider spending the rest of one's life with. He was too mercurial for that. Nonetheless, he was very attractive, not least because of his fascinating past. He had been around Asia for years, and his assured bearing showed that he was totally at home in this fascinating part of the world.

Fascinating was a mild term. Asia was alluring, mesmerising, on first sight. But she would wait a while to make a final judgement on Asia – and on Miles.

She usually found red-headed men uninteresting, even a little repulsive, but Miles was different. She definitely liked the way his hair curled over his very white high

(42)

forehead, though he tried to plaster it down. Not with some sticky gunk, thank God, but with water. Anyway, you wouldn't call his hair red. It wasn't carroty at all. More like copper, burnished copper, almost chestnut.

She also liked his aquiline nose, which was assertive, but not overbearing. The green eyes under his heavy eyebrows heightened his likeness to an alert eagle. How aggressive he would be she could not tell. He had, he said, taken her to Peking Nights because the bars of Wanchai were too raw. But the atmosphere in this night club was, to say the least, sensual, very provocative.

The stars of the floor-show were a pair of miniature flamenco dancers who looked like precocious children or perverted midgets. A refugee from political or criminal misdeeds in Europe, tiny 'Don Pedro', all in black, strutted like an inflamed bantam. His partner, slightly taller and half as broad again, clutched him as if she would engulf him right there in public.

The feral atmosphere was heightened by the musky perfume of the hostesses who were enticing their sweaty partners into the night. Negotiations conducted within were consummated elsewhere.

'Peking Nights is a respectable establishment,' the beldame proprietor had anxiously assured them. 'But I can't help what the girls do outside.'

Miles was clearly distracted – and not by the erotically charged atmosphere. Humphrey Enwright was ensconced three booths away, unseen in the dimness, but unmistakably identifiable by his booming voice. Having evidently attained the state he would describe as 'well lubricated', he was speaking alternately to an invisible male companion and an invisible hostess.

'. . . most beautiful . . . most astonishing object to come out of China for decades. Sorry I can't tell you more now. You'd be amazed . . . beside yourself with excitement – as a connoisseur and as a businessman.'

A pause while he downed a drink.

'Such dainty little hands. Pity there's only jade on them . . . should be diamonds. Oh, I am sorry . . . Did I spill whisky on you? Never mind. I'll buy you the finest brocades. And I'll replace the jade rings. Diamonds for every finger and emeralds for your toes.'

Soft baritone murmurs and soprano giggles replied.

'That man seems to be everywhere,' Sally objected. 'Always shouting.'

'Humphrey has never been known for his reserve.'

'What about all his big talk?' she asked distastefully. 'Does it mean anything at all?'

'Who knows?' Miles shrugged. 'Usually, no, not a damned thing. He has to brag to keep his whale-sized ego puffed up. Life keeps squeezing Humphrey's ego down to minnow size.'

'Can we go, Miles? The food was delicious, but I'm a little tired of the atmosphere.'

'You wanted to see Hong Kong at night.'

'I guess I've seen it. Let's go back to the hotel?'

Invitation or boredom? Miles could not tell. But he was just as pleased to leave Peking Nights and its unvarying scenes of commercial seduction.

Threading through the close-set tables, Miles glanced into a dark booth hung with red-glass beads to see Humphrey fondling a teenage girl. She might even be pretty beneath the white-and-red mask of make-up from which her soot-rimmed eyes peered, owl-like. Humphrey's male companion was K. P. Soong, the eldest son of Hong Kong's most respected art dealer. SOONG'S ART SHOP: ANTIQUITIES AND CURIOSITIES was neither the largest nor the grandest among the Colony's many dealers, but it was probably the most resourceful, and it was certainly the most reputable.

This, Miles reflected, is very odd. The Soongs prided themselves on their rectitude – with justification. Why, then, was young K.P. drinking with a notorious scavenger and charlatan like Humphrey?

Miles shrugged and returned his attention to Sally's light voice. Humphrey's business was Humphrey's business. All Miles asked of Fate was not to involve him again in Humphrey's dubious business.

Sally and Miles emerged into the maze of Causeway Bay east of hectic Wanchai. Behind iron-shuttered shop windows, mah-jong tiles clattered. Restaurants and eating shops solicited custom with neon signs. The few stores still open were hung with fringes of dried fish, fatty sausages, and big Yunnan hams. Hand written signs offered food packages for hungry relations in China. Furtive couples darted arm-in-arm down alleys to nearby boarding-houses, while sober citizens scurried homeward.

'Fascinating!' Sally exclaimed. 'So many people living so close together. And all these places to eat. Does it ever slow down?'

'Hong Kong's not strong on restraint or sensitivity or good taste. But it sure has a passion for living. Everyone's a glutton for life – and for money. Maybe because so many live so closely packed into such a small place, knowing deep down it can't last because . . .'

Miles stopped abruptly, amused and abashed by his own eloquence. He felt he was playing a part written for someone else when he waxed eloquent, just as he did when he was forced into performing heroics. Mock eloquent, he chided himself, surprised that Sally had brought on that expansive mood. Who would have thought she had touched him that deeply? He only lectured that way to someone he cared for or, to be honest, when he'd had a few drinks too many, which was hardly the case tonight.

Miles grinned, remembering one of the most discomfiting put-downs of his life. Fuelled by Martinis, he had been in full flight, brilliantly laying bare the subtle differences that separate the Japanese from the rest of mankind. A small, dark French woman had then spoken without perceptible irony, rather, it seemed, with puzzled Gallic respect for an intellectual high-wire act. She had asked simply: 'Mr Corrigan, are you what they call a wise old man, though not so old?'

They turned into a deserted street, all its shops and houses dark. A single neon sign glowed above the battered door of a grey stucco building beside an alley, which was itself half-lit by a street-lamp.

'What does it say?' Sally pointed to the green-and-red neon butterfly surrounded by Chinese characters. 'Oh, I see. Underneath in English . . . I guess you'd call it English . . . it says: *Many Patty Yung Girls!*'

'*The Butterfly Club*: *First-class Entertaining and Charming Hostesses*,' Miles duly translated. 'It's funny, that symbol . . . the butterfly. Rather like the hijackers' masks.'

'Too much so,' Sally shuddered. 'Not exactly but . . .'

'Not just that.' Miles was puzzled. 'I've seen it before. But where . . .'

A gong chimed, and the dark door beneath the neon sign opened. A small white object hurtled into the street, startling Sally and Miles. An instant later, he laughed. The white form prancing in the gloom was a small dog chasing its own tail.

The exuberant animal danced into the pool of brightness under the street-lamp – and Sally screamed. No puppy, it was a white cockerel with blood spurting from the severed stump of its neck.

Two men in dark-blue workmen's clothing erupted from the open door. The first fled as if in fear. The second pursued him, waving a shiny cleaver.

Miles saw that Sally and he were in the fugitive's way and pulled her aside. Nonetheless the running man side-swiped the stewardess and knocked her sprawling to the pavement.

The pursuer was upon them next. He swerved and ran full tilt at Miles, who dropped to all fours. The assailant fell over his crouched body, and the cleaver crashed onto the roadway.

Miles was up in the next instant, pulling Sally to her feet. His first instinct was to pin the assailant down, his second to protect Sally. He pushed her behind him as the disarmed assailant rose warily, dodging the kick Miles aimed at his kneecap. From the corner of his eye, Miles saw the apparent fugitive turn and dash towards him.

'Run!' he commanded Sally – and bent as if to tackle the man. 'Get away quick.'

The assailant waited just within the cone of light cast by the street-lamp, arms raised in the classic defensive posture of Chinese kung fu. One hand was cocked high in threat; the other protected his face. His vision preternaturally sharpened by danger, Miles saw the butterfly tattooed on the man's right wrist just before he hurtled into the thug.

Miles recoiled, slamming his shoe against his opponent's kneecap. The thug screamed and fell. But the second was coming in fast.

A whistle shrilled, and a voice shouted in gutter Cantonese: 'Hold it, you bastards!'

The assailants wheeled and dashed into the alley. A

slight Chinese constable carrying a heavy revolver followed in hot pursuit. A shot rang out from the alley, then another.

'My God!' Sally gasped. 'Oh, my God!'

'Thank God for the constable!' Miles drew her to him within the protective cone of light. 'And his gun!'

The constable emerged from the alley, holstering his revolver. The red tabs beneath the silver numerals on his shoulder indicated that he spoke some English.

'Motherfuckers got clean away,' he swore in Cantonese before demanding in broken English: 'Your name, gentlemen and lady? What happened?'

'Nothing . . . a misunderstanding,' Miles replied. 'I'll take the lady home now. She's been frightened.'

The constable was, however, insistent. It took him several minutes to write down their names and their room numbers at the Peninsula. He then demanded the full story of the incident, laboriously transcribing their brief account into his notebook.

Having complete that routine, he asked: 'You want file complaint?'

'Against whom?' Miles laughed. 'I'd never seen those men before and would hardly recognise either if I saw them again.'

The constable grinned and replied: 'OK, you go now. Maybe my inspector speak you tomorrow.'

Miles handed Sally into the red Mercedes taxicab, that had drawn up in expectation, its diesel engine ticking over noisily. While he directed the driver, she slipped her hand into his.

'That was terrible,' she said. 'Is Asia always so violent?'

'Hardly ever. You've had bad luck twice. We must've stumbled into a private fight. But it's over now.'

'I suppose we'll have to testify if the police catch them.'

'We won't,' Miles answered shortly. 'The cops won't catch them, and we won't have to testify.'

'We won't? How can you be so sure?'

'The constable made enough of a fuss to satisfy the ignorant foreigners. He will now make his report, carefully failing to mention that the muggers came out of the Butterfly Club. After all, he didn't see them come out. And that will be that.'

'Why,' she persisted, 'should he forget the Butterfly Club?'

How could he explain Hong Kong's internal workings without frightening Sally still further? Before Miles could speak, a memory, slowly crystallising, pre-empted his attention. The gaudy butterfly, he now remembered, was the symbol of the Green Lotus Lodge, a relatively obscure Triad gang.

The British indiscriminately called all secret societies 'Triads' after a precursor named Three Harmonies. Secret societies had originated as clandestine patriotic leagues organised in the thirteenth century to resist alien Mongol rule. They had subsequently grown into extra-legal quasi-governments in the disorder that so often afflicted China. Most had naturally fallen into crime to support themselves.

The efficient Communists had apparently broken their power within China, but had not quite destroyed them. Call them Secret Societies or Triads, such gangs were powerful in all Asian cities with large Overseas Chinese populations, as well as Hong Kong. Bound by blood-oaths promising fearful punishments for betrayal of the lodge, the Chinese quasi-Mafia was normally splintered into scores of lodges, which were often at dagger's point with each other. But they could, under threat, unite for mutual protection.

'Come back to earth!' Sally demanded. 'Why will the policeman forget the Butterfly Club?'

'Sally, if it weren't for the fact that foreigners were involved, he wouldn't even've bothered to take down the details. After all, nobody was hurt. No doubt he's getting a nice rake-off from the Butterfly Club . . . and duly passes a big chunk to his sergeant, who greases their British inspector. I'll bet we don't hear another word.'

'He did seem relieved when you refused to make a complaint.'

'He was damned relieved we hadn't fouled up his financial arrangements by getting ourselves hurt.'

'It's really different here,' Sally said in a small voice. 'Not like San Francisco!'

'It's not that different in San Francisco or Chicago!'

Horn blaring, the taxi emerged from the maze of side streets, and rolled along brightly lit Hennessy Road towards the Central District. The unsleeping activity of Hong Kong engulfed them. Night-labourers perched on rickety stools at outdoor food-stalls slurping bowls of noodles. Acetylene lanterns glared on the plastic, rubber, and wooden wares hawkers spread on pavements. Foreign sailors and British soldiers accompanied by clinging hostesses reeled from night-clubs towards convenient hot-bed hotels.

'Maybe not so different,' Sally conceded. 'But even San Francisco isn't so . . . so raw.'

'You're seeing the worst,' Miles replied. 'But we're on our way back to respectability.'

The green Star Ferries had stopped crossing the harbour for the night. Sally was delighted with the walla-walla, the small motor-boat that carried them to Kowloon for a single Hong Kong dollar each – seventeen US cents. Climbing the concrete steps of the pier, they strolled past the Edwardian red-brick railway station, its clock-tower a miniature Big Ben. The Peninsula Hotel, flanked by the eminently respectable YMCA, was a staid oasis, though the tumultuous neon artery called Nathan Road lay just around the corner.

Miles dangled their room-keys as they rose sedately to the fourth floor behind the impassive white back of the lift attendant. 'Hong Kong's sixteen worlds all in one,' he said. 'They only meet sometimes, usually by accident.'

'You're sure it was an accident . . . tonight?'

'Quite sure!' He overrode his own doubts. 'Last thing a Hong Kong thug wants is to get involved with foreigners. We're trouble, big trouble.'

He inserted Sally's key into the lock and tossed his own key into the air, catching it with a flourish. Two wizened faces peered at them before disappearing around the corner of the corridor. Neither of the night duty room-boys was a day under sixty.

'You've been wonderful, Miles,' Sally whispered. 'A knight in white armour . . . twice.'

Eyes cast down, she moved closer. When he kissed her she sighed softly. Slipping out of his arms she stood irresolute before the half-open door.

'Good night, Miles,' she said softly. 'I promised Jane I'd give you a sisterly kiss for her.'

She pulled his head down and kissed him again. Hardly sisterly, he reflected, his arms tightening around her.

'Well, just a quick drink,' she conceded. 'We deserve it. Your Hong Kong is a bit strenuous.'

He followed her into the big room with its easy-chairs flanking a coffee table, its big bed, and its lofty curtains. On the dresser stood a rank of miniature bottles of Scotch, the stewardess's prerogative.

'Make the drinks.' Sally kicked off her shoes. 'I won't be a minute.'

As he lifted a glass, she exclaimed in dismay, 'Oh, darn it. I've done it again.'

Completely unselfconscious, she lifted her long skirt, revealing black bikini panties – and a red abrasion on her right thigh. A smear of blood discoloured the tanned skin.

'I scraped it last night. Getting knocked down tonight hasn't made it better.'

'Better clean it up.' His voice was husky. 'Could get infected.'

'Please, would you . . .'

She led him into the bathroom. The clinging dress unfastened with a single button. As he had already surmised, she wore nothing beneath it except the bikini panties.

He knelt to dab at the abrasion with a dampened hand towel. She craned over her shoulder to watch, and her breast brushed his cheek in a velvet caress. The pink nipple was erect.

Wordlessly, he staunched the trickle of blood. Still kneeling, he slipped the panties down her legs. She stepped out of the garment to stand small, naked, and glowing before him.

He kissed the gentle swell of her belly and brushed his lips across the pale-gold triangle beneath. A sharp cry catching in her throat, Sally extended her arms, and he rose into them. They kissed long and deep.

'That's much better,' he breathed. 'Without the dress or the uniform.'

'I'm grateful, Miles,' she whispered. 'You look after me so well.'

While he shed his jacket, her hands were busy with his

belt. His shirt followed his jacket, he stepped out of his trousers and heard her breath come faster.

'You're better this way, too, Miles,' she breathed. 'So much better.'

They were on the bed, and Sally was kneeling over him. Her long hair brushed his stomach, and her tongue flicked out to touch him. Her nipples trailed across his thighs.

'So grateful.' She lithely twisted onto her back. 'You're so strong.'

He kissed each nipple in turn, but she cried imperiously: 'Now! I want it now.'

The scented moist grasp enclosed him. Her legs wrapped themselves around his waist, and he felt her urgent contractions as he slid deep within her.

'Now!' she cried aloud. 'Now!'

V

Awakening shortly after eleven in the morning, Miles stretched luxuriously and automatically switched on the bedside radio. He felt remarkably fresh, though he had strolled back to his own room through empty corridors only four hours earlier. He felt drained, but also buoyant and purified. His nagging conscience had not yet cut in – and he hoped it might remain disengaged this time.

They had made love with few words, her frank animal pleasure curiously innocent – as if she had never heard of the word sin. There was no depravity in Sally's unleashed inventiveness, only eagerness to give – and to receive. Miles promised himself he would never again indulge in the second favourite indoor sport of the American male in Asia: decrying the bossiness and the prudishness of American female participants in their favourite indoor sport.

Sally had cried out in pain when he gripped her bruised buttock hard, but she had taken her revenge. He reached over his shoulder to feel the weals left by her nails on his back. Only once had she spoken seriously. When they lay, her head on his shoulder and her leg cocked over his, passing a single cigarette from hand to hand, she had whispered to him.

'I guess you think I'm terrible,' she'd said. 'But I suppose all your girls say that the first time.'

'Not so many girls.' He evaded the question. 'You're delightful, and I definitely do *not* say that to many girls.'

'I know a lot more about you than you think, Miles. I *know* there are lots of other girls. But I don't mind. I couldn't, could I?'

'You're getting at something.' He laughed. 'Damned if I know what.'

'Miles, it's wonderful, just being with you. But there're no strings attached. I knew what I wanted, and I took it.'

'I wanted it too.'

'You sure hid it . . . right up to the last moment. You were the perfect gentleman – almost.'

'Sorry!' he murmured.

'Don't worry about Jane, my roommate. Ladies aren't gentlemen. There's no nonsense about not poaching.'

She drew deep on the cigarette and handed it to him.

'But seriously . . .'

He pulled hard on the cigarette but did not speak.

'I said no strings attached, and I meant it. I'd love to see you again, but I'm leaving tomorrow. So I'll just hope we'll meet again . . . soon. I'll be flying to Asia regularly now.'

'Look, no strings.' He held up his unfettered wrists. 'Of course I want to see you again . . . all of you, very soon.'

'We will, Miles, I promise. But you mustn't feel bound in any way.'

He smothered her words with a kiss. Later, just before opening the door, he declared softly: 'Next trip, Sally, or in San Francisco.'

The time-signal from the radio reminded Miles that it was morning and he was alone in his own room. Smiling at her repeated promise that no strings were attached to their love-making, he lifted the phone and dialled room service.

'Methinks the lady doth protest too much,' he muttered while waiting for papaya, caraway-seed rolls, coffee, and the newspapers. Sally is a lady, he mused, a frank and generous lady, neither inhibited nor prurient. Maybe a bit too frank for her own good. And she could easily become a habit, a persistent habit.

Their coupling had been joyous. Yet he now felt a stirring of the guilt invariably instilled by possessive American or British females, though not the faint revulsion aroused by Japanese or Thai girls who were too eager to please. It was only a flutter of guilt, a whisper of revulsion at his own unchecked sensuality. Maybe he was growing up; maybe he was reverting to adolescence. When his breakfast arrived, Miles irritably dismissed his cloudy introspection.

The big headline in the *South China Morning Post* read: HIJACKING FOILED: UNKNOWN PAIR DEAD. The story told Miles little new. There was fulsome praise for the captain, but no mention of his own role. The public relations officers of both Pan American and the Hong Kong Police had been discreet, as he had asked. The artistic and commercial respectability he so carefully nurtured would have suffered from reports of his role in thwarting the hijacking. Such notoriety could have recalled his intelligence role to some – and aroused suspicion regarding his present role. The newspaper had played down not only his part in the drama, but also its political implications:

The two gunmen who used the ingenious method of hijacking have not been identified. They carried South Korean passports issued in Seoul. But, the police spokesman said, checking with the South Korean authorities revealed that the passports were forged. Unless more is learned, their identities, like their motives, will remain a mystery.

Miles was content to leave it at that, a mystery he would like to see forgotten. Leafing through the *Hong Kong Tiger Standard* over his second cup of coffee, he told himself he should get to work.

A headline leaped out at him: MINISTERS MAKE DECISION IN PRIVY. Disappointingly, the story reported that Her Majesty's Privy Council had rejected an appeal by a Hong Kong criminal. He flipped through the paper: a delegation of Japanese industrialists had concluded that anti-capitalist China was a model for the Third World; food rations in Peking had been reduced again; and a Social Democratic American labour leader had warned against trading with Socialist China. He also learned that 'a month-old bride' had asked police to find her missing husband.

A small item on the back-page was headlined: EUROPEAN DROWNED FROM WALLA-WALLA. It read in full:

A 55-year old European was drowned last night after falling from a walla-walla in mid-harbour.

Chung Kit-hoi, operator of the walla-walla, told police that the European, who had drunk many drinks, engaged his walla-walla at Blake Pier at approximately 1.30 a.m., asking to be taken to Kowloon. After removing his shoes and jacket, the European had insisted upon performing a little dance on the fore-deck, though warned of the danger of the choppy sea. The craft was struck by a wave, and the European overbalanced and fell off. Chung said he circled, but was unable to find his customer in the dark.

A British passport found in the jacket's pocket identified the bearer as Humphrey Enwright of Tokyo, who arrived in the Colony yesterday.

Miles laid the paper down and lit a cigarette. He wondered who might feel profound sorrow at Humphrey's death, and he concluded regretfully that no one would. Almost everyone would react like himself: a twinge of regret at the passing of an odd phenomenon, much as he had felt when Clarabelle, the white pigmy hippopotamus at the Bronx Zoo, died of strangulation while attempting to swallow a tennis ball.

It was hard to be kinder. Miles was sad to see Humphrey go, just as he had been sad to see Clarabelle go. Each was an original, whose death hastened the day when all eccentricity disappeared. But no one had cared deeply about Humphrey Enwright as a human being, for almost everyone had looked on him as a freak of nature – sometimes amusing, more often irritating. Miles could almost hear Ambassador Sir Archibald Courtwright's indignant cackle. 'Mark my words, Leftenant Corrigan, Enwright will come to a bizarre end, a discreditable end.'

Humphrey's end was certainly bizarre, though not necessarily discreditable. A ludicrous man had died in a ludicrous manner.

Humphrey's lady of the evening might grieve for a few minutes – grieve at least for the gifts he had promised that she would now never get. She had certainly not received any gifts last night. At 1.30 in the morning, who could have found brocades, much less diamonds?

Half past one in the morning? Humphrey had not spent much time alone with his lady friend if he had drowned at that hour. Miles recalled that Sally and he had left Peking Nights at about 12.30. Though the incident outside the Butterfly Club delayed them, it was shortly after 1 a.m. when they boarded the walla-walla to cross to Kowloon. The harbour had been calm, not choppy. A few wavelets had slapped the wooden hull, but there was hardly enough motion to disturb the queasiest Chinese lady, much less Humphrey's ponderous composure.

How much had Humphrey actually drunk? If he were 'oleaginous', as he would have said, he might have essayed a jig on the walla-walla's fore-deck. Yet, 'oleaginous' but not 'sodden', his own terms for the final stage of intoxication, he would not have parted so early from his lady of the evening. When Humphrey was 'gloriously sodden', it took three men to haul his heavy body to bed. So inebriated that he deserted the dance-hall hostess, Humphrey would hardly have been sportive enough to turn a walla-walla into a dance floor. He would have been nearly comatose.

Miles reached for the telephone. Fearing notoriety, he had resolved not to inquire further into the attempted hijacking. But the scuffle outside the Butterfly Club had come afterwards. And now there was Humphrey's bizarre death.

The first incident could be disregarded. Even the second could be a coincidence. But three incidents in succession strained coincidence to breaking point.

Miles recalled the second hijacker's eyes lingering on Humphrey. If Humphrey were the target of the hijackers, the third parachute intended for him, the attack outside the Butterfly Club could have been more than attempted robbery. His own association with Humphrey must be known – and he himself might already be involved. In simple self-defence, he had to chat with K. P. Soong, whom he wanted to see in any event. Perhaps Humphrey's bizarre end had been discreditable after all.

SOONG'S ART SHOP: ANTIQUITIES AND CURIOSITIES was tucked into a corner of the old Gloucester Building near the plateglass windows of the Chinese National Aviation Corporation, which did not fly to Hong Kong. Having inherited the premises when they conquered the nation, the Peking regime now used them as a publicity and propaganda centre. The Soongs enjoyed that proximity; some of the curious passersby gawking at the Communists' displays strayed into their premises.

'But we're not like the tourist shops on the Kowloon side, just selling cheap things,' Old Man Soong would say as he knocked twenty per cent off the price of a common-place object. 'I offer beauty *and* quality!'

In the small room at the back of the shop, an amiably fierce Han Dynasty bear might be available for 8,000 Hong Kong dollars, a little over 1,000 American dollars. ('Only four Hong Kong for each year of his existence,' Old Soong pointed out.) A beautifully lined Ming Dynasty scroll might bring 6,000 Hong Kong dollars, about 800 US dollars.

Young K. P. Soong watched as Miles's eyes surveyed the back room. Mongolian and Tibetan jewel-boxes, prayer-wheels, and daggers were stacked on the rickety shelves beside necklaces studded with jade, coral, and turquoise.

'Just arrived last week,' K.P. said. 'We get a big shipment every time Peking stages a new movement to harass the bourgeoisie. Hoarded objects come out of cupboards – as bribes or fines. Peking then sells them to foreign bourgeois reactionaries for foreign exchange.'

Young K.P. was as briskly casual as the American undergraduate he had once been, his hair bristling in a crew cut. After his collection of Billie Holiday records, his most prized possession was a lilac-and-chartreuse Lotus Elan. His directness often distressed his old-fashioned father, but K.P. was wholly Chinese in his business etiquette. Only after two cups of tea and enquiries regarding mutual friends, did he strike a practical note.

'Miles, I'm afraid I've got nothing that'll interest you. Nothing special enough.' He rubbed his eyebrows with the back of his hand. 'Sorry if I'm a little incoherent. Last night was the first time I ever mixed Pernod and champagne. The last time too.'

'I wondered,' Corrigan replied, 'when I saw you.'

'Saw me?' K.P. was startled. 'Then you know I was with Humphrey Enwright. He was talking about some red-headed fellow. It must've been you. But I didn't connect . . . thought you hadn't seen him in years. So it was you he met on the flight from Tokyo.'

No expression of sorrow, not even conventional regrets. Such callousness was not like K.P., who could be disheartheningly sentimental behind his college-boy breeziness. K.P. could boast with honesty that he was the only artdealer in Hong Kong who had never charged a tourist more than three times the legitimate price. He was, perhaps, not terribly fond of Humphrey Enwright, who had never in his life dealt honestly with anyone. But he was far too punctilious a Confucian gentleman not to utter a word of regret at Humphrey's passing. Miles decided to be as direct as K.P. who, after all, did not boast that he had never lied to an art-dealer.

'K. P., don't you know Humphrey's dead?'

'Dead? What? How can he be dead? I left him at Peking Nights about one this morning and he was perfectly all right. A bit squiffy, but that's all.'

Miles pushed the *Standard* across the table, and K.P. murmured: 'I didn't see the English papers this morning.'

He read slowly, then folded the newspaper, and said deliberately: 'Poor old chap! What a filthy, cold way to die! I always liked him, Miles, though he was a scallywag!'

K.P. fished a jade cigarette-holder from his pocket and made a long business of lighting a cigarette. His hand shook slightly.

'I hadn't seen him for years before I bumped into him on the plane,' Miles said. 'He was overflowing with big talk about something portentous about to happen. Now his big coup will never come off. Well, he never cheated anyone who didn't deserve to be cheated . . . invite cheating.'

'That may be true, but his behaviour was often inexcusable,' pronounced K.P., the Chinese puritan. 'I suppose life wasn't easy for him . . . Miles, from the way he talked he was involved in a very big deal this time.'

'What did he want from you?'

'Hard to say. Between the champagne and the Pernod, I was pretty mixed up. But he obviously had two things on his mind. Something . . . he didn't say what . . . some object was coming out of China. He was asking whether any artists or connoisseurs had come from the mainland – or were coming out. He also talked about Montague.'

'Montague?' Miles exclaimed. 'Who's Montague?'

'You wouldn't remember. It was in Chungking in 1945, before your time. Cecil Edward Frederick Montague was a junior political officer on the staff of the Viceroy in Delhi. He often came over the Hump on courier flights. My father says those trips benefited Monty's collection much more than His Majesty's Government.'

'Monty!' Corrigan exclaimed. 'I do remember hearing about him. He and Humphrey were very thick. Humphrey used to say Monty didn't give a damn how he got hold of a piece – as long as he got it. What did Humphrey say about Monty this time?'

'He rambled, Miles,' K.P. recalled. 'How Monty'd come up in the world: Senior Political Adviser in the

Office of the British High Commissioner for Southeast Asia in Singapore. Humphrey seemed puzzled himself. He said many people were asking about Monty, but he didn't know why. And he wouldn't say who they were.'

'What about connoisseurs or artists coming out of China?'

'There's always a trickle, cultural missions en route to Southeast Asia, India, or Africa. Matter of fact, one's due next week – a delegation of painters to Indonesia.'

Miles brushed away the cowlick that fell over his forehead and asked: 'Anything else? Anything at all?'

'I'm still muzzy. But I remember now. Humphrey asked about Professor Turner Lee several times. You know Turner got into trouble at the beginning of the Communist regime, but then he went over whole-heartedly. He's living in Peking now, writing for the Communists.'

The young art dealer reached into a wall cabinet and brought out a bottle of Remy Martin cognac. Elaborately casual, he filled two tumblers and pushed one towards Miles.

'I'd heard not a word about Turner Lee for a year or so,' K.P. continued. 'But his daughter Hyacinth's living in Kowloon. She works for the British Council.'

Raising his tumbler, K. P. Soong said formally: 'Let us hope Humphrey has gone to a place where there are many beautiful things. Also many customers who want them badly – and don't care where the objects come from.'

VI

Sweaty throngs flowed through the narrow canyon of Queen's Road Central, jostling each other unmercifully. Miles gave way to the warning 'Hoo-hoo! Hoo-hoo!' of barefoot coolies, weaving under heavy wooden crates suspended from bamboo poles laid across their shoulders. He side-stepped beggars in rags and portly merchants in black silk. He dodged shop girls in knee-length Western skirts and maidservants in white tunics and black trousers. He gave way to muscular toughs in singlets and to British sailors who wore extravagantly bell-bottomed trousers and bore the marks of childhood malnutrition on their pinched faces.

A plump American tourist was industriously clicking the shutter of his Japanese camera. Miles's gaze followed the direction of the lens to note appreciatively that the side-slits in the skirts of silk cheongsams were three inches higher than last year. Preoccupied, he almost missed his turning, but at the last moment wheeled to toil up the stone stairs of a street so steep no car could climb it.

The Colony's best family-style restaurant did business under the gilded sign of the Golden Goose. A waiter in a soiled undershirt conjured up a steaming towel and a bowl of noodles with pork. Although not particularly hungry,

Miles knew he would be sorry later if he did not eat now. Better the casual Golden Goose than an alcoholic lunch at Jimmy's Kitchen, with the chatter of old friends making it impossible to think.

He poked at the tangled noodles with bamboo chopsticks. The Chinese could do anything with bamboo except extract atomic energy, and they would probably get around to that in time. He hooked a single strand and tried to pull it out unbroken, but it snapped before he could free either end from the skein.

The puzzle that confronted him was just as tangled. Since he could probably never prove his suspicions, he did not intend to try. Well, he wouldn't try *too* hard.

Yet he had to know whether he was himself under threat – and whether he should take evasive action. Regardless of whose hand had actually pushed Humphrey off the walla-walla, Miles surmised, a distant hand had pulled the long string that jerked him into the dark waters of Hong Kong harbour. The same hand had almost certainly pulled the hijackers' strings.

The manner of Humphrey's death further signalled that his last deal might in truth have been the big one he had chased all his life. If that big deal were still coming off, Miles might well profit from it.

Yet he hardly knew how to begin tracking it down. He had hooked part of the strand, but he could see neither end – and the strand would break if he pulled too hard. Presumably one end led to Monty – Cecil Edward Frederick Montague, Senior Political Adviser to Her Britannic Majesty's High Commissioner for Southeast Asia. The other end? Miles could not even guess, although somewhere along the strand were enmeshed not only the Green Lotus Lodge, but courtly Turner Lee, whose Confucian calm concealed much passion.

Miles remembered Professor Turner Lee from 1947, when the best and the worst in China had congregated in the Yangtze River city called Nanking, the southern capital. Turner was an idealist and a perfectionist, a conjunction virtually certain to make him or anyone unhappy. He, his wife, and two teenage children crammed into one room, he was hard-pressed financially at a time of raging inflation. The city in which he just managed to exist was already half-resigned to being conquered by Mao Tse-tung's People's Liberation Army.

Turner Lee posssessed twofold distinction as one 'returned from studies abroad', having attended universities in both the United States and England. He had also possessed a minor government sinecure. He brooded over more than fourteen thousand crates filled with China's art treasures, which had originally been packed, ready for flight from the Japanese, in Peking in 1936. Occasionally, he chose a scroll, a figurine, or a bronze for reproduction on a propaganda poster.

Like almost all Chinese whom young Americans considered 'good guys', Turner had been disdainful of the Nationalist government. Unlike most of those good guys, unlike almost all educated Chinese, he was not enticed by Communist promises. Basically apolitical, he was immersed in the other-worldly philosophy of Zen Buddhism, which inspired the misty black-ink paintings he loved. When he talked of his country's turmoil, he was equally contemptuous of 'those who are presently misruling China and those who will shortly misrule China'.

A brilliant connoisseur of China's masterpieces, Turner Lee scorned the 'daubs and squiggles' of Western abstract art – and entertained almost as little regard for Western realistic art.

'Abstract artists run away,' he had once expounded to

Miles over cups of strong *pu-erh* tea from Yunnan. 'They confront neither the human dilemma nor human nature directly. Instead they twist, turn, and evade both challengers. Yet the Zen masters, even at their most sublime, never parted with reality. Nor did they scorn the representational.

'So many Western painters never got beyond surface representation. But the Zen masters progressed from realism to the hidden secrets of the universe, the essence of life. Zen is mysticism with discipline, mysticism rooted in reality. A hill, a river, or a temple mistily seen expresses the logically inexplicable, the conventionally indefinable.'

Miles remembered that observation well. He had reconstructed the words from his notes after reading the recantation entitled 'Socialism and Zen' that Turner Lee wrote for the *Peking Literary Gazette* a few years later:

> Miles Corrigan was typical, a rapacious American
> vulture preying on Chinese culture. While
> pretending to be a connoisseur of art, he was actually
> stealing China's national treasures under the orders
> of American intelligence agencies co-operating with
> the traitors of the Nationalist Secret Service.

So much for the confused, idealistic young Naval lieutenant who had been trying to learn more about China's artistic heritage and trying just as hard to understand China's bewildering political upheaval. After that denunciation, Dr Turner Lee had kowtowed to his new masters:

> Socialist painting has attained the essence of the
> universe, though some persons, obsessed with
> technique, have criticised our new painters as crude
> and purely representational. Socialist painting has,
> however, finally attained the goal sought by Zen's
> eternal quest. We have now achieved the previously

impossible – and we see that the mysterious essence towards which the Zen masters strove was the welfare of the people. Under the inspired leadership of the Communist Party and Chairman Mao Tse-tung, Socialist painters have finally attained the ultimate because they put first of all the doctrine of serving the people.

Emerging from his recollections, Miles saw that he had finished the tangled bowl of noodles and the waiter was gesturing towards waiting customers. He paid the bill, reflecting that he would become as irrational as Turner Lee himself if he seriously tried to follow the old connoisseur's tortuous reasoning.

Instead, he telephoned Turner Lee's daughter Hyacinth at the British Council. Surprised yet pleased to hear from him, she happily agreed to see him that evening. He then set out on the round of business appointments arranged before his arrival.

However much the fate of Turner Lee and Humphrey Enwright intrigued him, whatever pot of gold might lie at the end of the rainbow he was chasing, the de Sola Gallery had to be stocked with new *objets d'art* now. If the gallery were bare, Miles de Sola Corrigan would find it very hard to indulge his expensive tastes.

VII

The clouds burst late that afternoon, and translucent cascades curtained buildings only fifty feet away. After forty minutes a slow drizzle settled in. When Miles stepped into a taxi after dining alone at Gaddi's in the Peninsula, the streets of Kowloon were shimmering ribbons of black silk studded with the jewel-bright reflections of neon signs.

The taxi-driver peered through his misted windshield, searching for 15 Kensington Mews. That short dead-end street in overwhelmingly Chinese-populated Hong Kong, palisaded by half-timbered Tudor bungalows, was as Chinese as steak-and-kidney pudding. Light shone from a window beside the red door of Number 15, and a small amah in white tunic and black trousers answered the bell. The thick plait of hair hanging down her back swayed as she led Miles into the house.

An unseen phonograph was playing Rimsky-Korsakov's 'Song of India' when he stepped through an arch into a room entirely hung with red silk. The curtains parted only to show a single ink-brushed scroll. Fine gradations of grey evoked, rather than depicted, a tiny village nestling beneath a many-cragged mountain.

A hint of incense hung in the air, and a bottle of Courvoisier VSOP stood on a low black-wood table. A woman in her mid-twenties lolled on a deep blue-silk sofa, a balloon glass in her hand. When she rose, the high slit in her tight black skirt showed a triangle of white thigh above her stocking-top.

'How do you like the stage setting?' She gestured expansively. 'A lover of the Orient should appreciate it. Some Courvoisier?'

'With thanks,' Miles answered. 'How are you, Hyacinth?'

'I'm fine, I suppose. Still pleased that you remembered me after all those years.'

She watched unblinking as he poured the brandy.

'I've never forgotten you, Miles,' she added. 'The idealistic young American who loved China . . . whose conversation my father so enjoyed. When I was a little girl, I used to call you *Mei-guo Sien-sheng* – Mr America. I thought you were wonderful.'

'I didn't know I'd made such a deep impression, Hyacinth. I'm flattered.'

'Of course, now I know it's all nonsense about American idealism,' she rejoined. 'And I know you're just a businessman. What do you want of me?'

'Just seeing you is worth the journey from New York.'

'As my father taught me to say, I am pleased that I find favour in your sight.' She poured more brandy into her balloon glass. 'What else do you want?'

'Only your excellent brandy.'

'Miles, don't play cloak-and-dagger games with me,' she directed. 'Tell me what you want.'

'I've hung up my cloak and my dagger. But I would like to talk about your father.'

'*What* about him?' Hyacinth set her glass down firmly. 'What do you want from him?'

'I'd just like to see him.'

'You can't,' she snapped. 'Do you remember what *ching-suan* means? Liquidation! Do you want to see him liquidated?'

'Of course not. But I hear he'll be in Hong Kong soon – and I'm afraid he's in danger. Do you remember Humphrey Enwright?'

She nodded.

'He died last night – murdered, I believe. Somehow, his death's tied up with your father.'

'You always bring trouble, the black bird.' Hyacinth brushed the back of his hand with her fingertips. 'You bring harm to others, but never to yourself. Like a diamond you cut anything, but can't be cut yourself.'

She took his hand in both of hers and held it against her cheek.

'Of course I remember Humphrey. But what possible connection can he have with my father?'

'Be careful, the diamond could chip.' Miles laughed. 'I'm not bringing trouble, only warning of possible trouble. I think Humphrey was killed because he was asking about your father . . . when he was coming to Hong Kong.'

'You know my father's coming to Hong Kong?'

'I guessed. But I don't know why or when.'

'You must *not* try to see him, Miles. Absolutely not. They're letting him out for a while, but the Communists are very suspicious. If he sees you . . . With your background, they'll be certain he wants to defect.'

Miles reclaimed his hand, poured himself a dollop of brandy and asked, 'Why let him out at all if they're suspicious . . . afraid he'll defect?'

'I can't tell you! I don't know! But you must absolutely *not* see him. Anyway, my brother won't let you.'

She sat up and smoothed her skirt over her silken knees. Unbidden, the little amah shuffled into the room in her cloth shoes.

'Ah Soo worries about me.' The mistress waved the maidservant out. 'She's very jealous.'

A flush like a pink pearl suffused Hyacinth's narrow face, rising to disappear under the curls that veiled her high forehead. Had the brandy made her flush or had he aroused complex emotions – anger, fear, or perhaps affection? Ignoring her cryptic remark, Miles took her hand again.

'I had no idea your brother was coming out,' he said. 'I only heard he was assistant editor of the *Ta Kung Pao*, the one they used to call *L'Impartial*.'

'He's coming along to watch Father – and to lecture me on my patriotic duty. Miles, please! You *must* leave them alone. You must *not* interfere.'

Miles sipped his brandy slowly. At length he drew a deep breath. It was going to be difficult.

'I don't mean any harm to your father or your brother,' he finally said. 'If only they felt the same about me. You saw what your father said about me in the *Literary Gazette*? Regardless of that, whatever game he's playing he's going to need help. Humphrey didn't amount to much, but someone took his life . . . Like it or not, I'm already involved. And you're better off with me on your side.'

'So you saw the article? Of course, you know he *had* to write it . . . Didn't really mean it.'

'But he wrote it,' Miles interposed. 'So the Lee family owes me something.'

'All right, I'll tell you what little I know,' she conceded.

'My father's with a cultural mission to Indonesia. He's stopping off in Singapore to deliver some scrolls to a wealthy collector.'

'Who?'

'I don't know.' Ostentatiously unemotional, she looked directly ahead. 'Peking only wants him to authenticate the scrolls. Who'd dare question his judgement? My brother's the watch-dog for Peking. They're staying with Morgan Tan, the rubber millionaire.'

She gulped her brandy and went on in the same flat tone: 'How could I know why Humphrey was killed? I do know it's nothing to do with the Lees. Father's mission, it's all on the up and up. No monkey business . . . Miles, you must *not* try to see him here. Just think, if anyone's in danger now, it's you. And you're a danger to him.'

Hyacinth folded her hands in her lap. Her expression did not change, but tears started in her eyes and trickled down her cheeks in two small rivulets.

'Now I've told you all I can . . . all I know,' she said. 'Ah Soo will put me to bed. You must go. But first kiss me. You used to kiss me goodnight in Nanking.'

Miles took the slight figure in his arms. The salty tears were real, though she was hardly a child now. Her lips responded to his gentle pressure, and the tip of her tongue darted into his mouth. Then her small fists pounded against his chest, pushing him away. He stepped back and turned to go, but she caught his hand.

'Miles, I've promised myself I'd take what I want!' Hyacinth's dark, secretive eyes opened wide. 'Whatever I want, if I *really* want it. Maybe I do, maybe I don't. But I'd like you to come with me.'

He followed her down a corridor, admiring her slender ankles and the sleek curves of her back outlined by her sheathlike cheongsam. Behind him, the amah's cloth shoes shuffled on the teak floorboards; before him, the musk-sweet scent of incense grew stronger.

Hyacinth led him into a half-lit bedroom, its walls concealed by pale-blue silk curtains embossed with the stylised Chinese character for happiness. A wide rosewood bed covered with a dark-crimson bedspread stood along one wall, its four rosewood pillars supporting a crimson canopy. The traditional Chinese marriage-bed was so high that a set of moveable steps stood beside it.

The furniture was all glowing pale-gold rosewood: a chest of drawers, a mirrored dressing table with gleaming brass handles, and two chairs cushioned in crimson silk. On a rosewood altar-table joss-sticks in a silver vase smouldered before a sinuous statuette carved in time-polished ivory.

'Kuan Yin, my patron!' Hyacinth indicated the statuette with a sweep of her pearl-pink fingernails. 'She's called the Goddess of Mercy. But you know she started millennia ago as a warrior demigod. So she's not wholly female: something between . . . something like me.'

Settling into a rosewood chair, Miles watched Ah Soo place a tray with the Courvoisier and two balloon glasses on the altar-table. The amah then closed the door and drew blue-silk curtains over the doorway. They were wholly isolated, almost as remote from bustling Hong Kong as if they were enclosed in the luxurious suite of an ocean liner. Completing the illusion, a concealed air-conditoner hummed softly.

Her cloth soles silent on the golden Tientsin carpet, Ah Soo opened the curtains on the far wall. The door thus revealed opened onto a bathroom walled with dark-bronze mirrors that reflected the outsize black bathtub sunk in the black marble floor.

'The previous tenant was a sybarite,' Hyacinth

explained matter of factly. 'Anyway, the concubine he kept here was a sybarite. So I now enjoy her comforts.'

Ah Soo turned the golden taps, and water began to flood the bath. She sprinkled pink powder from a blue-and-white porcelain jar into the water, and the scent of jasmine drifted through the suite.

'I told you Ah Soo likes to put me to bed.' Hyacinth smiled. 'She's from Swunduk, one of the professional amahs who never marry. They have different tastes.'

Miles sat silent, sipping his brandy and drawing on a cigarette.

'Nothing to say, Miles?'

'Nothing important. I'm very comfortable and very interested – though I'm wondering what role I'm supposed to play.'

'I'm wondering too. Anyway, Ah Soo likes to undress me. I thought you'd enjoy the ritual.'

The amah faced her mistress, her hands busy with the frogs that clasped the high collar of the form-fitting dress. She unzipped the diagonal closing, and Hyacinth stepped out of the black sheath. Ah Soo turned away, carefully folding the garment before placing it in an open drawer. Hyacinth stood motionless in a black slip trimmed with lace, an aloof smile on her pink-painted lips.

When the slip, too, was unzipped, Ah Soo flushed, and her tongue darted between her teeth. Miles felt his blood stir. But Hyacinth outwardly remained as unmoved as a young lady submitting to a dressmaker's fitting. It was, Miles reflected, a curious exhibition – and she was a curious kind of exhibitionist.

Ah Soo stepped behind her mistress to unfasten the diaphanous black brassiere. As she slid the silken straps over the ivory shoulders, her hands caressed the small, upright breasts, cupping their rotundity and trailing across their nipples. Hyacinth's pale-violet nipples rose in response to the caress. Her eyes sparkled, and her dreamy smile widened.

The amah laid the wispy garment away and knelt before her mistress. With deliberate pleasure, she slipped the black panties over the slight swell of slender hips, down rounded thighs and moulded calves. Eyes closed, Hyacinth submitted to the amah's gentle services. The black garter belt was unhooked, and the shimmering stockings rolled down her legs. She lifted each leg in turn to allow the amah to remove the stockings and stood naked. The delta between her thighs was almost hairless, its central parting clearly defined.

Still kneeling, Ah Soo leaned forward and delicately flicked her tongue between those lips. Her hands grasped Hyacinth's buttocks, and her tongue moved faster. But after a few moments, the mistress gently pushed the maidservant's head away.

'Miles, I thought you might enjoy watching.' Hyacinth spoke for the first time. 'But Ah Soo is disappointed.'

Slender hips swaying, Hyacinth lowered herself into the black jasmine-scented pool, her body gleaming ivory in the mirror-like water. Ah Soo knelt beside the sunken tub, hands busy with a soft cloth. She gently explored every crevice of Hyacinth's nakedness, lingering between the parted legs, stroking the yielding buttocks, and gliding over the distended nipples. Miles felt a swelling in his groin.

After a time, Hyacinth reluctantly rose into an enveloping, rose-coloured towel. Ah Soo patted her dry before dabbing her breasts and thighs with perfume. When Hyacinth's nakedness was draped with a rose-silk dressing-gown, she spoke again.

'The Japanese learned cleanliness from us Chinese,' she

observed casually. 'We must be absolutely impeccable before making love. Perhaps you'd like to bathe.'

Although Miles prided himself on his imperturbability, on being virtually impervious to shock, he had been startled and stirred by the languorous exhibition. He had also shared too many Japanese baths to hesitate at disrobing before two women. But he waved away Ah Soo's helping hands.

'Just as well!' Hyacinth laughed and climbed the stairs to bed. 'She'd do anything for you, but she wouldn't enjoy it. She's already burning with jealousy.'

The casual cruelty of Hyacinth's words disturbed Miles as he lowered himself into the scented water. She had candidly acknowledged her lesbian relations with the little amah. Merely because Hyacinth liked men as well as women was no reason for her to torment Ah Soo. He dismissed those thoughts and surrendered himself to the pleasure of Ah Soo's scrubbing his back. If she was rougher than necessary, there was pleasure in that too.

He climbed out of the tub and took a towel from Ah Soo, who averted her eyes. Towelling himself dry, he muttered thanks for the terrycloth robe the amah offered him. Hyacinth spoke briefly to Ah Soo in a dialect Miles did not know, and the amah left the room. As she drew the curtains before closing the door, she glanced without expression at the man who had usurped her place in her mistress's bed.

'If you'll join me with the brandy, I'll teach you an old Chinese game,' Hyacinth offered. 'Do you really *need* that robe?'

Miles's irritation at her highhanded treatment of the amah and even himself was overridden by curiosity. Hyacinth might be playing out a symbolic drama of revenge against the male sex. She was not only cruel to

Ah Soo, but appeared determined to humble him by taking absolute command. Yet whatever game she was playing, he, too, would play – for the moment, at least.

Still carrying his balloon glass, he mounted the step to the bed where Hyacinth shone ivory in the diffused light. She rose on one elbow, offering her lips in a quick tongue-darting kiss. Then she took the brandy from him and drew back.

'I'm keeping that promise to myself to take whatever I want,' she murmured. 'I want you.'

'I'm afire with curiosity, among other things. What's this game?'

'It's an old Chinese game called Bear Hunts Honey. You can be the he-bear first, then maybe I'll be the she-bear.'

She sipped her brandy and dribbled a few drops into the hollow of her throat.

'Hunt, bear!' she commanded. 'Hunt!'

Miles's tongue lapped the sweet drops of brandy. His mouth followed the trail of brandy she laid across her shoulder to the tip of a breast.

'Good bear!' she murmured. 'Clever bear.'

The trail led to her navel, and she wriggled in delight under his tongue's probing. Releasing the brandy drop by drop, the balloon glass hung over her arched belly and then moved lower.

'Lap, bear!' she commanded. 'Lap!'

Miles's tongue stroked her parted labia. Hyacinth writhed as his exploration grew bolder and his tongue penetrated deeper, lingering in flicking caresses.

'Good bear!' she gasped, opening her thighs wide. 'Come, bear, come!'

Later, she played the she-bear theatrically, snuffing loudly and following the brandy trail with deep-throated growls. Her ardent response to his renewed excitement belied her avowed lesbian inclinations. Their coupling was slow and luxurious the second time.

'It's a lovely game,' he whispered into her ear. 'Do you know many others?'

'Old Chinese game,' she murmured drowsily. 'Old Chinese game from Emperor's harem. The concubines experimented with each other . . . Hundreds of them, they got bored waiting for him.'

She was asleep. Miles gently disentangled himself and, while dressing, studied the ivory figure on the crimson bed. He felt a certain fondness welling up from the past. He also felt sympathy mingled with the exasperation inspired by a wilful perverse child. He let himself out, closing the bedroom door gently. Ah Soo was waiting to bolt the front door behind him. Her parting glance was malevolent yet, somehow, pitying.

Hyacinth Lee obviously inspired devotion, as well as evoking excitement by the wanton ingenuity with which she used her slender body. What other games did she play – in bed or out of bed? But his thoughts turned from Hyacinth to the Singapore rubber multimillionaire Morgan Tan when he stepped into the drizzle still falling on the darkness of Kensington Mews.

Hyacinth's father, Turner Lee, was planning to stay in Singapore with a man he despised. Morgan Tan had been Turner's class-mate at Peking University, and Turner had once described him as: 'A soulless Philistine, with neither moral nor aesthetic sense. He feels reverence only when contemplating a Straits Settlements five-hundred-dollar note.' Yet he was to be Turner Lee's host in Singapore – with the Communists' blessing.

'*Bieh-shar! Gan-bu jr yau jr-dau jer-ge jia-huor shr shei-yar!*'

Miles felt his arms seized from behind and saw the flicker of a torch as the hoarse whisper in a Peking accent entwined itself in his reverie: 'Don't kill him! The cadre just wants to know who this fellow is!'

His right heel lashed back, drawing an agonised grunt, and the grip on his arms loosened. His right hand knocked the torch tinkling to the ground. Following through, his shoulder flipped a body out of the way. He turned and began running, but saw in the next instant that he was racing towards the dead-end of the Mews. As he swivelled, a weight struck behind his ear – and he fell to the wet cobblestones.

Several minutes passed before Miles began to emerge from his doze, borne upwards by waves of pain. He fumbled for his lighter, while his left hand caressed the bump on his head. By the flickering light, he saw that his wallet lay open on the cobblestones. A black substance was smeared on his fingertips.

The assailants were thorough and relatively high-tech. Not content with the identification in his wallet, they had fingerprinted him.

Two separate groups, he concluded, were involved in the imbroglio into which he had wandered: the Green Lotus Society and Peking's agents, who were evidently watching over Hyacinth. The Green Lotus would hardly want his fingerprints, since they had no easy means to check them. But Peking undoubtedly had his prints on file.

If he were pitted against two separate groups of shadowy adversaries, he decided abruptly, discretion was not just the better course, but the only course. He had to get out of Hong Kong fast. And not only for safety. The action was almost certainly moving to Singapore.

VIII

'We plastered up every crack in the foundation, plugged every chink a cobra could possibly crawl through. But that night Mary heard the same slithering sound. I picked up my old Gurkha kukri and switched on the lights. Nowhere a snake to be seen, but the floorboards were rippling visibly.'

Rotund Alexander Cutler waved his beermug for emphasis. He was eternally curious, eagerly sniffing through Singapore's political maze and avidly collecting the macabre folklore of its Chinese and Malay inhabitants. He retold those tales with the theatrical zest he restrained in his reports for the staid British Broadcasting Corporation, which he served as Southeast Asia Correspondent.

'Alex loves his stories. But this was happening to *us*!'

Blonde Mary Cutler laughed. As ever, she seemed frail and ethereal in swarthy Singapore. Dark half-moons stained the fine skin under her eyes, which darted nervously from side to side.

'Like all gardeners, our old *kebun* is an authority on the supernatural. He said everyone knew our house had ghosts. Why else did we get it so cheap?' she continued. 'The ghost was sleeping on the roof of his own quarters.

So last week he asked his cousin, a famous exorcist from Rangan, to come down. This cousin chased the ghost away . . . right into *our* house. We're getting the exorcist down again this weekend. But *where* to send the ghost?'

The party swirled between Mary Cutler and the stolid teak sideboard, whose top was white-ringed from earlier parties. The basic Singapore selection was set out on the sideboard: brandy, gin, Scotch, and beer. An ice-bucket of Kelantan pewter was surrounded by ginger-ale, soda, Coca-Cola, Rose's lime juice, and boiled water in Gordon's Gin bottles.

Projecting on concrete pillars over the driveway, the room was vast, and the whitewashed ceiling was sixteen feet high. Nonetheless, cigarette and cheroot smoke hung over the guests like an evening mist. Though three doors and six windows were all open, four battered metal ceiling fans hardly stirred the fug. The cushions on the rattan furniture were covered with Indonesian batiks in abstract brown and blue patterns. Malay krisses with twisted blades hung on the walls, surrounding the two-handed samurai sword that occupied the central place of honour.

Two very young and very pink English subalterns seated on a rattan couch were arguing loudly. A small blue-black Indian woman no more than twenty-five or twenty-six in a red sari sprawled on a Tashkent prayer-rug at their feet, reading T. S. Eliot to a lean Malay with a wispy black beard.

'I know, John,' the stocky officer insisted. 'I saw it with my own eyes: they make Tiger beer and Anchor beer in the same vat, then put it into different bottles!'

'Nonsense, Dick!' snapped the second. 'There's a mellowness about Tiger which Anchor can't touch.'

'You were just as certain the map was wrong where it showed swamp,' Dick enunciated with barely controlled anger. 'And we spent two days floundering in the mud. You were just as sure you knew exactly where Ah Gee and his terrorists were hiding. But we never found them.'

Pained embarrassment flitted across John's face, and he said: 'My dear Dick, we agreed never to . . . After the wigging the adjutant gave me . . .'

'I *am* sorry. You couldn't help it. And it would have been madly exciting if you'd been right.'

The waves of the party broke over them, drowning their voices. Miles took Alex Cutler's arm and drew him towards the veranda.

'Can we talk before the next act of the circus?'

The correspondent's grin thrust his pointed black beard forward, heightening the Mephistophelean manner he cultivated.

'Miles, my performing animals're splendid . . . perform whether the ringmaster is present or not. There's nice distribution tonight. The older animals, mostly Limeys from the university, have trained the younger ones.'

Miles watched the oil lamps twinkling in the adjoining Malay kampong while he told his tale to the BBC Correspondent. Plump Alex was amiably slovenly. Yet not only his jealous colleagues, but even arrogant local politicians and condescending diplomats agreed that he was the best informed man in Southeast Asia.

'. . . after the attack, which I did *not* report, I felt Hyacinth was probably right,' Miles summed up. 'I was bringing danger on her head. Nor was I exactly joyous about danger descending on my head. So I came down here. The next act in this melodrama should unfold in Singapore – if it is a melodrama and not a farce. I'm worried about old Turner Lee. I can't see Chairman Mao letting him out unless the stakes are *very* high.'

Cutler quaffed the warm dregs from his beermug and

wiped his mouth with the back of his hand. He belched delicately and said: 'I assume you've come to me for background, as well as specifics.'

'What's your fee?'

'No fee now. Not till you find the mate of my Tang camel. Then we'll wipe the slate clean. As for specifics, I can have Professor Lee "frisked" when he comes through Customs tomorrow. He won't even know it's happened. We Brits still control the Special Branch.'

With automatic annoyance, Miles noted the inverted commas placed around the Americanism 'frisked' by Cutler's change of tone.

'As for the background, best come and listen to the animals. Your Professor Lee couldn't have picked a more dangerous time to come to our City of Lions. The opposing forces are deployed, and the battle for Singapore is about to start. Some of the leaders of the overt left and their camp-followers are here tonight.'

'What about the racial line-up?' Miles interposed. 'Still the same?'

'You really want me to go back to basics, do you? Yes, just about the same. The populace is about 1.2 million. Three-quarters are Chinese: the entrepreneurs, the bankers, and the shopkeepers. A sprinkling of British, who still run the place as a colony, though that's changing. Maybe ten per cent Indians: mostly clerks and professionals. And all the rest Malays, the sons of the soil who were dispossessed when the Sultan sold Singapore to Stamford Raffles a century and a half ago. As you know, Miles, Malays are policemen, drivers, and servants. All good Mohammedans, of course.'

'Just checking, Alex. And the political set up?'

'You'll see. Basically, the war in the jungle goes on up-country in Malaya. Chinese Communist guerrillas against the British. And here in Singapore, a welter of parties spread across the spectrum from the centre to the far left. All contending for power when the British leave. A number fighting to make that departure come quickly . . . with maximum humiliation to the old colonial overlords. But you can see for yourself.'

The group in the big room, whose teak floor sloped slightly on sinking concrete pillars, was more like a university party than a gathering of conspirators. It could have been Cambridge, England, or Cambridge, Massachusetts, except for the variety of races. Complexions ranged from the purple-black of South India through the cinnamon brown of Malays and the pale ivory of Chinese to the ruddy pink of British. Otherwise it was like any gathering of self-conscious intellectuals and would-be politicians anywhere.

Self-conscious mock-profundities and throbbing music were interspersed with adolescent profanity. Miles joined a small group around a lean, swarthy man wearing a belted safari-jacket of beige silk. A whey-faced blonde sat beside him, caressing his hairy hand, which lay in her lap meditatively rotating her buttocks against the sofa cushion.

'Paul da Silva,' Cutler whispered. 'Secretary-General of the Masses Operation Party – MOP to you. She's Janet Digby, a Londoner who sleeps with Paul, types for the Special Branch, and wants to marry a young Scots captain who's chasing terrorists on the Thai border . . . I'll leave you for a while.'

Intent on his own words, da Silva paused occasionally to drink from the glass in his free hand.

'. . . can't expect the British to *give* us anything. We must take what they offer and show our contempt for them at the same time . . .'

Miles looked speculatively at the pale English girl on the sofa. It sounded like an interesting relationship.

'Their ostensible concessions are intended to sap our will. They want to weaken our resolution so we'll accept their so-called liberal reforms. The British, in turn, obey their mock-democratic Yankee bosses. They offer us tinsel ideals and gold-plated handcuffs.'

Da Silva glanced round to reassure himself that his audience was attentive, sipped his whisky, and resumed: 'I deplore violence, and I weep at its consequences. But no revolution was ever made without violence. I fear Singapore's will prove no exception.

'The Universal Workers' Union speaks for the people. But the puppet government even questions the *bona fides* of our membership. We counsel moderation, but the people are growing angry.

'Then the arrests. Five men, simple Chinese workers, clerks and intellectuals, all arrested without cause. The people demand action. If the Chief Minister wants a general strike he'll get his general strike. How can peace-loving union leaders forestall violence? Injustice demands vengeance, and we cannot prevent such just vengeance.'

Paul da Silva paused, reclaimed his hand from the Englishwoman's lap to light a cigarette, and called to the Chinese waiter lounging against the sideboard.

'Boy, another whisky. Make it a double!'

After that imperious command, da Silva spoke again, his tone even more theatrical. He was, Miles realised, a compulsive orator, a man infatuated with his own words, who would speak whenever and wherever an audience offered itself.

'Remember, the students are with us. Students at Chinese-language high schools have turned their back on the mess of pottage offered by the colonialists and the

(86)

capitalists. Inspired by their great Motherland, they will fight shoulder-to-shoulder with the oppressed workers.

'All know that the ultimate enemy is not the decadent British, but the rapacious Americans. US monopoly capitalism encourages . . . incites . . . the Colonial Governor and his hand-picked Chief Minister with their puppets in the Legislative Assembly. The blood-stained Americans will commit any atrocity. But we shall prevail!'

An overbred English voice piped in the sudden silence: 'A stirring recital, Paul. As moving as your speech under the banyan tree. Do remember some of us English are good . . . some of us are with you.'

The lawyer sat silent, enjoying the adulation.

'Sometimes he almost frightens me,' confided the gawky Englishman to the slender brown-haired young woman who had come into the room beside him.

'Hullo, Tommy,' da Silva finally said without enthusiasm. 'How are you, Tanya? I'd hoped to see you here earlier, but now I must go.'

Blonde Janet Digby obediently rose and followed her master through the door. The room was suddenly silent, even the bearded Malay and the tiny Indian woman in the red sari relaxing as if a high-power circuit had been switched off. Released from the emotional tension, Miles turned to the newcomers.

'I'm Tommy Willing,' the Englishman drawled. 'And this is Tanya Tan.'

With detached interest, Miles noted her white-matte complexion and the faintly Oriental cast of her eyes.

'My name is Corrigan, and I sell pictures, and I'm an American,' he said. 'But I haven't eaten an underprivileged baby in years.'

Willing smiled nervously, and the young woman's eyes widened in silent reproach.

'I'm sure you don't, Mr Corrigan.' Tanya Tan's intonation was hauntingly continental. 'You're too well set up to breakfast on underprivileged babies. They're mostly skin, bone, and gristle. Anyway, some of us think not *all* Americans are beasts.'

She had somehow created an immediate atmosphere of intimacy that made Miles regret his aggressive words.

'Thanks for your kindness,' he said. 'Sorry about the outburst, but I was beginning to feel persecuted. A drink to seal our understanding?'

Tommy Willing had drifted off to hover like an ancient heron over the small-boned Indian woman in the red sari.

'Yes, please, gin and lime. I'm afraid my attitude's not typical. I'm tainted by bourgeois thought, as my friend Aziz would say.' Tanya Tan nodded towards the bearded Malay. 'You see, my father is Morgan Tan. Perhaps you've heard of him – the big, bad, bloated rubber capitalist.'

'My name really is Miles Corrigan, and I do sell pictures and statues in New York. I'm an exploiter too. I pay my artists nothing. Most are long dead.'

Miles glanced at the delicate high-bred ankles beneath her pale-blue dress. Despite the modified high Chinese collar, the loose bodice and the full skirt gave her a Russian air. He turned to the bottle-laden sideboard.

'What does Paul da Silva want?' he asked bluntly on returning. 'And who backs him?'

'The first question's easy. He wants power. As for the second, I can only tell you he's general counsel for the Universal Workers' Union. My leftist friends insist that UWU is a "popular movement". My conservative friends and my American friends insist it's a "Communist front".'

Again inverted commas, Miles noted. It seemed to be his night for people who voiced punctuation marks.

'I do know the UWU is the *only* effective union we've ever had in Singapore, the only union that ever got anything out of my father,' Tanya added. 'Anyway, Paul is determined to gain power through the Masses Operation Party. He's secretary-general, you know. He's madly learning Chinese so that he can talk to his supporters.'

She glanced at her wrist-watch.

'Mr Corrigan, I hope we can continue our talk some other time soon. I must go now.'

'May I take you home?' he blurted.

'I'm sorry. I promised Tommy I'd go to another party with his friends from the Colonial Government. We keep on good terms with all.'

She turned and was gone. Corrigan felt a glass pushed into his hand and turned to find his host beaming ghoulishly.

'East meets West in Singapore!' Alex wiped drops of beer from his beard. 'She's a good girl, Miles. But, I'm afraid, too much a combination of opposites to be happy. She told you who her father is?'

'She did.'

'She always does. She's obsessed with the old man. I can't tell if it's an unnatural attraction, or somewhat overdone filial affection or sheer hatred. Her mother was a White Russian governess in a very stuffy Swiss bourgeois family. It's questionable whether she and Morgan Tan were ever married. But that was another age, and besides, the poor wench is dead.'

Miles sipped his drink and grinned in appreciation. His host had given him marc. Alex *did* remember everything. He turned to say his thanks, but Alex had hurtled onto the veranda, where a British subaltern and a Chinese youth were rolling on the floor punching each other. The correspondent grabbed their collars, separated the combatants, soothed them with fresh drinks, and returned puffing slightly.

'The animals are in good form tonight. That started with: "I hope my cousins get you in the jungle, you cheap mercenary!" Now they're swearing they're the best of friends.'

He paused to pour a fresh mug of beer. When he spoke again, his tone was grave.

'Miles, they're not friends – and they never will be. The circus is getting out of hand. Singapore is a Chinese city, a volatile Chinese city. This time, it's serious. Someone wants those five "ordinary Chinese working-men" of da Silva's released. Someone's ready to turn the city into a bear-pit to get them released. But I'm puzzled. I simply can't see why the five're so important to the left.'

'A good pretext, Alex? For a demonstration of strength?'

'Maybe, but the risks are very high for the stakes. The deportees are cogs in the leftist organisation, just not that important. Besides, UWU and MOP aren't ready for a showdown yet, I'd swear it. Their organisation's not yet up to snuff. But the showdown's coming nonetheless!'

IX

The worst part of the hangover was not his throbbing temples or sandpaper tongue, though they were torture themselves. Those symptoms, which had persisted into late afternoon, came from mixing the beer, marc, and whisky abundantly provided by Alex Cutler. The worst part was the mental torment. Afflicted by profound depression, he felt totally detached from the external world and an overwhelming sense of futility.

Driven from his bed early by the hangover, Miles had already wasted most of the day. He had driven some fifty miles to Johore Bahru, the Sultan's capital on the northern shore of the narrow Singapore Straits, in order to view a highly touted collection. But it had proved to be nothing more exciting than late Ching copies of Tang and Wei figures – a difference of a thousand years and tens of thousands of dollars.

The old Cantonese owner had oscillated nervously between pride in the mediocre objects and hope of gain. Miles had finally escaped by pleading that the statuettes were so magnificent that none of his customers could possibly afford them. But the old gentleman had undoubtedly been wounded in both his passions, the aesthetic and the mercenary.

The only cure for a vile hangover that lingered into the stale end of a steamy Singapore afternoon was lots of liquids: cold beer taken internally and a swimming pool applied externally. Miles's rented Porsche was jaunty in its red paint, but hot, much too hot, to the eye and to the touch. Driving a Porsche was, for once, not a pleasure, but an ordeal, as much because of the scenes outside as the hot-box within which he sat.

Once serene Bukit Timah Road had become a daunting gauntlet since he last drove it a year earlier. Along the roadside, blue police Land Rovers, their windows shielded by steel grills, alternated with red riot-vans. Idling in slat-sided trucks, detachments of dark-skinned Malay riot police were accoutred with gas-masks, wicker shields, long truncheons, and rifles.

The factories lining the road were now miniature forts. Sentries in work clothes paced inside hasty barbed-wire barricades, bandannas tied under their eyes to hide their features. Bold black signs in Chinese and English draped fences and stretched across the road from palm tree to palm tree: WE UPHOLD DEMOCRATIC RIGHT TO STRIKE TILL OUR LEADERS ARE RELEASED! And ominously: IF NO RELEASE OF MARTYRS – GENERAL STRIKE!

Miles had known the strike was starting when he left downtown Singapore, but he was shocked by its rapid spread, which confirmed the fears of Alex Cutler, who was no alarmist. The BBC Correspondent had talked of conspirators 'turning the city into a bear-pit'. The foreboding of violence Miles felt in the air as he drove along the Bukit Timah Road was as real as the smothering heat.

Up country in Malaya the British were already fighting a new war. The enemy was the Communist-led Overseas

Chinese, many of whom had fought beside the British against Japanese invaders fourteen years earlier – fought at least as well and often better than British and Australian units.

Singapore, too, remembered the war against the Japanese. One of the fortresses the workers had now improvised was the gleaming white Ford Motor Car assembly plant where Lieutenant General Sir William Percival had surrendered his sword and His Britannic Majesty's Crown Colony of Singapore to the invaders. A little south of the Ford plant lay the stretch of road where five thousand Chinese volunteers had fallen in a gallant and desperate battle against the Japanese. That last stand was quite different from the mixed behaviour of their allies, which had occasionally been heroic, but was largely muddle and funk. The Chinese irregulars had fought to the death, hating the Japanese for the devastation they had already wreaked on China herself.

A Chinese Singapore, Miles reflected wryly, would never again resist an invader in defence of British rule, though it might rise against British rule. Past, present, and future were meeting on the Bukit Timah Road in a violent and potentially catastrophic collision.

Miles glanced at his watch, and pressed down on the accelerator. He would unavoidably be late for his appointment with Turner Lee at the Coconut Grove, which also had its memories. But, he hoped, not too late.

The red Porsche at length whipped through the mouldering iron gates. Only in Singapore, perhaps only at the ill-omened Coconut Grove, did iron moulder visibly. Driving up the curved driveway to the decaying, white-pillared mansion, Miles recalled the tales he had heard of the years when the boarding house was the headquarters of the Kempeitai, the Japanese Military Police, who were more brutal than the Gestapo. The old vaudevillian Bill Bailey who now ran the Coconut Grove – or, more accurately put, allowed it to operate around himself – still had trouble keeping Chinese employees. Almost all those highly superstitious souls in time heard the ghosts who walked by night, awakened by fearful shrieks from the old torture chambers – though both victims and tormentors had been dead for a decade.

Miles left the Porsche in the muddy driveway and returned to the troubled present. The day had begun with a telephone call from Alex.

'Your carrier pigeon flew in this morning,' the correspondent announced cheerfully. 'The boys gave him a good going over, I'm sorry, Miles, but he carried nothing extraordinary . . . A few scrolls of some value . . . technical and political literature on art . . . and the usual impedimenta: shaving kit, medicines, and so on. But absolutely nothing of special interest. When Customs got through with him, he was whisked off to Morgan Tan's house.'

The correspondent paused and Miles could hear the inrush of breath as he inhaled smoke.

'A peculiar pair, the intellectual commissar and the bloated capitalist,' Cutler observed. 'Even so, maybe you're on a wild goose chase . . . chasing up a blind alley!'

Miles was by no means sure that he was not on a wild goose chase. He had grown doubtful when he telephoned Turner Lee at Morgan Tan's residence. It was too easy.

The houseboy had cut him off when he asked in English for Turner Lee. But he had called again, declaring in Mandarin that he was the editor of Singapore's farthest left tabloid. Turner had then come on the line, remembered him immediately, and agreed to meet at the Coconut Grove that afternoon – all with no apparent hesitation.

Regardless, Miles was eager to see the old man again after seven or eight years. It was not just nostalgia tinged with affection and curiosity. He was due an explanation for the lies Turner had told about him in the *Literary Gazette*. His sophomoric streak might be asserting itself again, but he hoped Turner could explain the unprovoked attack. He had been very fond of the older man in Nanking, and he believed Turner had also felt some fondness for him. Could politics, Miles wondered, really extirpate *all* normal human feeling?

Whatever else had changed in Singapore, the Coconut Grove had not. It remained dilapidated, silent, and permeated with the sour stench of yesterday's beer. Miles walked through the deserted bar into the courtyard, his heels clicking on the terrazzo floor.

Decked out in a white-linen suit and white shoes, Turner Lee was playing with a Malayan brown bear cub, pushing bananas through the bars of its cage and dodging the animal's clumsy attempts to nip his fingers. He had not altered much, only grown more slender, his features fined down and his silvery aura more pronounced. Wiping his hands on his handkerchief, he came forward to greet Miles.

'I'm playing hookey,' he said. 'Just to see you again. Hyacinth . . . why must girls choose such peculiar names? Anyway, Hyacinth told me how kind you were to her in Hong Kong.'

Relieved that the volatile Hyacinth had been discreet, Miles replied: 'It's good to see you, Dr Lee. But I can't claim credit for kindness . . . just a worried warning.'

'Be that as it may, she was pleased. I must admit I myself have always felt you were one of the best among the all-knowing young men who came to save us Chinese from our own base nature.'

Turner Lee waggled his fingers promisingly at the bear cub, which was snuffling at the bars of the cage, clearly demanding that his benefactor return.

'Besides, I haven't seen anyone much lately,' he added. 'I've been cooped up. So I was particularly glad you called . . . Hyacinth said you'd seen what I was compelled to write about you. I know you want an explanation. But an old man chooses to assume you are also moved by some affection!'

Turner Lee spoke with the harsh Chinese frankness that so often startles the foreigner who is convinced that, if he knows anything at all about the Chinese, he knows they are devious.

Miles cursed his hangover, the heat, Singapore, and his own insensitivity. Turner had deftly deflected his indignation. He could not play the injured innocent, even though he would have been wholly justified. Also, there was Hyacinth, whom he had apparently pleased. There were other words, but *pleased* would do for the time being.

'Mr Lee,' he said, 'when I walked in here I was trying to decide to what I looked forward most – seeing you again, getting an explanation of your attack on me, or satisfying my curiosity as to what you're up to here.'

'I must admit I did say some harsh things,' the older man observed vaguely. 'They weren't *all* completely true . . . In fact some may've been completely untrue. Your curiosity, however, must remain unsatisfied. But I'd be delighted to give you a drink. Cold beer seems the universal panacea here. Perhaps, in turn, you can tell me a little about the world I've missed seeing the last few years.'

A barefoot Chinese youth, chubby in a soiled undershirt and stained white-drill shorts, slapped two tall glasses onto the rattan table. After counting out change with frowning concentration, he seated himself on a wicker stool in the corner of the courtyard and retired behind a Chinese tabloid. Miles automatically read out the banner headline: AMERICAN IMPERIALISTS ONCE MORE INVADE CHINA'S TERRITORY OF TAIWAN.

'It's ironic you Americans are so opposed to the Chinese People's Government.' Turner Lee continued after the interruption. 'In Nanking, you bright young sparks used to cry out: "Look at all this misery. If only these Nationalist bastards would do something! To hell with democracy! There has to be blood-letting!" Now you've got what you wanted. The Communists *always* act vigorously. Yet Americans are unhappy. I must admit it puzzles me.'

'It's never struck me quite that way,' Miles muttered evasively. 'But certain universal human values do appear to have perished in China.'

'Undoubtedly!' Turner replied. 'Perhaps, unnecessarily. I must admit it that as an old man, I find it all rather trying . . . extremely trying. This new era is for the young.'

'Some of the young aren't wildly enthusiastic about the People's Government!'

'Perhaps. Still, there are so many of us Chinese – young and old. As for myself, I must admit to great fatigue. So much activity! So much in vain!'

'Spinning their wheels, you mean?'

'Quite, though I haven't heard that graphic American idiom in a long time. Nonetheless you practical Americans should rejoice. Dams are built; children are inoculated; railroads are repaired and extended; steel mills are rising; and farms are consolidated for efficiency.'

'Quite a trick,' Miles objected, 'to make hardworking Chinese farmers even more efficient.'

'To the contrary. I must say there's much room for progress in farming: chemical fertilisers and insecticides, more efficient irrigation, widespread mechanisation . . . As a Chinese, I rejoice at my country's new strength, though as a human being I grieve that so many individuals are sacrificed for the masses. As an unreconstructed bourgeois aesthete, I fear this frantic assault on the material world will actually remove us further from reality. Perhaps we don't really know where we're going. I'm confused.'

Miles's assessment of this new Turner Lee was also less than clear. Such apparently candid self-revelation might be meant to veil the old man's meaning. In any event, it did. To talk so openly and so critically, Turner must either be very secure or very frightened, almost beyond hope. But which?

The older man absently signalled for more beer. While waiting for the barefoot youth to move, he rose and poked another banana through the bars to the bear-cub.

'I never wanted the Communists – and they know it,' he then resumed. 'They've never forgiven me my American friends, my fuzzy aesthetics – or my years at Harvard. They believe those years were a sybarite's delight, if not an outright orgy.

'Actually, I ruined my stomach at Harvard. I went into a teashop on my second day. I was confused by all the strange food. Finally, I pointed at the watercress-and-crabmeat sandwiches. Do you know I lived on watercress-and-crabmeat sandwiches for six weeks?'

Miles knew the quaint tale was true, although he had been dubious when he first heard Turner talk about that eccentric diet. Later a friend of his mother had recalled at a dinner party in New York the little Chinese who lived on watercress-and-crabmeat sandwiches until directed to the baked beans and brown bread that were to be his staples for the following month. He did not speak of the coincidence, for Turner's words, so long pent up, were in full spate.

'They'll never forgive me my American friends. Are you Americans better at forgiving? What about you, Miles? Can you forgive what I wrote?'

'I don't know, Dr Lee. But I'm delighted to drink beer with you. I suppose I was a little avid in those days.'

'Miles, my article didn't say you were avid. I said you were the agent of a vast American conspiracy to loot China of her art treasures. Actually, you *were* a bit of a looter. I must admit I sometimes found it hard to distinguish your love of beauty from your acquisitive instinct.'

'Maybe I was a minor-league looter. But an agent of a vast conspiracy?'

'Politics, my boy, politics! I had to write their way to survive. But you must admit you and your friends did spirit away some beautiful objects.'

Turner was in full flood, the sluice-gates open after a decade when he could not utter a word without fear.

'Still I've learned not to condemn . . . I've given up absolute moral judgements. In China now there is bloodshed, carnage, and much suffering. But every dynasty has come to power through violence and cemented its greatest works with blood. Ruthlessness . . . even cruelty may be necessary. Human suffering stamps every great human achievement like a master painter's seal.'

The grey-and-white figure rose arthritically and shuffled across to poke another banana through the bars of the cub's cage. He resumed when he was again seated at the rickety table.

'Paradoxically, each dynasty created its greatest art when it began to decay, shortly after attaining its apogee!

'The orchid is most beautiful when faintly overblown. Perhaps out of human suffering and brute materialism great beauty will emerge again. Yet I must admit I can see no justification for a young dynasty's seeking to impose its will – and its suffering – on outsiders.'

The last sentence had a harder ring than the previous rambling. Miles had never subscribed to the popular belief that the Chinese are devious. The Chinese, he felt, had in good part acquired their reputation for deviousness by saying exactly what they believed. Candour was a good way to deceive both self-anointed experts and excessively subtle diplomats in any age. But Miles could not make out what the old aesthete was really saying now.

'Moral judgements only have their meaning against specific circumstances,' he temporised. 'Present excesses in China are in no way justified by anticipated future benefits. By the same token, I cannot condemn what is done in Peking because it is *not* done in San Francisco. Regardless, one aspect of Peking's behaviour is totally unjustifiable – suppressing art and literature.'

'Yes, it's sterile just now,' Turner Lee half-agreed. 'But most plants bloom better after vigorous pruning. Our great Tang dynasty rigorously suppressed innovation, particularly the new cult of Buddhism and its art. But the Tang produced our finest writers. Also . . .'

Turner Lee stopped abruptly and sipped his beer. His expression was for once easy to read. Like a chess master he was considering his next move.

'Also, out of the decay of the Tang came the most fragrant legend of all,' he finally said. 'I mean Yang Kuei-fei, the sparrow-plump concubine who turned an emperor's head and almost destroyed a dynasty by her rapacity. Yet this girl, this cunning miss who was the catalyst of decay, inspired some of the greatest writing and painting China has produced.'

'And new Yang Kuei-feis will do the same?'

'Of course not!' the old man snapped. 'The essence of Yang Kuei-fei was her capriciousness, not her calculation. These new women are different. They'll inspire no poems.

'You recall Po Chü-yi's epic about Yang Kuei-fei, *The Everlasting Sorrow*. One of our greatest works, written by a poet who, we would say today, possessed a social conscience. Yet Po Chü-yi, the social critic, hymned the tragedy of the corrupt Yang Kuei-fei.

'His epic inspired other artists. How many painters became intoxicated with Yang Kuei-fei through *The Everlasting Sorrow*! Her glittering career, beginning when she was carried naked, wrapped only in a shawl, across the snow-covered courtyard to the Emperor's bedchamber by a giant eunuch . . . her abuse of power . . . and finally her death at the hands of mutinous troops. How many painters have used these scenes to express the high emotion of their own lives.'

Heels clattered on the terrazzo floor, and a young Chinese burst into the courtyard. He was the image of a youthful Turner Lee, frailty become wiry strength, wilted shoulders proudly erect, silvery aura shining black.

'Miles,' the older man asked, 'do you remember my son, Ying-nan?'

The young man acknowledged the introduction with a brusque handshake. Turning on his father, he spoke in imperious Mandarin.

'*Dieh-dieh, wo-men dzai wai-guo. Bu ying-gai* . . . Father, we're in a foreign country. You shouldn't go wandering around by yourself. I was worried, searched for you, until the chauffeur told me he'd taken you here. Who is this foreigner?'

'He is a friend, an American friend,' Turner Lee replied in English. 'And he understands what you say.'

Young Ying-nan Lee turned to Miles. Hostility mingled with curiosity, as if he had just become aware of Miles's existence.

'It is not right that my father should go away without telling me on our first day in Singapore,' he said. 'In these times, a Chinese patriot should not be speaking to people such as you. Come, Father, we must go.'

With that reprimand, confidence drained from Turner Lee.

'Goodbye, Mr Corrigan,' he said and drifted out of the courtyard in the wake of his strong-willed son.

Miles was more puzzled than he had been at any time since meeting Humphrey on the airliner. He had hoped for enlightenment. Instead, Turner Lee had left him a mess of intimations, innuendoes, and nuances more tangled than any bowl of noodles. He sighed, ordered another beer from the chubby youth, and decided to call Tanya Tan.

X

Miles wondered whether frustration and bewilderment were to be his lot in Singapore. He could normally understand the Chinese – at least part of the time. But he was now having extraordinary difficulty in understanding anyone, Chinese or otherwise. His talk with Turner Lee had only deepened his perplexity. The old connoisseur remained an enigma cocooned in a myriad tissue-paper-thin hints regarding his attitude towards Peking and his mission for Peking. Miles concluded that he was not any closer to penetrating the puzzle posed by Humphrey's bold talk and murky death. If anything, he was further from his goal than he had been when he started.

Tanya Tan was another mystery. It was perhaps her Russian half, her Slavic capriciousness, that so perplexed him. He simply could not get a fix on Tanya. She had said on the telephone that she would be delighted to see him, adding that she was free that evening. But she had refused his invitation to dinner that same night. She would, she had said, prefer not to see him until lunch the next day. At least she was not totally indifferent to him, puzzling though she was.

Standing side-by-side at the serving-counter at the front

of the Padang Restaurant, they now contemplated the rosy-shelled prawns, the sautéed beef coated with shredded coconut, the egg-plant in chili sauce, and the cold fried-eggs dotted with red pepper. Tanya, who knew Singapore so well, said she had never been to the Padang before.

'I'm told it's the only Malay restaurant in Singapore, maybe all Malaya,' Miles observed.

'Most Malays can't afford restaurants,' she interjected. 'Anyway, this style of cooking is from Padang in Indonesia. It's Sumatran, not Malayan.'

'It's also supposed to be great for a hangover breakfast.'

'Breakfast?' she remarked primly. 'This is my lunch, a late lunch. In the House of *Tan Tan* everyone breakfasts at seven. We're devoted to good health and good works.'

They seated themselves at the round marble-topped table, where the waiter was stacking dishes of white rice and red curries.

'And what's *Tan Tan*?' Miles asked.

'Mr Corrigan. All right, *Miles*. You can drop that admonitory hand. Maybe you don't eat underprivileged babies for breakfast, but I can't believe you don't know *Tan Tan*.'

'Honestly, I don't. Though it sounds like some kind of gambling.'

'That's fan-tan,' she laughed. '*Tan Tan*'s not gambling . . . It's a sure thing. The best commercial bet since somebody invented caskets – and of even less practical use. *Tan Tan* pills're taken by every Overseas Chinese household for every conceivable complaint. My father keeps several thousand underprivileged young girls busy compounding *Tan Tan* in dingy warehouses. The pills are mostly camphor, with a sprinkling of rhinoceros horn. You must have seen our trademark . . . an aggressively virile rhinoceros. They may not do much good but, my father assures me, they don't do much harm either. Of course, they've done the Tan family a lot of good.'

'Thanks for the lecture,' Miles said. 'I'll remember next time. You know, a beer would do me a lot of good right now.'

'This restaurant is strictly Moslem,' she reminded him. 'We'll have to make do with iced coffee.'

The bite of the coconut-milk curry was, however, clearing his head. For the tenth time since young Ying-nan Lee had reprimanded his father like an officious nanny, Miles considered that interrupted conversation. Turner was clearly far from senile, and Turner had been telling him something. But exactly what? Still, two points seemed to emerge: first, Turner still had no use for the Communists; second, he was, for some reason, obsessed with the romantic figure of the Tang Emperor's concubine, Yang Kuei-fei.

'What,' Miles asked Tanya impulsively, 'do you know about Yang Kuei-fei? You resemble her, though your figure's better.'

'Plump, minor noble lady of bewitching beauty who clawed her way up, leaving the royal prince, her husband, to become his father's concubine and almost empress.' Ignoring the heavy compliment, Tanya replied in a credible imitation of telegraphic style. 'Provoked revolt by enriching and ennobling hundreds of her relations . . . Revolt almost destroyed the Tang Dynasty . . . Lost her head . . . And became perpetual inspiration to soft-headed male poets and artists . . .'

'. . . inspiration to poets and artists!' Miles mused. 'Let's go. I've got a job for you.'

A battered black miniature taxi, its seats covered with genteel white duck, bore them through the afternoon heat to the domed Edwardian building which housed the tall bookshelves of the Raffles Libary.

'Why, Miles, I could have spent the evening with you after all.' Tanya laughed when they stopped before the section labelled ART. 'You *really* are interested in my mind.'

'Time for other things later. Right now there's work to do. You take the Chinese, I'll take the English. I want to see any and all references to Yang Kuei-fei and painters.'

'You take the Chinese,' she commanded, selecting a thick volume. 'I'll take the English.'

He could not help looking up from pages thick with the dust of disuse when she reached for a new volume and the thin cloth of her blouse stretched taut over her breasts. But he immersed himself again in his own reading; Chinese was the devil if you didn't read it every day – and he no longer did. After almost two hours, Tanya raised her eyes from her twelfth volume.

'It would be helpful if I knew what you were looking for,' she complained. 'Every reference to Yang Kuei-fei I've found, her posturing, her colouring, her tastes, every single one you've rejected. Do *you* know what you're looking for?'

'Not exactly. Only that it's mysterious and elusive, something very strange.'

Tanya sighed and began turning the dusty pages again.

'Is this mysterious enough for you?' she asked five minutes later. 'The greatest painting inspired by Yang Kuei-fei has not been seen since the Mongol conquest of China in the thirteenth century. Copies exist, but not the original. Strangely enough, the inspiration for that painting came almost three centuries after her death, not till the mid-eleventh century. Here, look at this passage yourself.'

The most poignant and most evocative tradition relating to Yang Kuei-fei and the brush [Miles read] is the story of Wang Lung, called the Dragon King because of that pseudonym, with which he signed all his works. Wang Lung, who flourished about 1050 A.D. at the height of the Sung Dynasty, was obsessed with Yang Kuei-fei. He painted innumerable portraits of the Immortal Concubine.

Obsessed, he clothed his own favourite concubine in the costume of the Tang Dynasty and addressed her as Exalted Imperial Highness, making obeisance to her. The painter became so possessed by the legend that he finally called himself Hsüan Tsung after the great emperor of the Tang who was Yang Kuei-fei's lover.

His own concubine had learned well the behaviour of a haughty, capricious Imperial Concubine, particularly disdain for a humble artist. She was, therefore, slow to show the deference due his belated self-elevation. In a fit of rage characteristic of his mania, when the concubine addressed him familiarly, Wang Lung snatched up a two-handed sword and hacked her to death.

His homicidal rage was succeeded by immense contrition. Laying out a fresh piece of silk, he painted with preternatural energy a scroll in tribute to the woman whose mangled corpse lay at his feet. He signed the painting with a brush dipped in her congealing blood. Then, throwing himself upon the same sword, he died.

The scene he chose encapsulated his obsession: Yang Kuei-fei at the moment of her death, when 'she shone forth lily pale between tall avenues of spears to die.' He inscribed that verse from Po Chü-yi's masterpiece, *The Everlasting Sorrow*, on the painting, which is one of the greatest masterpieces in the grand panorama of Chinese painting.

The original became a treasure of the Sung Court. But its history ends abruptly with the Battle of Hong Kong in 1278, when the invading Mongols defeated the last Sung army and a faithful retainer jumped from a war junk with the boy emperor clasped firmly in his arms to drown. Persistent rumours maintain that the painting was recovered by a Mongol commander. But no further reliable references to the masterpiece appear in Chinese annals.

Fortunately, the painting is not unknown to the present day. At least three Sung court painters made copies of the scroll known as *The Everlasting Sorrow*. Later, the famous Chin family, professional forgers who flourished at the end of the seventeenth century, made several copies of the copies. One copy was in the Summer Palaces outside Peking when they were sacked by French and British troops during the second Opium War. None, however, quite caught the passion of Wang Lung who was mad with regret.

The vanished original was reputedly a transcendent triumph of the painters' art. Love, power, passion, and madness all contributed to this great achievement, signed in blood, painted amid blood, its spirit stained with blood.

'Does that satisfy your need for mystery and drama?' Tanya asked softly. 'Even the copies, the forgeries, are wreathed in mystery.'

'It's certainly hair-raising,' Miles replied. 'I'd love to see . . . I suppose, I should say, I'd love to have seen that painting.'

'Enough of painting. You can now buy me that drink you promised. I've been thinking about the most appropriate drink and the most appropriate setting. We'll have

Singapore Slings at the Raffles Hotel. An imperialist drink in an imperialists' hotel for an American imperialist.'

'I never hear that drink before . . . Singapore Sling.' The waiter looked puzzled. 'I go ask barman.'

Five minutes stretched into ten, but the waiter did not return. Miles excused himself and strolled across the faintly seedy lobby to the tiny telegraph counter. He wrote out two cables, after each one tearing off the half-dozen blanks below and tossing them into the wastepaper basket, a precaution born of habit. One was addressed: Professor Thomas Morninghurst, Art Department, Columbia University, New York. The other went to: Dr John Suggs, 76 West 85th Street, New York. Returning to the table, he found both the waiter and the bartender in attendance, both adorned with smiles.

'I never before hear this drink,' said the bartender. 'But I find it in this book.' He flourished a stained copy of the *Esquire Bar Guide*. 'You want drink all these things mixed up together?'

The two white-coated Chinese watched apprehensively as Tanya sipped the drink.

'Taste all right, Mem?' the waiter asked. 'Not make sick?'

'Very good!' she assured them, but in an aside to Miles: 'Just like raspberry syrup.'

As he sipped, she suddenly said: 'Perhaps I shouldn't, but I simply must ask: *Why* this mysterious interest in this mysterious picture?'

'I don't really know,' he answered. 'With luck, I'll be able to tell you in a few days. Look, Tanya, could you please find your own way home? There's someone I must see right this minute.'

Miles dashed through the marble-floored vestibule into the muggy afternoon. Tanya slowly finished her drink, neatly tucked her cigarettes into her handbag, and gracefully rose. On the way out, she too stopped at the telegraph counter. While the clerk counted the words in her message, she dropped her handbag. Stooping to pick it up, she scooped out the blank sheets Miles had thrown into the wastepaper basket.

XI

Morgan Tan was entertaining.

Ignoring the odd plebeian Austin or Chevrolet with regal disdain, the Rolls Royces, Cadillacs, Mercedes, and Lincolns rolled under the white portico. They discharged European diplomats and businessmen wearing white dinner-jackets with their ladies in print-cotton frocks, as well as portly Chinese rubber barons accompanied by much younger ladies, diamonds glittering on their throats and wrists, who wore long silk cheongsams with high side-slits. Solemn houseboys in white jackets directed the guests through the marble-floored entry hall after greeting them as was appropriate in Malay, English, and three Chinese dialects.

It was a small party, quite intimate for Morgan Tan. No more than fifty guests would sit down to four round tables in the family dining-room. In the main dining-room, no settings adorned the blackwood table inlaid with mother-of-pearl which, as Morgan Tan often remarked with dignified pride, could seat a hundred and fifty 'without touching elbows'. The big dining-room was closed, its ten air-conditioners silent, its glass-fronted floor-to-ceiling shelves dark. Only an occasional automobile's headlights struck glints from the silver and gold vessels that could serve three hundred. Nor were the Ming vases, the Han figures, the Sung celadons, or the tortuously carved Manchu Dynasty jade animals on view that evening.

Morgan Tan was, as he himself affirmed, a man of refined taste and modest manners. Not for him the ostentatious public display of wealth beloved of lesser millionaires. He spoke tolerantly but with a disdainful undertone of the former coolie, now worth twenty million American dollars, who had just given a dinner for three thousand on the grassy padang at the centre of the city. Five hundred golden-brown suckling pigs had turned over open fires in a mass sacrifice to the God of Wealth. Not only the Overseas Chinese elite, but the leading lights of the European community had been present. Fortunately, few of the non-Chinese understood their host's Hokkien dialect when he carelessly began his welcoming speech: 'Ang mao . . .' meaning roughly: 'Red-haired foreign devils . . .'

Morgan Tan was no arriviste to parade his new wealth. His grandfather who, he admitted proudly, had come to Singapore as a coolie, had amassed the family's first few millions. His father, who made tens of millions, had also been the unchallengable doyen of the Overseas Chinese community in Singapore.

Morgan Tan had subsequently compounded his father's fortune many times. Complacently confident of his commercial acumen, he wished to be renowned as a connoisseur, a patron of the arts, and a benefactor of education. Extensive research had turned up three or four aspiring scholars and one middle-ranking official among his revered ancestors. Those men had flourished three to four centuries earlier, before misfortune reduced the Tan family to the penury that had forced his grandfather to leave their impoverished Fukien fishing village for Singapore. Culture, Morgan Tan nonetheless affirmed proudly, ran in the family.

Wearing a sharkskin dinner jacket with star-sapphire studs and cufflinks, Morgan Tan greeted each guest in his own language – not only the Chinese of Peking, Shanghai, and Amoy, as well as English and Malay, but French and German too. His dark regular features were lit by the flash of white teeth when he smiled, and his erect figure bowed gracefully. Beside him, his daughter Tanya glowed, her pale throat rising swanlike from the cowl collar of a long dress of iridescent Laotian silk embroidered with stylised silver birds. The crimson depths of her bracelet of massive rubies were reflected by the serpentine ruby pin in her hair. Her elder half-brothers, all immaculate in sharkskin dinner-jackets, chatted stiffly with their father's guests.

It was, nonetheless, a small party for close friends. Most of the guests greeted each other by first name, and hardly half the normal complement of forty servants was in attendance. As a matter of course, the servants poured champagne. But it was a discreet Krug, rather than the Dom Perignon the House of Tan dispensed when the master wanted to impress strangers.

'A few intimate friends, just to keep in touch,' Morgan Tan said repeatedly. It was not his fault, he would explain if pressed, that the roster of his intimate friends altered as commercial and political circumstances altered.

'After all,' he would often add, 'an invitation would only embarrass old friends whose fortunes have declined so that they cannot at least make a pretence of reciprocating. One must be of the elite to mingle comfortably with the elite.'

Morgan Tan spread his arms expansively, his sapphire

(113)

cuff-links flashing, as the introductory courses were placed on silver-rimmed turntables on the round mahogany tables. In this company, there was no need for the usual explanations to newcomers on the proper way to hold chopsticks. Nor need he call attention to the gold clips in the shape of the Chinese characters invoking longevity and prosperity that both ladies and gentlemen were given to secure their napkins. They knew he expected them to keep those clips to remember another pleasant evening at the House of Tan. Some had collected several dozen – no fortune, but still a tidy sum for a British civil servant.

Morgan Tan beamed as the servants bore in the first of the main courses to follow the bountiful appetisers. Fresh whelk and abalone flown from Hong Kong that day were presented in porcelain serving-bowls nestling in sterling-silver tureens shaped like the mollusc's own shell. Silver ladles filled the guests' bowls, which rested in gilt-filigree holders.

'I remember, Monty, how much you like whelk,' Morgan Tan said in his dry, precise English. 'I hope you'll like it this way, Cantonese style with a touch of Amoy flavouring.'

The Englishman seated at the host's right raised his eyes from the table and smiled with thin red lips under a sweeping ginger moustache speckled with grey. He had been avidly calculating the cost of the shellfish. At least 70 pounds sterling for each whelk or abalone, about 150 American dollars. As for the tureens, each must have cost 500 pounds originally, say 1,250 US dollars; their value was now at least double.

'Delicious, Morgan,' he responded 'I haven't had a super treat like this since we last dined with you.'

'My pleasure, Monty,' the host replied. 'I only regret we don't see each other more often.'

'I've been so busy, travelling so much lately.'

The Englishman's faded-blue eyes swivelled to watch a waiter bearing sharks-fins soup in a gilt tureen Cellini himself might have shaped into the simulacrum of a killer shark.

'Everyone knows how busy you are with Asia so unsettled. What would Her Majesty's High Commissioner do without the counsel of his Senior Political Adviser?'

'I'm not so important, Morgan. Just trying to help out!' Cecil Edward Frederick Montague replied to the liturgical Chinese flattery with liturgical British modesty.

'But why talk of dreary politics?' Morgan Tan asked. 'Have you met Professor Lee, Professor Turner Lee?'

'Know his name, of course,' answered Montague. 'Delighted to meet him at last.'

'Professor Lee knows more about Sung and Yüan painting than any other living authority. I hope we can have a talk with him after dinner. He's brought some new scrolls which may interest you.'

The unvarying ritual of the dinner ran its formal course. Great steamed fish, glaring myopically from their pools of sauce, signalled the approaching end. The fish were followed by soup in tall cylindrical winter-melons, which heralded the arrival of the ritual noodles for longevity and the dessert of sweet sautéed lotus stalks.

Morgan Tan deftly detached Cecil Montague and Turner Lee from his chattering guests, who were sipping their first brandies. He felt no embarrassment at cutting favoured guests out of the herd. All his guests knew he was above conventional constraints.

Their hands cradling enormous balloon glasses of brandy, the chosen pair followed their host into his study.

Its five hundred square feet were the smallest of his six reception rooms.

Morgan Tan and Cecil Montague drew on Havana cigars, exhaling blue smoke with ostentatious appreciation. Turner Lee smoked a Lucky Strike with quick, birdlike gestures.

The English diplomat was tall and thin. Despite his fifty-two years, he was as awkward as a schoolboy who has not yet learned to control the new length of his arms and legs. His high strung disposition was camouflaged, though not wholly concealed, by a façade of heartiness, and his left arm, shattered by a mortar-shell in Burma, was supported by a black sling. He looked extremely distinguished when he relaxed.

The Chinese connoisseur was short and very thin, visibly worn by sixty-six years of hardship and peril. Though the black-leather chair almost enveloped him, his nervousness was revealed by the rhythmic jiggling of his right leg. Yet he conveyed a fundamental impression of serenity drawn from his family's millennia of Confucian self-discipline and Confucian self-confidence. Somehow, his restrained demeanour diminished both his ebullient host and the aggressively jaunty Englishman.

'A super party,' Montague said. 'But your parties are always super.'

'Good of you to say so, Monty,' the host answered. 'I know you're not being polite . . . not just "using guest-words" as we say in Chinese.'

'I *do* mean it . . . truly!'

'I won't use guest-words either,' Morgan Tan continued. 'I won't waste valuable minutes in formalities. Professor Lee is pressed for time, and I expect a vital call from London in an hour.'

'I'm sorry time is short.' Montague was suddenly suspicious, fearful of being forced to make a decision or, worse, a commitment. 'Is this a matter of business?'

'No, Monty, not in the usual sense.' Morgan Tan laughed expansively. 'Not your kind of business or mine. We won't talk about the fate of millions of persons or hundreds of millions of dollars. This is more important than business or politics. I want you to see a few pieces I'm thinking of acquiring.'

'Sorry, old man,' Montague smiled in relief. 'I misunderstood.'

'My fault, really. I'm damned edgy nowadays, got too many things on my mind.'

'These are difficult times, Mr Montague.' Turner Lee tonelessly made his first contribution to the conversation. 'Difficult everywhere.'

'Quite, Professor Lee,' Montague responded. 'But we'll manage. We'll all manage, I'm sure.'

'Before I forget, Monty,' Morgan Tan interjected. 'Before we view the new scrolls, there's one little thing I hope you'll do for me.'

'Yours to command, old man. I'm always at your . . .' Greed and suspicion contended in Montague's reply. 'But what is it?'

'The last time the High Commissioner honoured my house with his presence, he admired a small thing of mine. It's nothing of importance, only a Sung celadon bowl. Naturally, I didn't want to embarrass him.'

'Quite properly!' Montague bestowed judicious approbation. 'Quite right!'

'Later, I prevailed upon him to allow me to lend him the bowl,' the host continued. 'I know it will give him much pleasure.'

'Just a loan, eh?' Montague said blandly. 'I'm sure His Excellency will be pleased.'

'No hurry about returning it, of course,' Morgan Tan added as three heads bent over the silk-brocade box in which the fragile, flower-embossed bowl glowed. 'I know H.E. likes time to savour beautiful things.'

'. . . and women!' Montague guffawed, just restraining himself from nudging his host with his elbow.

'A fine piece,' Turner Lee said unenthusiastically.

'And now the *pièce de résistance*!' Morgan Tan rose to slide open a mahogany panel on the wall. 'I'd like your advice, Monty.'

'Flattered, I'm sure,' the Englishman replied.

Turner Lee, too, rose, entranced once again by the two paintings that glowed in the indirectly lit recess. Mounted on silk scrolls, they were roughly of a size: three feet wide by five feet long.

The painting on the left depicted a figure in flowing pale-green draperies. It was neither positively female nor positively male, though an impression of femininity dominated. The features were serene, but the smile on the full lips seemed troubled, as if pitying endless human sorrows.

'An early Goddess of Mercy,' Turner Lee explained. 'Probably mid-Tang, about 750 AD. Note that she hasn't quite completed her transfiguration from the male to the female mode. An outstanding picture. I've only seen two or three comparable Kuan Yins.'

Morgan Tan sketched a half-bow and asked: 'And the other, Professor Lee?'

'Magnificent, some of the finest brush work I've ever seen. But, alas, a copy. A copy of some value, but still only a copy. I'd unhesitatingly place it between 1690 and 1730. Just which one of the gifted Chin family of forgers painted this copy, I cannot say.'

Mesmerised by the second painting, Montague leaned

forward. More literally representational, it was more attractive to Western taste than the first.

A squad of soldiers, distinguished by the character *yung*, meaning 'brave', on their breastplates, was drawn up in two lines facing each other. Their long lances caught the last rays of the sun, which was a red orb just visible behind jagged mountains. A bountiful female figure wearing an oyster-coloured gown drooped in the foreground, head bowed, tears glistening on opalescent cheeks. A male figure in Imperial-yellow robes sat dejected on a rock in the background, his head sunk in his hands.

'By God, that's a beauty!' Montague exclaimed. 'You can feel the sorrow and the grief . . . the splendour, too.'

The Everlasting Sorrow,' Turner Lee said slowly. 'The moment the Tang Emperor Hsüan Tsung surrendered his only love in order to preserve his realm. His own troops demanded the death of the Imperial Concubine Yang Kwei-fei – and the Emperor was forced to comply.'

'Otherwise, he'd have lost his head and his throne, as well as his lady love,' Morgan Tan interjected. 'So he made the only sensible decision. He had hundreds of other concubines.'

'But only *one* Yang Kwei-fei,' Turner said softly. 'Po Chü-yi wrote his epic work around this moment: *The Everlasting Sorrow*.'

'Now I recall it,' Montague boomed. 'Stupid of me to forget.'

'You have much to think about nowadays.' The host automatically applied the salve of flattery.

'Morgan, they're both magnificent. I'd say take both,' Montague advised, adding archly: 'That is, if you can afford them.'

Morgan Tan ignored the heavy humour. There could be no conceivable question that he could readily afford anything he wanted. Unspeaking, he studied the scrolls through a heavy magnifying glass.

'Well, Professor Lee, Mr Montague agrees with us,' he finally said. 'Our taste seems to be the same. We'll talk price on the Kuan Yin again if you wish. But 100,000 of the US dollars your principals seem to prefer seems right to me. As for the other, I just don't know.'

'It's your decision, Mr Tan,' Turner Lee answered. 'As you know, I'm not a salesman. I'm just a messenger with some knowledge of art.'

'Of course, Professor, of course!' Morgan Tan placated the connoisseur. 'It's just, as you say, hard to put a price on the Yang Kwei-fei.'

'I am authorised to offer the Yang Kwei-fei at a *very* low price, almost ridiculous,' Turner Lee said tentatively. 'The copy's authenticity cannot be established absolutely, although I am all but positive. Still, it's not a certifiable painting. Since you want the Kuan Yin, I'm authorised to offer the Yang Kwei-fei for 150,000 Straits dollars, say, 50,000 American dollars.'

'Straits 150,000,' Montague exclaimed. 'That's a good round figure to a poor civil servant. But it *is* magnificent. I can just see it hanging in my cottage in Kent . . . But it's madness even to think about it. I'll be retiring in a few years – and every penny'll count. No, not for me . . . I only wish I could if you don't want it, Morgan.'

'You like it that much, Monty?'

'By Jove, I do! It's perfection.'

'Why don't you buy it then?' Morgan Tan asked negligently.

'I can't . . . Couldn't possibly afford it. Matilda would give me hell. School bills're almost overdue . . . and all that.'

'Look here, Monty!' Morgan Tan spoke with quick

(120)

decision. 'I don't really want the Yang Kuei-fei. It wouldn't fit into my collection, not a copy. In fact, I'd advise you not to touch it. It's not up to your standards.'

'Your standards are different to mine, you know.'

'Hardly that different,' Morgan Tan responded automatically. 'But, then, you really want it?'

'Yes, but I'm afraid . . .'

'Monty, this is embarrassing,' Morgan Tan said slowly. 'It's hard to say even to an old friend. Still, we are such old friends . . . Why don't you take it? An interest-free loan, we'll call it.'

'It's tempting, very tempting,' the Englishman mused. 'One perfect scroll to remind me of the East when I'm put out to pasture in Kent. Very tempting, but no . . .'

'Monty, I insist!' Morgan Tan's whim solidified into granite. 'You'll offend me if you refuse.'

'But, Morgan, really . . .'

'I insist.'

'How long to pay?' the Englishman asked. 'Might be years, you know, several years.'

'Quite all right, Monty,' Morgan Tan answered. 'Just think of the pleasure it will give me to give pleasure to an old friend.'

'Well, I suppose, I could, if . . .'

'Done, Monty, done,' Morgan Tan said conclusively. 'It's yours!'

'What about security, old man?'

'Security between old friends? I only need your word.'

'I couldn't do that,' Montague objected. 'There must be something on paper.'

'If you insist, you can write me a simple promissory note specifying repayment not fixed. No time limit and no interest. I don't want you to get into a fix.'

'Seems more than fair to me,' the Englishman answered. 'Damned generous.'

He gazed possessively at the scroll, avidly taking in the subtle colouring and the dramatic postures.

Morgan Tan smiled at his friend's passion.

'If you can't tear yourself away, I'll ask Professor Lee to write out the note. More convenient if it's drawn to him, though I pay.'

Rapt in contemplation of the painting, the Englishman abstractedly nodded agreement.

'Just one other thing, Monty,' Morgan Tan remarked. 'Please don't say anything about this scroll for a time. It's all on the up and up of course. But publicity could embarrass Professor Lee and his principals.'

'Quite understandable,' Montague agreed readily.

'Then I'll send it to you tomorrow. It's too cumbersome, too conspicuous for you to carry tonight.'

'It can't be too soon for me. My thanks, Morgan, a thousand thanks. Matilda will love it too. If not, I can talk her around. Thank you, Morgan. I'm truly grateful.'

XII

Miles slammed the black handset of the telephone into its cradle. Leaning back in the plastic swivel-chair, he glumly contemplated the heap of soiled clothing in the corner of the room the Ocean Park Hotel's brochure ambitiously described as 'a spacious patio-suite overlooking the sea'. The entire staff had walked out two days earlier, 'to demonstrate our complete sympathy for our fellow toilers of the Universal Workers' Union.' Since then, nothing had functioned properly, despite the sweaty efforts of Michael Tong, the proprietor, his wife Ivy, and three amahs too old to be intimidated.

Neither fraternal solidarity nor revolutionary fervour, but bald intimidation had transformed the Ocean Park's bustling corridors into deserted tunnels. The cheerful room-boys and waiters did not want to go, they had said, apologising to the Tongs and to the guests. But they feared for the lives of their families if they did not obey the cold-eyed young terrorists from the Chinese-language high schools. Killer Squads, the underground Malayan Communist Party forthrightly called the seventeen to twenty-year-olds who murdered opponents on command. They *were* moved by revolutionary fervour, as well as by

Chinese nationalism hardly distinguishable from sheer racism.

'Your fat tips from imperialist foreigners won't do you any good when you're lying dead in the gutter,' the students had warned. The staff hardly needed that additional tip. They had decamped.

Knowing that the boys and the amahs would have preferred to stay on, holding themselves aloof from politics, was little consolation.

Miles bundled his dirty laundry into a cupboard, but the elastic mass seeped out, forcing the door open. In a muggy climate, where one wore cotton and might change three times a day, unwashed laundry accumulated as implacably as did masses of dusty files in a government office.

Even worse, the telephone service had gone from execrable to catastrophic. The Ocean Park was proud of having a telephone in every room, but the instruments had no dials. A total breakdown might almost have been preferable to waiting five to ten minutes for that amateur operator, Ivy Tong, to respond. She invariably reached three wrong numbers for every right number — and inadvertently cut off most conversations at critical junctures.

For two days now Miles had been trying to arrange another meeting with Turner Lee. The vicissitudes of the Ocean Park's switchboard were compounded by the stubbornness of Morgan Tan's servants, who deliberately misunderstood and, in the end, always declared that Professor Lee was out.

Miles had just suffered the final indignity. Friendly and courteous as always, Turner Lee had finally come to the phone. But, after a half dozen words, Miles heard his son's voice.

'Father,' Y. N. Lee had shouted. 'Who is that?'

A soft reply – and the handset was firmly replaced.

Miles resigned himself. It was obvious that he would not be able to arrange a second meeting. It was clear that the last person Turner's watch-dog son would let him see again was Miles de Sola Corrigan. His frustration was, however, brightened by one ray of light. Tanya Tan had agreed to meet him for dinner when she, rather than a houseboy, picked up the telephone.

Whistling tunelessly, he pulled on his last clean sport shirt, a violently patterned purple-and-brown batik he did not much like. After vigorously attacking his stubborn dark-red hair with a stiff Kent brush, he pushed a wad of Straits dollars into his pocket and slammed the door behind him. A shower of plaster fell from the damp ceiling onto his head and shoulders, quashing the mildly malicious satisfaction he had derived from that gesture.

The East Coast Road hummed companionably under the tyres of the red Porsche. On Miles's right, the sea glittered in the encroaching dusk, and the off-shore islands of Indonesia in the distance were enchanted violet islets. On his left, the long bungalows of the wealthy, as imposing as the main house of a Westchester estate, alternated with Malay kampongs, where hundreds were crammed into stilt-legged huts of woven palm leaves. He had chosen the rendezvous at Bedok because it was far from the centre of the city, where knots of militant strikers and students taunted police patrols. It was even farther from the Bukit Timah Road, where the activists skirmished with riot squads. If peace still reigned anywhere on the uneasy tropical island that evening, it would be among the open-air foodstalls of Bedok by the sea.

Tanya was waiting for him, sipping a Tiger beer, the Colony's ubiquitous drink. She was poised like a visitor from another world on a rickety metal chair at a round metal table outside Hok Kee's Beer and Sea Food Delights Restaurant. The many-coloured lights in the trees gleamed in her lustrous brown hair and cast glowing abstract patterns on her full-skirted cream dress.

A row of white-capped *hadji* knelt at her feet as if in supplication to tiny terracotta braziers, gently fanning the charcoal flames under long sticks of satay. No one had ever satisfactorily explained why the *hadji*, devout Moslems who had made the pilgrimage to Mecca, should monopolise the trade in tid-bits of chicken or goat skewered on bamboo and served with a piquant peanut sauce. Miles had reconciled himself to never quite fathoming such trivial mysteries of the East, as well as the reason for Bedok foodstall proprietors' devotion to outsize acetylene lanterns that cast a blinding white glare, when they could just as easily use electricity.

Tanya came forward to meet him, the light of the half-moon glinting in her hazel eyes. Smiling in evident pleasure, she extended both hands.

'How clever of you to think of Bedok, Miles. I haven't been here in years.'

'A change from your father's banquets or the Elizabethan Grill.'

'And a change from Raffles Place or the Bukit Timah Road. They're swarming everywhere, "the enraged students and workers," as Paul da Silva calls them. Everyone's gone mad tonight. They stopped me twice to make sure I wasn't an imperialist foreigner. One nice boy carrying a wicked looking mattock even advised me to turn back. But I was determined to come . . . strike or no strike.'

'I'm glad you did, very glad. But what about getting home?'

'Oh, I'll manage. The name Tan is still a good password. But let's forget politics. I'm going to gorge myself, eat all the greasy things I haven't had in years.'

'Maybe I'd better take you home right now! The danger . . .'

'You'd be in much greater danger than I. They're after red-haired devils like you.' She laughed and pointed. 'Look at the enormous crab on that table. I want that.'

Putting his fears aside, Miles played to her light mood and ordered a bountiful meal: crab baked in salt, prawns steamed in their shells, fried fish with a tart red sauce, and thin noodles garnished with lobster. She attacked the food with gusto, as he did after the pallid ham sandwiches served by the moribund Ocean Park Hotel. They ate like hungry children, hardly exchanging a word. Half an hour later, they leaned back replete from a table heaped with crab and prawn shells.

'Not bad.' Sighing with satisfaction, Tanya wiped her hands on a hot towel. 'I can't remember when I've eaten so much. You have a bad effect on me.'

Ruefully contemplating the spots on his last clean shirt, Miles smiled and said: 'A *good* effect. What's wrong with a healthy appetite?'

Later they walked along the beach, her hand resting lightly on his arm.

'Let's sit here.' She pulled him down. 'Right here.'

'As good a place as any!'

'Better!' She did not release his hand. 'No one here knows us, and no one who knows us knows we're here.'

'It's a strange place.' He felt a welling up of tenderness for her. 'Practically the southern tip of continental Asia. And all hell is breaking loose a few miles away. Sitting here, you'd think peace was universal, the birthright of all men and women.'

'It is! It would be if . . . if only politicians would leave us alone.'

Tanya leaned back on her outstretched arms, her gaze fixed on the lemon-yellow half-moon above the slumbering South China Sea.

'Miles, I don't belong here any more than you do,' she said softly. 'Sometimes, at a moment like this, I feel at home in Singapore . . . at peace. But I'm afraid I'm really European emotionally. I always feel more at home in Europe . . . just before I get homesick for Singapore.'

'And China?' he asked gently. 'Do you feel homesick for China, too?'

'Not really, not in myself. Not till my father delivers one of his lectures on the glory of being Chinese. Then, I suppose, I'm half-proud of being Chinese – and half-angry at his demanding that I *must* feel Chinese.'

She laid her hand in his again and spoke emphatically: 'It's not *my* fault I'm not Chinese. It's *his* fault! It's not *my* fault my mother was Russian and I went to school in Switzerland. What does he expect me to be?'

'I could hardly know. All *I* want you to be is yourself. I wouldn't alter anything about you. Not your character or your eyes or your little toe.'

She smiled at him, her pensive mood abruptly altered.

'I'd alter nothing.' He strove to sustain the light, trifling note. 'Not a jot or a tittle.'

'I've always wondered exactly what jots and tittles are. Do you wear them, eat them, or look at them? Do you wash them every morning?'

'Whatever they are, every jot and tittle of yours is perfect.'

'Even though I'm so mixed up?'

'We're all crazy mixed-up kids nowadays,' Miles answered seriously. 'I'm just as bad as you.'

'Don't be silly!' she commanded. 'I'm a Eurasian. I'm between two worlds, part of neither. How could you know how it feels to lie awake nights wondering whether you *really* exist? Do you ever feel you may not really exist at all because you have no people . . . because you're an alien wherever you go?'

'The Irish-Jewish combination is almost as volatile,' he observed. 'My father was a tough New York Irish cop who became a flamboyant trial lawyer. His father was an immigrant bricklayer. My mother came of the old Portuguese-Jewish aristocracy of New York. Aristocrats to themselves, though many others, WASPs who came a century later, thought they were just a fancy kind of kike.'

He paused, lit two cigarettes, and handed her one in silent intimacy.

'It's not the same!' She took the white cylinder abstractedly. 'Not at all!'

'Nothing's exactly the same as anything else. But there are similarities. Look, you're *you* . . . no one else . . . not your mother's daughter or your father's daughter, but yourself. Tonight, especially, you're *only* you. And I'm very glad of that.'

'That's nice, Miles. Nice of you to say so.'

She leaned closer and brushed her lips against his cheek, as light as the touch of a butterfly's wing. He squeezed her hand.

'I mean it . . . totally,' he affirmed. 'Tonight there's only you. You may be a mixture of many things, but, above all, you're you.'

'For tonight, perhaps,' she said softly. 'But tomorrow, tomorrow when we're apart again, I'll be a collection of fragments again. At least you have a country. I don't even have that.'

'A country? I suppose I do. That country is a collection

of fragments itself, but, somehow, it holds together. I'm also an art dealer – by pure chance. My uncle died an unrepentant bachelor and left me a gallery. It was particularly known for French Impressionists and, of all things, Russian icons.'

'How did you come to Asian art?'

'Hardly an original story. Language school in the Navy, then duty in China and Japan. And suddenly, I was in the Oriental art business.'

'The fragments all fit together now, don't they?'

'Maybe because I've let them come together. Maybe you should do the same thing. Not fight . . . just let things come together.'

'I'm drifting, anyway, not fighting. It's easy to drift. I'm too comfortable to exert myself. Maybe I need to believe. Maybe I need an obsession.'

'Not a jot or a tittle,' he repeated, 'would I alter.'

'Well, perhaps, not tonight, at least.'

His arm around her shoulders, they kissed gently. She withdrew first, but only an inch or two.

'Miles, we're like children huddling in the dark.'

'Pretty grown-up children, Tanya. And this wonderful moonlight's hardly the dark.'

He kissed her again lingeringly, then pulled her to her feet. They were moving much faster emotionally than he expected. And physically? That remained to be seen, but he was, surprisingly, in no hurry.

'Speaking of the dark,' he said. 'This is no night to stay out late. The phantoms of the night are real, not imaginary.'

'Must we leave, Miles?'

'If you insist on going home alone.'

They kissed briefly before Tanya squeezed into her small blue Fiat and darted south, her horn tootling a high-pitched farewell. Gazing at the sea, Miles meditatively smoked a cigarette. At length, he slipped into the red Porsche and drove slowly along deserted roads to the darkened hotel.

The deserted lobby was dimly lit. Lifting his key from its hook, he saw that almost all the other keys still hung in place. The Ocean Park had been virtually vacated when the frightened guests fled – south to the airport or north to Malaya.

'Mr Corrigan, I'm glad I caught you.' Michael Tong, the portly proprietor, emerged from his office. 'You have two cables. Badly delayed I'm afraid. They only came in an hour ago.'

Miles tore open the familiar blue-and-white envelopes of Cable and Wireless. A strike alone could not halt those swift couriers, only a major catastrophe like a flood or an earthquake.

MILES: YOU MAY JUST HAVE SOMETHING [the first read]. IT IS NOT ESTABLISHED POSITIVELY, BUT THERE IS GOOD REASON BELIEVE ORIGINAL REPEAT ORIGINAL EVERLASTING SORROW BY WANG LUNG WAS STORED IN PEKING IMPERIAL COLLECTION. SINCE COLLECTION NEVER PROPERLY CATALOGUED, IT MAY HAVE SAT FOR CENTURIES. ALL TRACES DISAPPEARED AFTER 1860 SACK OF SUMMER PALACES. IF EXTANT, CONSERVATIVELY WORTH QUARTER MILLION. THREE CHING DYNASTY COPIES KNOWN TO EXIST, THOUGH PRESENT LOCATIONS UNKNOWN. COPIES WORTH TWENTY THOUSAND TO FIFTY THOUSAND. INCIDENTALLY, LEGEND HOLDS ORIGINAL BRINGS GOOD AND BAD LUCK TO ALTERNATE POSSESSORS. WRITING SPECIAL DELIVERY WITH DETAILS OF DATING PAPER AND SILK. MY NORMAL CONSULTATION FEE. THIS CABLE CHARGED YOUR ACCOUNT. GOOD HUNTING. REGARDS MORNINGHURST.

Miles Corrigan smiled with satisfaction. He might, after all, not be chasing a will-o'-the-wisp. Then he laughed. It was characteristic of old Professor Morninghurst, the leading American authority on Chinese painting, to answer definitively – and to spend a few more dollars in cable charges to remind him that he was paying not only a consultation fee but the cable charges.

SIGNATURE EXTREMELY LIGHT [the second cable read tersely]. RUSTY BROWN FADED AND FLAKED IF TRULY HEMATIC. SUGGS

Miles stuffed the cables into his pocket and pushed open the swinging door to the dimly lit corridor. Whistling in time to his jaunty tread, he began the quarter-mile hike down the corridor. The hotel, Michael Tong regularly complained, had been planned as a military hospital – and sketchily adapted by a lazy architect. The corridors radiating like spokes from the central lobby were fine for guests with strong legs. The layout also provided privacy in widely separated rooms. But it was hell for the staff, a most uneconomical design for a hotel.

Portly Mike Tong normally ended his complaint with a hopeful question: 'Don't you know someone who'd like to buy a beautifully laid out, highly profitable hotel in fine condition?' For the last week he had omitted the question. No one was investing in a Singapore that tottered on the brink of civil war.

Miles was, however, not concerned with Mike's troubles. He was too pleased with himself. His impulsive decision to come to Singapore might well turn out to be highly profitable.

The Everlasting Sorrow. He could all but hear the poet's lines: 'When she shone forth lily pale, between tall avenues of spears to die.' China's official records spurned such lyricism as unworthy of self-disciplined Mandarins. Yet occasionally the passionate romanticism of the Chinese shone through such puritanism.

The scroll in question, if there *were* a scroll, was, of course, not the original. Peking would never let out a national treasure of enormous intrinsic and historical value. Perhaps, however, it was one of the old copies. At least 20,000 American dollars on the open market, if he could get hold of it. And he knew one collector who would pay twice that to complete his array of scrolls from every historical period. More like 50,000 to 60,000 dollars when that client heard of its gory origin.

He tossed his key high in the air and caught it with a flourish. He was delighted, far more excited than even the prospect of such a coup warranted. And why?

Tanya! There was also Tanya. Even more than anything else, perhaps even more than the painting, there was Tanya!

Miles was as exhilarated as a sophomore after a first date, but he could not gainsay his own feelings. At least, she clearly did not dislike him. That was enough for the moment. He whistled loudly, improvising arpeggios and trills. Tanya of the hazel eyes, the matte-white skin, the glowing hair, and the subtly rounded body.

With a flash of dismay, Miles realised that his thoughts were only faintly carnal. That was not at all like him, who normally loved in haste and left hurriedly. For a moment, the whistling stopped in alarm. He shrugged off his forebodings. What would be, would be, he told himself unoriginally. Besides, there were so many obstacles he need not fear getting inextricably involved.

'*Gaudeamus igitur.*' In a subdued baritone, Miles sang the old student drinking song 'Let Us Rejoice!', lingering over the bitter-sweet words. Why not rejoice now? Old age would come, but it was still far away. He boomed '. . . *Post molestam, senectutem, Nos habebit humus.*'

A distant tenor replied like a distorted echo: 'Said the tinker to the duchess . . . With his dirty kidney-wipers and his foreskin hanging down below his knees.'

Startled, Miles paused, but the elusive tenor came no closer. The singer must be out on the beach, whence sounded the uninhibited words of 'The Duchess and the Tinker.' Grinning, Miles softly joined the chorus as he slipped his key into the lock and swung open the door.

'*Hoi-yah!*'

The explosion of breath warned him an instant before a hard hand chopped at his neck. He twisted and raised a defensive arm, but the blow brushed aside his defence and hammered just below his jaw. Even partially deflected, the pain cut like a scimitar. He slumped to the floor, head and shoulders just within the room, legs sprawled into the corridor.

Miles felt himself rolled over by rough hands. Two faces floated before his eyes inside rainbow rings of pain. The hands plucked at his shirt.

'*Oi, nei-ya! Gam mat yeh?*' the tenor voice cried out in bad Cantonese. 'Hey, what the hell are you up to?'

Startled, Miles's assailants dropped him, and his head thumped on the rough coir matting. His eyes not quite focusing, he saw thin legs in khaki knee-socks race past him. An instant later, he heard a shot, then another.

Miles closed his eyes, happy to lie unmoving and uncaring for a moment. Thrice in one week, he reflected inconsequentially before the grey mist that had followed the many coloured whirling before his eyes became impenetrable blackness.

He woke to see an odd figure bending over him. Elongated and lean, it wore ballooning khaki shorts and khaki tunic whose shoulder-straps bore the single star of a sub-inspector of the Singapore Police Force. A revolver was clasped in its right hand.

'How are you?' the now familiar tenor voice asked. 'Can you make it to the bed with a little help.'

Miles nodded assent and tottered towards the bed, leaning on the sub-inspector's arm. The blankets had been stripped away, and the mattress had been slashed. His vision clearing, he saw that the room had been ransacked. Every drawer and suitcase lay open, and a torrent of soiled clothing flowed over the ruined furniture.

A glass approached his lips, and he automatically drank. Neat brandy. His benefactor was clutching an enormous balloon glass.

'Cutworth's my name, Basil Cutworth,' the tenor voice declared. 'Couldn't let them rough up my singing partner. Do you know "The Ball at Kerriemuir"?'

'Yes, but not right now, please.'

Miles realised that his rescuer was happily and thoroughly drunk.

'Well, if that's the way you feel . . .' The tenor voice was hurt. 'I might just as well go back to my beach party.'

'Appreciate it . . . fine song,' Miles said. 'But not right now, please.'

'Of course, my dear fellow. Stupid of me. You won't feel like a song just yet.' Effusively apologetic, Basil Cutworth poured himself another enormous dollop of brandy. 'Good job they didn't break the bottles.'

He paused to look around the room before speaking again.

'A right mess they've made. And got clean away in the mist. No point me calling in. All personnel're on riot duty.'

'Thanks,' Miles said. 'Could you get hold of Mike Tong, tell him I need another room?'

'Of course.' Cutworth drained his brandy and poured himself another before leaving. 'They won't come back, but do lock the door.'

Miles painfully swung his legs over the side of the bed. Leaning on the wall, he studied the wreckage of his belongings. His attaché case lay in the far corner, its contents strewn on the floor.

When he bent to pick up the case, pain shot through his neck and shoulder. He groped in the lining behind the accordion file built into the lid. The copies of his own telegrams were still there. He slipped the replies beside them before turning the stud that looked like another rivet securing the file.

'What else could they've been looking for?' he wondered aloud. 'Must've been the cables.'

XIII

Although the matter was routine, Cecil Edward Frederick Montague was disturbed. He was at ease with the procedure for dealing with visitors who refused to reveal their purpose beforehand, having carried out the drill repeatedly for several years. But the voice on the telephone had been hard – mocking, indeed almost hectoring. He was better accustomed to the oily tones of those seeking to sell secrets or wheedle favours.

He was, therefore, mildly disturbed, although all the precautions were in place. His rawboned wife Lady Matilda and their two pert daughters were not at home. They were splashing in the swimming-pool of the Tanglin Club, shielded by the bye-laws' exclusion of all non-Europeans except Club servants and baby amahs. A Chinese plainclothesman waited for them in the parking lot, idly watching the Malay drivers who squatted at their unending high-stakes dice game. The Security Officer of the High Commission for Southeast Asia insisted that no British dependent leave home without an armed plain-clothesman in attendance, as long as the 'disturbances' continued.

Cecil Montague was devoted to his eleven-year-old twin

daughters, though hardly devoted to his sour wife. He was weary of her complaints, and he found her bony body anything but erotic, indeed repelling. She had already done her part by bringing him the rapid promotion due to a son-in-law of a former Viceroy of India who was also competent and personable – and he would now dearly love to be rid of her.

Besides, she would not bring him an additional penny. The family property was entailed on her brother, the heir to the family title. In any event, her father, the Earl of Underwood, detested his son-in-law.

Nothing would please Cecil Montague better than sloughing off Lady Matilda. Unfortunately, there were the girls to consider, not to speak of the opinion of the smug little world in which he moved. There was also a knighthood to think about – and the lucrative sinecures it would bring on his retirement.

A second plainclothesman waited in the servants' quarters behind the house, and three Malay constables guarded the gates. Since the matter might be sensitive, the plainclothesman would see the self-invited guest only if an emergency arose. He, like the constables, could be summoned by a bell-push in the arm of Montague's chair. A revolver was tucked under the cushion, but Montague was not concerned about his own safety. He had been born without the capacity to feel physical fear, as his two Distinguished Service Orders and his shattered left arm attested. The harsh voice had, however, hinted at more complex perils.

'Since it's a purely personal matter,' the lawyer called Pritchard had suggested, 'you may prefer to see me at your home, rather than your office.'

Cecil Montague had strolled down to the Central Records Office himself, rather than call attention to his interest by having his personal assistant fetch Pritchard's dossier. But the dossier had told him little.

Working as a junior solicitor in the venerable law firm of Copplestone, Heath, White, and Company, when the Japanese invaded Hong Kong, George Pritchard had fought bravely. Surviving three years of forced labour in the coal-mines of Honshu, he had returned to Hong Kong after the war. After attaining a senior partnership, he had divorced his Scottish wife to marry a Chinese woman twenty years younger than himself. Regarding Pritchard's second wife, the file noted baldly: 'Background unknown.'

Pritchard had, however, represented the Peking government in its suits to reclaim the fleet of Chinese civil airliners that landed at Hong Kong's Kaitak Airport just before the Nationalists' collapse. He was also retained by several firms that traded with nearby China. But many Hong Kong lawyers were involved with Peking one way or another.

Otherwise, Pritchard's record was almost insipidly conventional: the usual clubs; the usual corporate practice, which had made him rich; and the usual indiscretions with his friends' wives and dance-hall girls. Nothing out of the ordinary at all.

Nonetheless, Montague started when he heard tyres crunch on the gravel driveway. He did not like receiving visitors who held the initiative. Normally, he would fix the conditions of a meeting – and dominate the conversation.

The blurred photograph in the file had not prepared Montague for Pritchard's appearance. Short and plump, pouter-pigeon chest thrust forward, he strutted rather than walked. His seamed cheeks were fiery red, and immense black-rimmed spectacles perched on his jutting nose.

'Mr Montague, so good of you to see me,' the remembered voice grated. 'I'll take no more than a few minutes of your time.'

Montague waved him to an armchair, asking : 'Whisky?'

'With just a splash of soda, please.'

Neither spoke while Montague mixed two dark-amber drinks. The silence continued while Pritchard swallowed half his whisky in a single draught. Like wily wrestlers, each man was waiting for the other to lunge first.

'As I told you,' Pritchard finally broke the impasse, 'my firm is Copplestone, Heath, and White.'

'I know the firm.'

'Then you know our reputation. No need for long introductions.'

'Not necessarily.'

'Odd we've never met. Lots of mutual friends. Dickie Little, Rob MacIntosh, and Hector Stewart send their chin-chins. I told them I might be seeing you if I found myself in Singapore.'

'Good chaps,' Montague replied coolly. 'I knew them in the war. Freshen your drink?'

'Yes, please.'

Pritchard disposed of his second whisky almost as summarily as he had his first.

'I didn't come here to reminisce, pleasant though it is. A small matter of business, Mr Montague. A minor matter I wouldn't normally bother with. But, since I found myself in the neighbourhood . . . I'm sure we can clear it up easily.'

'I hope so.' Montague was fractionally more relaxed. 'It's really too hot today for business.'

'Don't know how I survived before air-conditioning. But I was younger in those days.'

'Weren't we all?' Montague smiled.

'You know, I remember my first night in Singapore in the mid-30s,' the lawyer rambled. 'Came ashore with the officers off the old *Caronia*. What a night! We raced down Orchard Road at four a.m., pulling the coolies in their own rickshaws.'

'Done it myself, Pritchard. We were young and foolish.'

'So we were Montague, so we were.' The plump lawyer's laugh was as gritty as coal sliding down a chute. 'But, I suppose, we must to business.'

'What can I do for you?'

'A small matter, as I said. My client finds himself embarrassed. Can you let me have the 50,000 American dollars for that picture within the next few days?'

'What picture?' Montague was genuinely puzzled. 'What client?'

'That scroll. What's it called? Yes, *The Everlasting Sorrow*. Rum sort of name.'

'Your client, you say?' Montague was shocked. 'Why doesn't Morgan Tan ask me himself. Besides . . .'

'There must be some misunderstanding. Morgan Tan's nothing to do with the matter. My client is Professor Turner Lee, a representative of the government of the People's Republic of China.'

'Turner Lee! He had nothing to do with the arrangement. Morgan Tan assured me his name on the note was only a formality.'

'I'm sorry, old chap. I know nothing of Tan's involvement, as I said. But that's the law for you . . . all formalities. My client holds your note for fifty thousand gold dollars – and he needs the money. Tried to dissuade him, myself, but his government insist on payment.'

'Insist?' Montague exclaimed. 'Insist? They can't. It's an indefinite note . . . no call date.'

'Indefinite *either* way, Montague.' Pritchard's voice

hardened. 'No definite date at all, you're quite right. By the same token, my client can call your note when he pleases.'

'But Morgan Tan said . . .'

'It's nothing to do with Morgan Tan, as I've told you.'

'You want fifty thousand American dollars by . . .'

'By the day after tomorrow. Otherwise, regrettably, my client insists we must take action. There's no use arguing with him. I tried, but no joy!'

'Day after tomorrow,' Montague objected. 'That's frightfully short notice. I'm afraid I simply can't . . .'

'I'm afraid you'll have to. Needs must when the devil drives, Mr Montague. Though you won't find us unreasonable.'

'Damned unreasonable!' Monty exploded. 'A damned fraud I call it! I'll get hold of Morgan Tan. He'll set you right – you and your precious client.'

'Tan's up-country, out of reach on a rubber plantation. And the matter's out of his hands.'

'Well, I simply can't! I won't, and that's that!' Montague declared. 'Frankly, I don't have the ready cash. Everything's tied up. Besides, this is practically blackmail.'

'That's a harsh word, Mr Montague,' the lawyer replied. 'But have it your own way. We needn't even go to court you know . . .'

'What *are* you saying?'

Pritchard's weathered face glowed a deeper red. Without a word, he poured himself another whisky and splash.

'Freshen yours?' he offered insolently. 'You look as if you need another.'

Montague angrily shouldered the smaller man aside and poured himself a double whisky.

'We needn't go to court,' the lawyer repeated. 'There's

a suspicion of corruption – a whiff of something rotten – about this matter. Why should Professor Lee, which means the People's Government, make you a virtual present of a valuable scroll? That's what I ask myself. Why a note-of-hand with no fixed date – and no interest? Above all, why the ridiculous price, fifty thousand US dollars? That scroll is worth more than a hundred thousand sterling – at least a quarter of a million US. *What* have you been up to, Mr Montague?'

'Damn your impudence!' Montague exploded. 'Get out!'

'If you wish . . . But I'll be back.'

'Oh, sit down, man!' Montague conceded wearily. 'Sit down and let me think.'

'You should know,' Pritchard continued relentlessly, 'that the government of the People's Republic are distressed that a Chinese national treasure should have found its way into the hands of a senior British official. Hotheads in Peking are talking of diplomatic action . . . a public protest.'

'Let them protest! The deal was on the up and up. You've acknowledged Turner Lee is their agent – and he sold me the scroll. I'm not responsible for Peking's differences with its own agents.'

Montague's voice gained assurance as he spoke. He was truly in the clear. He leaned back, coolly sipping his whisky and soda.

'And the money?' Pritchard punctured his complacency. 'When do we get the money?'

'Look here, Pritchard, I simply can't raise the ready cash,' the diplomat replied evenly. 'But surely the answer's simple. You can have the scroll back in exchange for the note.'

'I'm afraid it's not that simple. Things have gone too

far. My instructions are clear: the cash day after tomorrow
. . . or else.'

'Why?' Montague exclaimed. 'Why not have the scroll
back?'

'Don't know myself, old man.' Pritchard's gritty voice
softened in sympathy. 'I don't understand their thinking
. . . never have. Maybe they reckon the treasure's been
tainted by falling into the hands of a foreign imperialist
agent. I heard that term used. But only God knows what's
going on in their twisted Oriental minds. I'm afraid it's
the money . . . or else.'

'Or else what?'

'Exposure, I presume. But that's up to Peking – not
me. They reckon you could be as pure as the falling snow,
but any breath of scandal . . . Collusion with the enemy,
it's called. Any breath of scandal would, shall we say, not
do you a great deal of good.'

'I tell you I don't *have* the money. Do they want to ruin
me?'

'Maybe they do. They're vindictive devils. And they're
not too happy about the way things're going in Singapore.'

'Singapore?' Montague asked blankly. 'Singapore? Why
they started the disturbances.'

'I've heard angry talk about repressive measures. They
seem to think you're behind them.'

'They flatter me.' Montague forced a laugh. 'Tell them
they're wrong. I'm not pushing the hard line. Quite the
contrary. Can't you ask them to take the scroll back and
wipe the slate clean?'

'Afraid not, Montague. Damned sorry, but it's out of
my hands.'

Pritchard tossed back his fourth whisky and splash and
rose to leave. Montague meekly followed him to the front
door.

'By the by, deadline's midnight the day after tomorrow,' the lawyer added. 'And also . . . By God, I almost forgot. There is a possibility of what they call an arrangement, some other quid pro quo.'

'What, for God's sake?'

'Don't really know, old man. I'm just a messenger boy.'

'What *could* it be?' Montague pleaded. 'Give me a hint.'

'Sorry! Haven't the foggiest idea. By the by, I'd erase the tape of our conversation. Couldn't hurt me, you see. But you . . .'

Montague slowly closed the door on that parting shot. He felt he was closing the door on all his hopes for the future. How could he possibly escape this cunning trap?

He could not even reach Morgan Tan, who had unwittingly lured him into the trap. Morgan Tan, the shyster had said, was unreachable up-country in Malaya. Unreachable, perhaps, to a private citizen, but not to the resources the High Commissoin commanded. Montague exhaled in relief. Morgan Tan would straighten out the misunderstanding or put up the cash. Fifty thousand US was a flea bite to Morgan Tan.

'I want Mr Morgan Tan,' Montague instructed the duty operator at the High Commission. 'Try the Gold Palm Plantation in Kedah. This is an official priority call.'

He mixed another whisky and soda and subsided into the armchair. Why had he been so worried? Why had he allowed the shyster to come so close to making him panic? Morgan would solve the problem with a snap of his powerful fingers. After all, Morgan owed him several favours. He leapt up when the telephone jangled.

'Hello,' he said, 'hello, Morgan. How are . . .'

'Sorry, sir,' the operator interrupted. 'Mr Tan is not available. They don't know when he'll be back.'

'Well, keep trying,' Montague snapped. 'I *must* speak with him.'

It would be all right, he assured himself – of course it would be all right. Nonetheless, he extracted from a desk drawer the latest statement from his bank in London.

The figures were uncompromising. He was £9,521 overdrawn, almost 25,000 US dollars, an astronomical 75,000 Straits dollars. Still, the bank manager's accompanying letter was understanding: 'No difficulty is foreseen in maintaining the overdraft against appropriate payments of interest.' But, equally, the bank 'could not entertain any application for additonal advances.'

Montague's gratuity, due on retirement, would handily cover the overdraft – even provide another 15,000 pounds. But retirement was still three years off. He had built all his plans, based all his investments as well, on that date. If he were forced out of the service without the gratuity, without a pension, he would be ruined. Everything he had worked for would collapse. And as for the scandal!

He glumly acknowledged that he was threatened by a major scandal. The gutter press would go mad with joy at the opportunity to blackguard the Earl of Underwood's son-in-law. However innocent he knew it to be, this transaction would not be forgotten after no more than a ritual reprimand, as would a lesser transgression. This would be far worse than the 'whiff of corruption' the shyster had gloated over. A charge of wilful betrayal of trust, even treason, was in the air. It would ruin him totally, leave him penniless and ostracised.

But everyone, Montague comforted hismelf, everyone, even the High Commissioner, accepted small presents. All the more reason, a relentless inner voice replied, all the more reason for them to make an example of him in order to protect themselves. Besides, no one else was on the verge of precipitating a severe diplomatic protest, an international confrontation. Sino-British relations were already strained without such a disaster.

His masters would sacrifice him without thinking twice. They would happily sacrifice him – with a maximum of publicity, since his disgrace would prove their own rectitude. Morgan Tan was his only hope.

The telephone in the bedroom Cecil Montague did not share with his wife rang at 1.15 a.m. Morgan Tan's voice was weary. Reedy and faint over the long wire to northern Malaya, it nonetheless conveyed his irritation. This was not the most propitious time, Montague knew despite the fog left by the whisky he had drunk while pleading with the operator to find Morgan Tan. But he had no other hope.

'Morgan,' he said. 'Morgan, old man, how are you?'

'Tired, Monty, very tired. It's been a long drive. What can I do for you at this time of night?'

'Oh, just a small misunderstanding, Morgan. But I had to tell you about it.'

The thin voice replied over the clicking of the telephone relays: 'What's the problem?'

'Morgan, there's been a misunderstanding about the note.'

'The note?'

'You do remember? The promissory note I gave you the other day.'

'Oh, yes, that note. But, Monty, you didn't give me the note. You gave it to Turner Lee.'

'That's just the problem, Morgan, old man. A chap came round, a lawyer representing Lee. Said he had to have the money by this time the day after tomorrow.'

'Oh!' The voice was cool. 'And?'

'I know you can straighten it out. Remember, you said the note was just a formality. Can't you get it back?'

'I'm afraid it's proved more than a formality. Turner Lee's son refused to accept my money for *The Everlasting Sorrow*. He agreed only to accept payment for my own scroll. I'm afraid you do owe Turner the money.'

'Oh!' Montague was deflated. 'But can't you . . .'

'Just a thought, Monty. You can still solve the problem even if you don't have the cash.'

'Yes?' Montague asked eagerly. 'How?'

'Why not simply give the scroll back?'

'That's just it. They don't want the scroll. They want the money. And, Morgan, I don't have the ready cash.'

'That's a pity, Monty, a great pity. But I don't see what I can do.'

'If you can't get the note back, Morgan . . . I hesitate to ask . . . but couldn't you take my note for the fifty thousand? I'd pay up later.'

'I'll think about it, Monty. But, offhand, I don't see how I can interfere. If they want the money from *you*, they must have their reasons. I could, of course, let you have the money, though I'd hate to imperil our friendship by lending you more money. But I must think of my relations with others. Not just the objects I occasionally buy from them, but our business relationship. I simply can't offend them. Still, I'll think about it.'

'Please do . . . And do remember, please, that it's just forty-eight hours.'

'I'll see what I can do, but I'm not optimistic. Good night, Monty. I'm sure you'll work it out. I have confidence in you. Good night.'

Cecil Montague replaced the handset numbly. He could plead no more, for it was obviously pointless. He had used that mock-sympathetic brushoff too often himself to mistake a harsh rejection for the candy-floss in which it was wrapped.

What was the arrangement, the quid pro quo at which Pritchard had only hinted? He had to know. It was his only hope of avoiding bankruptcy and disgrace.

XIV

As always, dawn broke early on Singapore. The molten copper sun rose from the South China Sea in a bravura display. Gold, pink, and violet rays ignited the fronds of the tall palms, transforming thousands of trees into gigantic Roman candles. The sunrays gilded the domes of public buildings and glowed softly on the ruddy-tiled roofs of shops and private dwellings.

But the air itself was sodden and dull. Sleepers awakening were offered no sparkling morning draught, but only the stale dregs of yesterday. By noon the streets would be superheated into a vast sauna. Intermittent cloudbursts would not cool the city, but would transform it into a steam-room.

Dark-skinned Malays awoke in palm-thatched huts to another day of dispirited lounging. Golden-skinned Chinese awoke in concrete shop-houses, their nerves already on edge. Even well-to-do Chinese and privileged Europeans emerged from air-conditioned bedrooms to breathe the effluvia of an old sewer: raw disinfectants, stale urine, and decaying plants.

Mercifully, the Senior Political Adviser to Her Britannic Majesty's High Commissioner for Southeast Asia still slept in his rumpled bed. Cecil Montague had collapsed into dream-haunted slumber at three a.m. He twitched uneasily in the humid bedroom each time the softly clanking fan completed a revolution, for he conscientiously despised air-conditioning as unhealthy. His alcohol-fumed breath stirred his straggling moustache, and he tossed from side to side on sheets sodden with perspiration.

Some twelve miles to the east on the eastern edge of Singapore Island, Miles awoke in the cool dimness of the patio suite next to his own ravaged room. His body protested with pain as he eased himself upright and leaned against the pillow.

Adhesive-tape cocooned the purple-black bruises on his shoulder, extending over his torso. The hotel doctor, half awake at two in the morning, had spun that cocoon as a precaution against the possibility of a greenstick fracture of the collarbone or broken ribs. He had instructed Miles to visit the General Hospital for an X-ray later that day.

Still lethargic from the sedative the doctor had prescribed, Miles lifted the telephone to order breakfast. Although few guests were in residence, he would wait for at least half an hour for the skeleton staff to bring the food. Idly, he switched on the bedside radio.

'. . . have ordered mobilisation of all police reserves. I repeat: All police reservists will report immediately to their duty stations. The government have explained that the mobilisation is purely precautionary. No major disturbances are anticipated. I repeat: No major disturbances are anticipated, and workers are urged to report to their places of employment as usual. This is Radio Singapore. I return you now to Melodies for Morning.'

In the clapboard classrooms of the Motherland Middle School, young Chinese girls and boys jeered gleefully at the announcement. They had awakened long before dawn, rising decorously from their pallets on the floor of the improvised dormitories. Their natural decorum was reinforced by the strict segregation of the sexes enforced by squads of Morals Guardians, who were drawn from the most politically conscious older students. Those vigilantes patrolled the campus, alert equally against any impropriety and any unusual movement by the Malay constables who were massed outside the locked gates.

Most constables had slept restlessly in riot-vans parked in nearby side-streets. They were ordered to watch the school compound, but not to interfere with either movement in or movement out – 'as long as action is not absolutely necessary to keep the peace'. The school grounds were private property, and the adults of the School Management Board, intimidated by the youngsters, had warned the government against trespassing. British police superintendents had clamoured for permission to drive the students out of the compound and send them home before violence broke out. Chief Minister Patrick Wee of the semi-autonomous government formed by his Democratic Alliance Party under British supervision had refused his permission.

'Our children are ill, not bad,' Chief Minister Wee had told the Police Commissioner, who was still a Briton. 'We must cure them with kindness and understanding. We must *not* inflame them with harsh punishment to further violence.'

Not even flirtatious glances between boys and girls had disturbed the puritanical student leaders. The students' passions were all political. They were wholly dedicated to 'supporting the workers' just demands'.

The two thousand students in the Motherland Middle School and an additional thirty-five thousand in other

Chinese-language schools were the designated 'spearhead of the revolution,' the weapon wielded by a small group of militant cadres who answered to Peking. Though the Overseas Chinese students in English-language schools were apathetic, the students in Chinese-language schools were political shock troops. The idealism of youth bound those adolescents to the resurgent Chinese People's Government, which claimed to be creating a perfect egalitarian society – and to be making China a great power again. Feeling themselves oppressed now, as in the past, by the Colonial Government, the students fought ardently against the established order. Their Chinese patriotism and their racial solidarity were transmuted into revolutionary fervour.

Students was, however, a misleading term. Many were in their late teens, and a number were in their twenties. The elite were organised into the Killer Squads that terrorised the city. The adult cadres who were their secret generals also controlled the United Workers' Union and dominated the Masses Operation Party. Through their children the prosperous Overseas Chinese bourgeoisie were drawn into the conspirators' net. But the students themselves were the knife at Singapore's jugular – and the knife was poised to thrust.

The students had already spent three days in voluntary incarceration, awakening each morning with the hope of action that day. But they had not yet been ordered to sally into the city. Morals Guardians, only their eyes visible above knotted handkerchiefs, kept the gates and patrolled the inner perimeter to prevent communication with distressed parents. The students had been promised action this fourth day.

RELEASE OUR PRINCIPAL! The slogan was painted on a bedsheet hung above the main gate. Other slogans draped the barbed-wire barricades: OUR PRINCIPAL IS A PATRIOTIC MARTYR! NO ILLEGAL DEPORTATION! OPPOSE IMPERIALIST, POLICE-STATE OPPRESSION!

Similar signs hung limp on the woven-wire fence around the Metal Box Company's plant sixteen miles away on the Bukit Timah Road. Barricaded inside, workers had little to do but paint signs and sneer at the Malay constables on guard outside.

HAIL THE PATRIOTIC UNITY OF DEMOCRATIC WORKERS AND INTELLECTUALS! a large placard proclaimed in ragged Chinese characters.

The English versions were more explicit: A LIVING WAGE FOR A LIVING MAN! CAPITALISTS DRINK OUR BLOOD! GRANT OUR JUST DEMANDS! One theme dominated the workers' slogans, as it did the students': NO ILLEGAL DEPORTATION! RELEASE THE PATRIOTIC MARTYRS! RESTORE MR THE SAM-LOK AND HIS FOUR HEROIC COMRADES!

The workers' strike had begun with vague demands for general benefits. Forty thousand students had then mobilised in support of the workers. The generalised protest had finally crystallised into opposition to the deportation order against Principal The Sam-lok of the Motherland Middle School and four union leaders. All five had been incarcerated in Changyi Jail. But they had smuggled their orders out during the night with the help of a Malay warder who was 300 Straits dollars richer for his daring – and cherished a promise of 'forgiveness for serving the imperialists when the people come to power.'

The explicit orders had been drawn up after long deliberation among the 'five martyrs', whom the complacent government had placed in a communal cell. Two principles dictated by the clandestine Malayan Communist Party dominated their council-of-war: The cause needed more martyrs! The deportation order must be reversed!

The strategy was simple and deadly. Workers and students were to converge on the iron-grill gates of Government House, the residence of the British Colonial Governor. They would demand the prisoners' immediate release, which the government could grant only by abdicating its power. The conspirators had concluded that the police could be goaded into striking back viciously, thus giving the campaign the martyrs it needed. If a single student were killed or even seriously injured, overwhelmingly Chinese Singapore would rise up in outrage at the barbarism inflicted on its children by Malay mercenaries directed by British imperialists.

Throughout the tense fourth day an impasse prevailed along the barricades at both the Metal Box Factory and the Motherland Middle School. Worker activists and student vigilantes glared over their handkerchief-masks at stolid Malay constables. The workers shouted slogans and convened political study classes. The students sang patriotic songs like Peking's anthem 'Arise' and pranced through revolutionary folk-dances. Occasionally, a Lincoln, a Cadillac, a Rolls, or even a Chevrolet stopped before the main gate, and a tearful mother called across the barbed-wire, in vain begging her child to come home. Fathers were more practical and took out political insurance by pressing money on the Leadership Committee, which sat in continuous session in a clapboard hut just inside the gate.

A steady exodus over the back-fences of both schools and factories was not observed by the police. Designated activists slipped out one by one and seeped stealthily through the steamy streets towards Government House. Meeting, they assembled on a hillock a hundred yards from the gates.

At 3.10 p.m., when Singapore dozed in the greatest heat of the day, stocky Gurkha riflemen in starched white uniforms stood at attention before twin sentry-boxes flanking the gilded gates of Government House. Their stubby bayonets were fixed to the muzzles of their rifles, but their rifles were not loaded. The Gurkhas' function was ceremonial. But four red vans as big as railway cars had been parked since morning in the oval plaza before the gates. Inside them waited the riot-squads, the cutting edge of government power.

At 3.12 p.m., a blue police Land Rover skidded to a halt in the plaza. A burly British police superintendent with a flushed face jumped out and drummed his swagger stick against the leading red van. The long lugubrious face of Sub-Inspector Basil Cutworth popped out of the hatch atop the cab.

'Basil!' the superintendent screamed hysterically. 'Basil! They're coming! Follow me!'

At 3.13 p.m., the vans were in motion, lumbering forward like enraged elephants. Their sirens shrieked in the silence of the tropical afternoon, and their warning bells clanged. Engines whined in distress when excited drivers clashed their gears.

At 3.15 p.m., the police and the militants met in a side-street flanked by an iron picket-fence to keep pedestrians away from a sheer cliff. Grinning Malay constables tumbled out of the vans, eager to charge the Chinese who were their ancient enemies and the ruthless exploiters of their race. The constables' rifles were slung on their backs, but they flourished their black wicker shields and their three-foot-long billy-clubs in gleeful anticipation.

At 3.16 p.m., the policemen recoiled, shocked by the youth and the peaceable behaviour of the illegal gathering they had been ordered to disperse.

The students in their twenties who headed some nine hundred demonstrators carried placards demanding: RELEASE THE PATRIOTIC MARTYRS! The remainder of the procession strung along the picket-fence declined from apparent innocence to pathetic vulnerability. Most of the white-clad boys and girls were between thirteen and seventeen, but a hundred-odd bewildered seven-year-olds trotted at the procession's tail. Gathered separately some two hundred yards away, several hundred workers watched in silence.

At 3.17 p.m., the British superintendent roared at the student leaders, ordering them in English to disperse immediately. Now on foot, Sub-Inspector Basil Cutworth pleaded with the superintendent to use the vans' loud-speakers. The superintendent shook his head in angry refusal to play the customary five-minute warning recorded in Chinese, Malay, and English. He would not once again be reprimanded for hanging back, as he had been reprimanded after the race riots set off by Islam-intoxicated Malays three years earlier.

At 3.18 p.m., voices piped in slurred Mandarin: 'What did he say? What do we do?' Student leaders ignored those questions and raised their fists in ironic salute. They then led their followers in the Mandarin chant: 'Unity is strength!' The superintendent thrust out his hand in command – and the Malay constables charged. Sub-Inspector Basil Cutworth trotted disconsolately behind his men.

At 3.19 p.m., the two groups collided. The chanting halted, and the somnolent afternoon was still for an instant. The abrupt silence was broken by the grunts of

Malay policemen swinging billy-clubs at unprotected heads and by the screams of young Chinese girls. A few students half-heartedly fought back, but most stood passive.

At 3.21 p.m., the two groups recoiled from each other. Inflamed by the violence, a constable twisted a boy's head as if to tear it off. Other constables flailed with their heavy boots at youths prone in the gutter with hands clasped over their heads. The superintendent lashed out with meaty fists – and Sub-Inspector Cutworth shook his head despairingly.

At 3.22 p.m., Basil Cutworth issued the only order he was to give that day on his own initiative. Fifteen constables smartly whipped a heavy rope around a clump of students and tied the ends to the picket-fence. Curiously inconstant in purpose, the police were trying to prevent the dispersal they had originally ordered.

By 3.26 most of the students had pelted away from the slower-footed constables, and the workers had drifted into the side-streets, throwing rocks as they left. The plaza and its approaches were empty except for panting policemen, twenty-two captive students being bundled into the riot-vans, and fourteen students writhing on the hot pavement.

The encounter had taken no more than sixteen minutes from impulsive inception to inconclusive end. But the police had their prisoners – and the movement had its martyrs.

Small groups of students and workers roamed the streets of Singapore well into the heat-charged dusk. Some collided with police patrols and retreated slowly, hurling bricks and stones. The police charged time after time, trotting awkwardly on their short Malay legs like furious bulls pursuing agile matadors. They could neither catch the rioters nor halt the vandalism.

The flames from overturned automobiles lit the gentle violet dusk. Their youthful bravado inflamed by hatred, students were burning 'imperialist' vehicles. A gleaming Mercedes limousine carrying a plump Chinese millionaire was waved on. But students pounced on a tiny Austin-7 driven by a lean Indian clerk and overturned it with glee. The driver scuttled unmolested into the shelter of a side-street while the assailants beat his car into scrap with iron bars.

As casually as they had tossed coins the day before, laughing students flicked matches at the liquid dripping from the ruptured fuel tank. On the seventh try the petrol caught, and a gout of yellow-red flame lit the students' delighted faces.

A police patrol ordered to enforce the recently pro-claimed curfew clumped around the corner in heavy boots. The students threw a few valedictory rocks before drifting into the darkness.

They found fresh amusement three blocks away. Rais-ing their iron bars high, they converged on a stately Chrysler Imperial that was threading the maze of side-streets towards broad Orchard Road. The grey-haired chauffeur braked in fright. The street was too narrow to turn, and an awkwardly parked truck blocked the road fifty feet ahead.

In the cushioned interior of the Chrysler, Turner Lee awoke with a start. He looked accusingly at his son, who sat impassive by his side.

'What is it?' he demanded. 'What's happening?'

'Just some students, Father. Don't worry!'

'I told you we shouldn't come out tonight!'

'It was necessary, Father. We cannot always choose.'

The chauffeur poked his head out of the window.

'Imperialist lackey! Running dog!' Faces shadowed by the gloom, their shirts shining white, students hurled invective at the grey head.

'Where do you come from?' one demanded in Mandarin. 'And where are you going?'

'On the people's business,' the chauffeur replied in the same language. 'The Chinese people's business!'

'More likely an old goat of a lecher returning from a couch of delights,' a student jeered.

Closing on the Chrysler, the students raised their iron bars to strike. Their leader shattered the side-window with a single tap and demanded again: 'Where are you going?'

'The House of Tan,' the chauffeur said softly. 'We are returning to the House of Tan.'

The leader waved his followers back and pondered silently for a moment.

'Pass!' he finally said. 'And be careful.'

The Chrysler resumed its stately progress.

'You see, Father,' Y. N. Lee said. 'I told you it would be all right.'

The limousine slowed again, attempting to manoeuvre around the truck that projected into the road. Finding that he could not squeeze past, the chauffeur tooted his horn peremptorily.

As if at a signal, six figures appeared out of the gloom. They were not students, but older men in workers' blue who moved with the heavy, menacing grace of professional thugs.

The foremost wrenched open the back door of the limousine. The men did not touch the chauffeur and ignored young Y. N. Lee. But scarred hands with swollen knuckles grasped Turner Lee and bundled him out of the car like a rag-doll. In the glow of the headlights knives flashed, and the butterfly tattoo of the Green Lotus Society fluttered on the thugs' wrists.

Turner Lee lay unmoving on the wet asphalt. Forty-eight seconds had passed since the Chrysler's horn tooted to demand free passage.

XV

Miles eased his arm out of the black-silk sling and painfully peeled off his sweat-soaked shirt. His face was pale; black shadows lay under his red-rimmed eyes; and his nostrils were pinched with strain.

'A hell of a day!' He spoke aloud to the empty room while filling a balloon glass with marc. 'First this damned shoulder, then the riots – and finally poor old Turner.'

He lit a cigarette and settled into the armchair. The radio, forgotten since morning, was playing a Bach concerto, the measured chords at once inspiring and reassuring.

'A hell of a day!' Miles said again and resurrected from his memory a line in Po Chü-yi's epic *The Everlasting Sorrow*: 'Trampling the failing limbs under the war-horses' hooves, the rabble army took its brute revenge.'

The words were uncannily apposite, he reflected, rubbing the back of his neck. He himself had now been attacked four times in all, twice in Hong Kong and twice in Singapore. Humphrey Enwright had died in the dark waters of Hong Kong harbour, and now, it appeared, Turner Lee, too, would die. Yet Turner had not been assaulted because of the scroll; he had been savaged by a random convulsion of the riots.

Miles had seen the attendants bring the old man into the casualty ward as he was about to leave the hospital. He had already waited for hours, gone out for a drink, and returned to wait two more hours before the harried radiologist assured him that neither a rib nor a collarbone was broken, just badly bruised.

Turner's slight form had been smeared with blood and filth, but his wise old eyes had been strangely serene. A dazed Y. N. Lee walked beside the stretcher. Uninjured physically, he was manifestly in shock. He did not speak.

After stitching up the old man's wounds and ordering a plasma transfusion, the Chinese casualty surgeon whispered: 'Your friend should live. His wounds are grave, but not mortal. Still, he's very frail . . . very old.'

Miles had sat beside the old man, hoping Turner Lee might find some comfort in his silent presence. Turner had spoken faintly before the attendants wheeled him away.

'Enlightenment, Miles?' he had whispered. 'Who knows? But perhaps I shall know soon.'

'Nonsense, Turner,' Miles had replied. 'You'll be fine in a few days.'

'You were never . . . never . . . very good at . . . Insincerity is not your . . .' After a long pause, the thready voice had resumed. 'Look after things for me, Miles.'

'What things, Turner? What do you want me to do?'

'Just . . . look after things. The scroll, you must know . . . and Hyacinth, of course.' Turner's voice had trailed off as the sedative took effect.

I'll call tomorrow, Miles now told himself. No, this morning. It's well past midnight. At least, he's got a chance. I'll call in the morning to find out how he is. Nothing else I can do!

Miles was a little surprised at how deeply the casual

cruelty of the attack on Turner Lee had moved him. The old man's courage touched him, of course. But, even more poignant, it was like watching his own father humbled and broken. The old man's affection and the trust he had shown at the last moment stirred Miles profoundly.

He had wondered at his own reaction during the long drive from the hospital through deserted streets. The only other vehicles were police Land Rovers whose sirens wailed a dirge for the ravaged city and, also, for the small bloodstained figure of Turner Lee. The old connoisseur's wounds cried out against the brutality that always seemed to usher in radical change – the brutality lamentable even when change was essential. The old China Turner Lee represented had been ruthlessly used by the new China – and then cast aside cynically.

'Oh, to hell with it,' Miles said aloud, lifting his glass. 'Stop brooding, pal!'

He was becoming maudlin, driven by fatigue, by the progressive shocks, and by the marc itself. Turner Lee was just one more among the many victims of Asia's cruelty whom he had seen over the years. It was foolish to overdramatise the incident.

Miles knew he would not sleep immediately despite his fatigue. He must first purge his mind of the turmoil of the day. The Bach concerto was calming him, and the fiery marc would in time blur all feeling. Half-asleep, he started when loud raps on the door broke his reverie.

Kam, the aged night watchman, stood outside the door, the smirk on his brown face framed by the innumerable wrinkles on his cheeks.

'Missy come see you!' His smile revealed bare gums. 'I say too late. She say no too late.'

Tanya strolled casually into the room. A tan raincoat was belted tightly about her waist above a long filmy white skirt, and she carried a black-velvet evening purse. Her vermilion lipstick was the only colour in her pale face.

'I've come for a drink, Miles.'

'You're always welcome,' he answered lightly and bundled a stack of newspapers off the sofa before pouring a large marc for her.

Tanya drank half and shuddered convulsively. She said: 'This is powerful stuff!'

'It's supposed to be. It's good for whatever ails you.'

Her eyes looked into the distance; her movements were jerky; and her left hand was so tightly clenched that her vermilion-lacquered nails dug into her palm. If her speech had not been so normal, Miles would have judged her the second case of shock he had seen that night.

'Nothing ails me . . . nothing at all,' she asserted. 'I'm fine. It's just been a long day . . . a very long day.'

Her eyes narrowed and focused on the black sling that supported his left arm.

'You, too, Miles? What happened to you?'

'Nothing serious. Only a slight misunderstanding.'

'With whom?' she demanded. 'When?'

'Last night . . .'

'And you didn't call me?'

'I didn't want to bother you. Anyway, I don't have the right to . . .'

'Miles, *I* have the right to ask. I claim it. You should have called. You already bother me just by being you. What happened?'

'Just a bad strain, the doctor says. I got knocked about a little. What about yourself? You always look lovely to me, but I've seen you looking better.'

'Just a long day, as I said.'

'Then why don't you take off your coat and relax? The

air-conditioning's good, but it's not all that cold. Or is your blood so thin?'

'I'll keep the coat, thanks. It's not thin blood, but a thin nightdress.'

'Nice of you to come prepared to spend the night.' He kept his tone light. 'I'm flattered.'

'Oh, Miles.' Her eyes were no longer distant, but liquid with unshed tears. 'It's been a *very* long day.'

'Tell me.' He sat beside her on the sofa. 'It's been a very, very long day for all of us.'

She rested her head on his good shoulder, and tears seeped beneath her closed eyelids. He tightened his arm to bring her closer, momentarily dismayed by the overwhelming concern and tenderness he felt for her. Rote consolation fell from his lips, but, he realised with a further shock, those hackneyed words welled from deep springs.

'Why do we speak in clichés when most moved?' He mused aloud. 'Why does strong emotion sound like a B-movie?'

'But still comforting.' Tanya smiled. 'Very comforting.'

'I'm glad,' he said softly. 'Tell me about it . . . when you want to.'

'Miles, I know I'm overwrought.' Her lashes veiled her eyes. 'Everyone's overwrought tonight. But this . . . this is betrayal.'

'Betrayal?'

'The only word . . . the only possible word. My father was the foundation of my life, a tower of strength. But, Miles, he's *evil*!'

He did not speak, but stroked her shoulder, marvelling at how fragile it felt under her raincoat.

'You know how I feel as a Eurasian. I'm torn in two sometimes. My father was always my consolation. Don't

(166)

feel isolated, he would say, because you're not. You have my love, he'd say, and all my support. Besides, Eurasians were the pioneers of a new world, blending races and cultures into new harmony for the future. It was a proud role.'

She sipped from the balloon glass, shivering when the spirits seared her throat.

'Look, he'd say, how he had reconciled two worlds, never forgetting his Chinese heritage, yet comfortable with the West. His business dealings bridging two worlds. To embody and understand both cultures, that was nobility and power.'

'And now?'

'And now, I've learned that he . . . that my father betrays all trust, betrays both cultures. He has even destroyed one of his own people . . . one of his Chinese brothers who is also one of his oldest friends.'

'Turner Lee?'

'You know?'

'I guessed, just now. But don't say any more if it's going to upset you.'

'Give me a little more marc.' She dabbed her eyes with a tissue. 'I'm all right. Now is the time to tell it. I want you to know.'

Tanya shivered again, but her chin was firm.

'We all sat up late last night. On the way to bed, I stopped by my father's study. I was worried, afraid the terrible day had exhausted him. The door was ajar, just a crack. I heard his voice raised.

'*He's not dead?*' my father shouted in Mandarin. *Not dead, but in hospital? You know he could connect me with that blasted picture. Even that fool Montague would finally realise we couldn't use the note if I could be tied to it. He would never dare himself. Montague would never call our bluff. But Turner could . . . and would. The whole thing's an empty bluff if he lives. Why won't the old man die?*

'I stood with my hand frozen on the doorknob. A placating murmur answered my father's tirade. I couldn't make out the words. I was just creeping away quietly when the telephone went. My father answered.

'*Dead?* he said in English. *How terrible! How terribly sad. When?* There was a pause, and my father added: *Yes, of course, I'll make the arrangements. At least he didn't suffer too much. Thank you for calling. Goodbye.*'

'Turner is dead?' Miles interrupted. 'I feared so. It must've been only minutes after I left him.'

'I'm afraid so. He was a nice old thing.'

'Very decent . . . usually.' Miles was shocked, sorrowful, and angry. 'Weak, but very nice.'

'I'm sorry. He was your friend.'

'A special sort of friend.'

'I'm almost finished.' She was more composed. '*Well, we're both lucky*, my father said, speaking Chinese again. *The old man just kicked off. Didn't say anything, just drifted from coma to death. There will, I suppose, be the expense of a tremendous wreath. But Peking can pay for the funeral – and we can proceed as planned.*

'The other voice said clearly: *You see, Mr Tan, it has worked out well. An artistic job the Green Lotus lads did, though we shoot thugs like them in China. And it looks as if the police killed him. Couldn't be better!*'

Tanya freed herself from Miles's arm. She lit a filter-tip cigarette with a chunky silver lighter and blew out a plume of grey smoke. Her voice was cold and controlled when she resumed.

'He chuckled, Miles. My father actually chuckled, and he said: *Well, it's all worked out beautifully. You'll understand my earlier concern, I'm sure. I must not be compromised, not even for this operation.*

'The other man answered: *Of course, Mr Tan, you're much too valuable. Peking deeply appreciates your sacrifices.* And my father chuckled again and said: *It's an honour to serve. It's my patriotic duty.* He sounded like a fanatic. His patriotic duty! When I think of his accounts in Switzerland that no one knows about but me, not even my brothers. His patriotic duty! To kill an old man . . . a sweet, harmless old man who was one of his oldest friends.

'I'll finish quickly. *Let me have the note*, my father said. *It'll be safer here. And tell Pritchard to go ahead. The road is clear.*

'I was horrified. I stumbled up to my bedroom, undressed without thinking and lay down. But I couldn't sleep. My father was a monster – and everything he'd told me was a lie. He belonged only to *one* world – the old cruel Chinese world. Everything he'd said about my being the child of love, a pioneer of a new world, everything was a lie. He doesn't love. He only hates.'

Miles drew her into his arms again. She lay back, her eyes cold.

'Tanya!' He chose his words with great care. 'What is said may be true, though the speaker is false. Your father spoke good sense, even if he doesn't believe his own wisdom. Don't torment yourself any more.'

She stirred impatiently and spoke again in the same detached tone.

'There's not much more to tell. I lay awake for hours, wondering what my father was doing . . . and hating him. I never knew I could hate anyone as I hate that man . . . I wanted to hurt him. Then I remembered his asking for the note . . . how he'd stressed the note all the time. If it

(169)

was so important to him, I could hurt him most by taking the note.

'I waited till everyone was asleep, and I crept downstairs to his desk in my bare feet. I found the promissory note tucked into an envelope among discarded newspapers and magazines. I *knew* it would be there. He always talked about Poe's *Purloined Letter*, saying the best concealment was no concealment.

'I was afraid to get dressed . . . afraid someone might catch me before I could get out, so I threw the raincoat on and came to you.'

Tanya plunged her hand into a pocket of the raincoat and pulled out the promissory note Cecil Montague had signed to Turner Lee. She thrust the paper at Miles, holding it between forefinger and thumb as if it were unclean.

Miles slowly read the spidery handwriting in which Turner Lee had written his own death-warrant: *I promise to pay to Dr Turner Lee, his heirs or assigns, the sum of US $50,000 (fifty thousand American) in exchange for the scroll known as* The Everlasting Sorrow, *payment to be made on no fixed date, but at the convenience of the concerned parties.* The signature was *C. E. F. Montague.*

'A simple document, but deadly,' Miles mused. 'No wonder they'll kill for it. To risk involving your father almost directly . . . that's a bold step. It must be something *very* important they're after. I wonder . . .'

'Miles,' she interjected fiercely, 'whatever they're after, you must stop them. My father must *not* benefit from Turner Lee's murder. You've got the note. Can't you take it to Mr Montague and get the picture back? My father will be furious . . . frustrated. That's what I want.'

'And that's why you came to me?'

'Not the only reason, Miles. Maybe not even the main

(170)

reason. But a big reason. That's the truth. From now on I must be completely honest, not tell half-truths and half-lies like my father.

'Miles, he used me against you. He told me to see you and watch you. I even took him the telegraph blanks you threw away at Raffles. He said you were planning to cheat Turner Lee.'

'And you believed him?'

'And I believed him!' Tanya acknowledged flatly. 'I had no reason not to believe him. But I've come to you now.' She laughed. 'After all, I had to go somewhere – and you were convenient.'

'Complete honesty from now on? Nothing hidden?'

'Complete honesty, Miles darling, nothing hidden.'

Turning her back, she untied the belt and let the raincoat fall from her shoulders. She wore a long filmy peignoir over a nearly transparent nightdress. Slowly she turned to face him.

He gasped at the revelation. Her breasts were high, and her waist curved gently to the swell of her hips. Glimmering through the translucent folds, her belly swelled sweetly to the lustrous triangle between her thighs.

Tanya let the peignoir drift off her shoulders and raised her arms. Miles slid the nightdress over her arms and let it fall to the sofa.

'Complete honesty,' she smiled. 'Nothing hidden at all.'

Miles took Tanya into his arms with exaggerated gentleness. Her breasts pressed softly against his bare chest, the nipples tense. He fought down his body's demands. This coupling must be neither frankly animal like Sally's joyous sensualtiy nor perverse like Hyacinth's inventiveness.

The next instant he forgot all other women and everything else in his absorption with Tanya. They explored each other's bodies languorously, intense but unhurried, as if time had stopped for them alone.

'Maybe this is love,' he whispered as her fingertips traced an intricate pattern on his chest. 'True love.'

'Not maybe,' she whispered in reply. 'I *know* this is love.'

She was less wary of expressing emotion in words than he, and her bold hands stroked his thighs purposefully. Blood pounding in his ears, Miles watched Tanya's slow movements reflected in the mirror.

He gasped with pleasure when the searching fingers of his right hand found the smooth slope of her back and buttocks. Gently, he drew her down, feeling the velvet length of her against his naked body. She lay quiet for a moment before pulling away, her breasts brushing his chest.

'Just lie back!' she commanded. 'I want to make love to you. And I don't want you to hurt your shoulder.'

He obediently relaxed on the cool sheets. Her tenderness was a benediction, blessing him and absolving him of all previous encounters.

Exultation lifted him from the bed, and he heard her cry out from a great distance. Transcending all normal sensation, he felt his own explosive release at the same instant as hers. After a small infinity, she dropped gently to lie upon him.

'That was the first time,' she murmured, 'the very first time it ever happened, my love.'

'Nothing hidden, absolutely nothing,' he whispered. 'You are my love.'

XVI

'You've got to admit it's a funny name.'

Tanya laughed and stretched luxuriously in the late-morning sunlight that shone through the Venetian blinds to cast a barred pattern on the rumpled bed.

'Tanya Tan! It's almost as bad as Jerome K. Jerome or Evan Jones Evans, a chap I actually knew at Cambridge. I might as well be called Mary Maryland. I think I'll change it.'

A premonitory twinge of alarm distracted Miles's attention from the precise adjustment of his red-and-green striped silk bow-tie. He turned from the mirror to regard the young woman curled sinuously under the sheets like a replete tabby cat.

'What are you thinking of changing it to?' He played to her whimsical mood. 'Lili Lin?'

'Perhaps Giselle de Ballantier. When I was a little girl, I decided French names were very feminine – yet independent . . . strong. French is really a woman's language. How would you like that?'

'Not much! I think you ought to keep Tanya Tan. It's a very pretty name. You should stick to it . . . While you're brooding, how about a Bloody Mary?'

'Keep it always, Miles?'

'Well, maybe not always!' He side-stepped. 'But for a while yet.'

He filled two tumblers with the red liquid in the glass pitcher and crowned them with wedges of lemon. The trays with the sparse remains of their late breakfast lay on the table in the entry hall. The scene, Miles suspected, might be too cosily domestic for his long-term comfort.

The night together had been splendid, though brief. Both had been exhausted: she by emotional storms loosed by her discovery of her father's perfidy; he by his injuries and, like her, by the mounting tension of Singapore's day of riots. They had both fallen asleep shortly after their leisurely yet intense coupling.

The morning held its own perils. Miles had awakened to a sense of well-being unknown to him after such a first encounter, a sensation compounded of joy and tenderness. Excessive tenderness could be his undoing. Nonetheless, he now stooped to kiss her softly.

Tanya tugged gently at the bow-tie and said: 'I bet I could get you to untie it a lot faster than you tied it.'

Miles wanted nothing more than to join her again in the big bed. Sadly, he could not. He had to make his move immediately – be it a move entirely for himself that would at the least allow him a glimpse of the scroll, or, he conjectured vaguely, a move for Singapore to help calm the upheaval.

He did not know precisely what he would do, but he could now act. Nor was he sure of his own emotions, although he had been reflexively evasive when Tanya prattled archly about changing her name, presumably to his.

Beyond the affection for her whose depth he was still discovering, he was, above all, surprised that he felt none of the disgust, almost self-loathing, that normally afflicted him after the hectic hasty couplings that occurred too frequently in his life. Yet his heritage was not only Jewish guilt, but Catholic guilt as well.

Miles did not, for once, feel he had sinned. That remission was still remarkable in itself in the year 1955, when the Western world had not cast off its Judaeo-Christian inhibitions and granted itself permanent absolution for all the sins it no longer recognised.

What, he wondered, did his untoward reaction mean? Or portend? Now *he* was being coy, if only with himself.

'You're a fop, Miles Corrigan.' Tanya mocked his self-absorption. 'Not only the tie. I could also get you to unbuckle that fancy matching belt in a big hurry.'

'Very easily. There's nothing I'd like more. But what do you propose I do with that little bit of dynamite you brought along last night?'

'Oh that!' She was reluctant to discard her playful mood. 'I suppose we'll have to do something about it. But must it be right now?'

'Sooner the better. They'll be looking for you.'

'Well, they won't find me so soon. No one could possibly guess I came here.'

'I hope so . . .'

'Miles,' she interrupted, 'fop or not, you look very handsome in that costume. But what about me? It's a sunny morning in Singapore. A raincoat's not quite the thing. But I can't go out like this.'

Tanya dropped the sheet she had been holding under her chin. The perfection of her pearly breasts and the tender little crease at her waist were still a revelation to Miles. But he answered lightly.

'You *could* go out like that. It would attract a lot more attention than a raincoat. You'd cause a sensation. They'd call off the demonstrations to come and look.'

He, too, was keeping it light, Tanya realised, as if they were both afraid to show their true feelings. She was virtually certain she knew how Miles felt, even if he might not yet know it himself. Still, she was afraid to show too great emotion too soon, although she'd teased him by hinting that they should make it permanent.

Yet was she absolutely certain how she truly felt? It was all too sudden and too overwhelming. Also somewhat equivocal.

Tanya was acting as if she had already overcome her revulsion at discovering that her father had lied treacherously all his life – to herself, to everyone. Yet it would be ages before she forgot her betrayal by the man who had been the bedrock of her existence. That hurt might never heal completely. But she would mourn the death of her illusions when she was alone. She would not allow her distress to intrude into her relations with Miles.

Relations? What relations did they really have? So far, only sexual relations – and a common taste for badinage.

However Miles might really feel, what made her so sure that her feelings for him were not just a reaction to her own distress? Still, they could hardly say she had gone to Miles on the rebound. A woman did not rebound from a father to a lover.

Did she not? From one powerful emotion to another, from one extreme to its opposite, was certainly a rebound. If she were on the rebound, how could she be so certain her feelings for Miles were not synthetic?

Simply because she *knew* they were real and not synthetic. She had been strongly attracted to him the moment they met. The cut of his jaw and the high forehead with the unruly copper hair falling on it; his cocky self-confidence and his lithe movements. Women were not supposed to be moved so much by physical attractiveness, but she was. Besides, he lived in two worlds, as she did herself: Asia and the West simultaneously.

She could never marry a Chinese. The Chinese man's assumption of total proprietorship and his expectation of total obedience was medieval. Anyway, she found few Chinese men physically attractive.

Marry a European? Possibly, but she might always feel he was condescending to her in his ignorance of her Chinese heritage. Besides, European arrogance could be just as withering as Chinese arrogance.

Of course, Miles was a European. A Caucasian, she should probably say, since he was an American. But he was a Caucasian who knew as much, perhaps more, of China and Asia as she did, an outsider who loved Asia, but could assess its sometime deceptive glamour objectively. His mixed heritage was hardly as burdensome as her own. But they were, nonetheless, both outsiders by blood as well.

Still, what was all this about marrying? Marriage simply didn't come into it, certainly not yet.

Aware that he was looking at her quizzically, wondering about her long silence, Tanya said light-heartedly: 'If I can't go out like this, you'll just have to do something about both our problems: the little packet of dynamite and my wardrobe. It's so nice to be helpless – and to be looked after.'

'You'll be well looked after.' He leered dramatically. 'Time after time.'

'I can hardly wait. But you should really get the note to Cecil Montague just as soon as you can. Let *him* destroy it.'

'And the picture, love? Does he get to keep it?'

'It's not really his property.' She pondered. 'Is it?'

'Not till he's paid for it. That's just about the only sure thing in this tangle. It's *not* Montague's property. God knows whose it is.'

'Not my father's,' she said fiercely. 'Not his at all. I imagine it really belonged to Turner Lee. So it definitely must belong to his son Y. N. now.'

'Not so definitely! You know, Turner told me to look after things – the scroll among them. He told me, *not* Y.N.'

Why tell Tanya that Turner had also charged him to look after his daughter Hyacinth? Besides, Y. N. had been in no condition to listen to, much less to comprehend, his father's instructions.

'You're not saying it now belongs to you?'

'I wouldn't say that.'

Miles deliberately diverted her attention. Desire to possess *The Everlasting Sorrow* had not merely entered his mind, but had lodged there.

'Anyway, the responsibility's mine. Turner made me responsible. So I can't turn it over to Montague or even Y. N. till I know exactly what's been going on. For one thing, we still don't know how your father planned to use the note.'

'I suppose you're right, darling,' she conceded. 'All right, then. First, some clothes for me. Then we'll whip out our magnifying glasses, shine up our daggers, don our cloaks – and find out what's really going on. Give me a pen. I'll write down some sizes.'

'Can't I just . . .' He cupped his hands. 'Well, show them?'

'No, you can't. You have very clever hands. But it's more practical to give some sizes. I'll make a list.'

'You'll want something nondescript,' he advised. 'Also

big sunglasses and one of those floppy straw hats the amahs wear to keep off the sun.'

'I can see,' she laughed, 'I'm going to be a vision of loveliness.'

'You'll just have to depend on my bad taste.'

'Anything but that. Go to Town and Country on North Bridge Road and ask for Mrs Tan. She's no relation . . . You can trust her.'

'Are you sure?'

'Quite sure. Now, come and kiss me before you go.'

He sat on the edge of the bed, her warm naked back beneath his palms. Her lips moved softly under his, and her tongue darted. He began to press her down. But she wrenched her head aside and slipped from his grasp.

'I told you,' she laughed, 'that I could have the fancy bow-tie off fast if I wanted to. But not now. The sooner you go, the sooner you'll be back.'

Walking down the interminable corridor, Miles whistled under his breath. He grinned when he realised the tune was 'Arise!', the old marching song of the Chinese Red Army.

Michael Tong, portly and perspiring behind the reception desk, smiled broadly when Miles asked: 'How's it going?'

'Much better, Mr Corrigan. The waiters and roomboys are trickling back to work. You saw we finally got your laundry done. And the disturbances should be over soon.'

'Don't bet on it. By the way, do you have a couple of plain envelopes?'

Miles carefully printed addresses and strolled to the far end of the parking lot to drop the envelopes into a cylindrical red postbox. Climbing into the Porsche, he revved the cold engine repeatedly before taking off in a splatter of gravel. It was bad driving, but it was sure to attract attention to him – and away from the hotel where Tanya was hidden.

North Bridge Road was not its usual stream of cars, trishaws, trucks and bicycles. On the five-foot way behind the monsoon ditch, pedestrians jostled each other in their normal unyielding manner. But motor traffic was much lighter than usual on the steaming asphalt of the commercial artery, where you could buy anything from a lacquered pressed duck to an original Balenciaga ballgown. The few vehicles moved even faster than normal, avoiding the blue police Land Rovers with grills covering their windshields.

Miles slipped the Porsche into a narrow parking place and got out. Pedestrians and shopkeepers were also behaving abnormally. The bony Indian watchman in front of Hop Huat's Gold Shop was alert, his shotgun firmly clasped in his hands. He usually lay at ease on his rope-net bed, the shotgun beneath it. Plump Chinese matrons in loose flowered pyjamas did not linger to gossip, but made their small purchases of fish, vegetables and meat briskly. Knots of students in white shirts and white shorts strutted along the covered pavement; it was barely three feet wide, but Singapore called it the five-foot way. The students were isolated. The other pedestrians drew away as if they carried the plague bacillus.

Intent on the spectacle, Miles walked right past the unassuming entrance of the shop called Town and Country. Turning abruptly, he collided with a middle-aged Chinese whose shaven head glistened with sweat. The powerful man wearing a torn singlet and dirty blue shorts ploughed ahead muttering imprecations in the Hokkien dialect.

Miles shrugged. His absent-mindedness would not

spark another riot. This was just normal Singapore bad temper.

A sweet-faced woman with a harsh voice responded when he asked for Mrs Tan. She took Tanya's list and sent two chubby saleswomen scurrying to collect the articles. They finally came to fourteen parcels.

'You'd think she was planning an expedition to the South Pole,' Miles joked.

'It's all necessary, Mr Corrigan, absolutely necessary.' Mrs Tan smiled. 'At least she thinks it's all necessary.'

'Well, if she says so . . . Now, what's the damage?'

He reached into the inside pocket of his jacket, but did not find his wallet. Without alarm, he tried other pockets. It would not be the first time he had thrust his wallet into the wrong pocket in haste. But it was gone.

'Look, I'm afraid I don't . . .'

'So I see.' The proprietress smiled. 'For a minute, I thought you were doing a hornpipe. You must have forgotten your wallet. I can put it on her account.'

'I'd appreciate it.'

'Certainly. You know, when I was living in Shanghai everything went on account. Young European men about town never collected their salaries. They could sign for anything – rickshaws, restaurants, White Russian princesses, even church collections. The chit-holders would collect from company cashiers at the end of the month. Anything left over, their cookboys took to run their households. Often there was nothing left. The young men ran up tremendous debts that way.'

'Sounds like fun,' Miles observed breezily. 'Can you add a phone call to the chit? And is there a phone that's not as public as the one on the counter?'

Mrs Tan led him to a minuscule office at the back of the shop.

'You'll be quite private here. I hope all's well with Tanya.'

'So do I.'

It took only three minutes for the hotel switchboard to put the call through to the room. That was a new record. Maybe Mike Tong was right, and things were really improving.

'Miles!' Tanya's voice brightened. 'What a pleasant surprise. I knew you couldn't bear not talking with me for so long.'

'That too, Tanya. Unfortunately, there's more. We've been playing the fool.'

'What's gone wrong, Miles. Why are you worried?'

'Maybe nothing, maybe a lot. I just had my pocket picked . . . my wallet lifted. I made a big show of leaving the hotel. And, at least, I've proved they're after me. So my room's the worst possible place for you right now. How did you get to the hotel last night?'

'My car, naturally. I could hardly walk or find a taxi at that time of night.'

'Where's your car now?'

'Where I left it, I suppose. In the hotel parking lot.'

'Oh, that's great!' He groaned. 'Just great!'

'Where should I have left the car – under a bush or buried on the beach? What's wrong?'

'You're an amateur at this game – and I'm getting careless,' he explained. 'I'll bet they've either got you staked out now – or will within an hour.'

'You mean they know where I am?'

'If not now, very soon. Leaving your car in the parking lot . . . you might as well have put up a signboard. You may have a little time. But once your father finds out the note's missing . . .'

'And then?'

'You know him best. And then?'

'He'll be furious . . . enraged. He can't stand anyone's interfering with his plans. But his darling submissive daughter . . . he'll be three times as angry.'

Miles wanted to alert her, but did not want to frighten her. Concluding that a little fright would make her more alert, he said: 'Your father has to prove to his friends in Peking that his loyalty to them transcends *all* other loyalties. Maybe by making an example of you. You've got to get out right now. Where can you go?'

'There is Maggie Wong,' she said hesitantly. 'I thought of her last night before deciding to come to you, and decided you were more interesting. Maggie's father is a big bug among the Nationalists and violently anti-Communist. Three Alsatian guard-dogs and two bodyguards patrol the Wongs' compound. Maggie would probably be best. I'll call her . . .'

'Don't call. Just get there. Take the room-key with you . . . Don't leave it at the desk. Walk along the beach, not the road, till you're opposite the taxi-stand. Don't take the first in the line . . . and neither a Chinese nor an Indian driver. Get a Malay driver. What's Maggie Wong's phone number?'

'It's 272823,' she said in a small voice. 'Miles, will you be all right? Be careful!'

'We'll both be all right if we move fast. Now git!'

He hung up and loped through the shop, leaving the parcels on the counter and Mrs Tan just opening her mouth to protest.

XVII

That same afternoon, Cecil Edward Frederick Montague, CMG, OBE, DSO (bar), MC, Senior Political Adviser to Her Britannic Majesty's High Commissioner for Southeast Asia, faced his moment of truth. Like a maddened bull challenging the matador who tormented him, Montague himself provoked the confrontation. He could no longer wait for the deadline the lawyer George Pritchard had set for twelve hours later. Physical courage Cecil Montague had never lacked. But his psychological reserves and his financial resources were both heavily overdrawn.

For thirty-four hours, he had desperately tried to evade the nets cast around him. His wealthy father-in-law detested him, so that door was closed – and double-locked. He could not ask his wife for money; he had already spent twice over the funds she had entrusted to him. Only clever bookkeeping and inspired lying had so far concealed that misappropriation. If she should find out, the sour bitch was quite capable of suing him, exposing him to the world. Lady bloody Matilda was no bloody hope.

Banks were useless, since he could offer no collateral. He had tried every possible private source, which in Singapore meant Chinese sources, the wealth of the

Sephardic Jews having trickled away. However splendid their titles, his British friends did not command large sums. Unlike the independent Chinese entrepreneurs, they were only the custodians of funds belonging to their firms.

He had been offered fleeting hope several times during his search. But invariably the price in future favours had been intolerable. Indeed, the price had been impossible for him to pay – not because of any moral squeamishness on his part, but because they believed his power to be far greater than it was.

Convinced that a corrupt senior official could totally ignore regulations, as had corrupt Imperial Mandarins, the Chinese millionaires had been courteous, almost obsequious. They had also been implacable.

'Why so little, Mr Montague?' one had offered. 'Take a hundred thousand gold, a quarter of a million if you like.'

But every one had made it clear that an unsecured loan for an indefinite period would be forthcoming only if he placed his influence wholly at his benefactor's command. If the Chinese bought a man, he was their servant, virtually their bond-slave, ever after. Knowing he could not deliver what they would demand, Cecil Montague had even tried Morgan Tan again – to be rejected with syrupy sympathy.

He could turn to no one else for a loan. But a single bright ray pierced his gloom. One phrase resounded in his mind, offering hope at the same time as it heightened his fears.

'Just a small quid pro quo,' Pritchard had suggested. The implication was assuredly that he need perform only a single action, not be permanently enlisted in the service of Pritchard's masters in Peking. Then he could, presumably, keep the scroll, as well as regaining the note he had so casually signed. In an optimistic moment, he decided he would insist on retaining the scroll – and also on securing a receipted bill, in return for that 'small quid pro quo.' That would quash the threat of subsequent blackmail.

Of course, he would do nothing dishonourable, but the quid pro quo was likely to be marginally acceptable. After all, they were not fools in Peking.

Montague was exhausted by his own emotional turmoil when he had finally lifted the telephone, suspended between fear and hope. Pritchard had been surprised at the call, since the deadline was still several hours away. After a show of reluctance, the lawyer had agreed to come by that afternoon. The two men sat in the same positions in the study they had occupied a day and a half earlier.

'I'll hear what you've got to say, Pritchard.' Montague was determined to dominate the conversation this time. 'But I'll make no promise, no commitments, till I've heard you out.'

'Can't find the money, eh?' Pritchard rejoined silkily. 'Sorry about that, old boy.'

'By no means. I could find the money if I wanted to.'

'Well, it comes to the same thing, don't it? You *could* find the money, but you've *not*!'

'I didn't say that.' Montague felt the initiative slipping from his hands. 'I only said I'd listen to your proposition.'

'Proposition?' the pouter-pigeon solicitor asked blandly. 'What proposition?'

'You did talk of a quid pro quo, didn't you?'

'Oh that! Yes, I suppose there is a possible quid pro quo. But it's such a small thing you'd hardly call it a proposition.'

'What is it, man?' Montague's pale-blue eyes protruded, and his splendid ginger-grey moustache drooped dejectedly. 'For God's sake, what is it?'

'Rattled, old boy?' the lawyer inquired solicitously. 'Don't be . . . There's no need for alarm. It's only a small thing, as I said.'

'Well, what is it? If you've got something to say, for God's sake spit it out!'

'Actually, I can tell you between us . . . in confidence . . . that I'm rather relieved. When I saw you last, I didn't know what they wanted. But it's such a small thing, I don't see how you can object.'

'Fine! But what is it? Stop playing cat and mouse, damn you!'

'Sorry, old man. Thought you'd be pleased to know it was so minor. You know, I still can't make these people out. Simply can't see why they're making such a meal of it.'

'If you'd just tell me . . .' Montague said icily.

The little lawyer tossed down his whisky. He leisurely lit a fat Burma cheroot and fussily made sure it was drawing well before speaking again.

'It's really nothing . . . nothing more than your job. That's why I'm so surprised. But you know our yellow brethren. They never do anything straightforwardly if they can find a roundabout way.'

'What *is* it?' Montague gritted through clenched teeth.

'I won't keep you in suspense any longer. Sorry if I meandered. It's very simple, as I said . . .'

'Yes! Spit it out, man!'

'You know about this deportation business? Some obscure headmaster and three or four labour leaders.'

'It is unlikely *I* wouldn't know when every coolie and schoolboy in Singapore does . . . And half of them are tearing up the streets in protest?'

'Don't get your back up, old man. Just wanted to be certain. But to the kernel: My clients do not want to see those five men deported.'

'Why do they feel so strongly?' Montague's professional curiosity prevailed momentarily over his personal apprehension.

'I'm not absolutely certain . . . can't speak for them. My own feeling, for what it's worth, is they're embarrassed . . . gravely embarrassed. These deportees're small potatoes . . . very small potatoes. But deporting them could embarrass the People's Republic of China.'

'How so?'

'You must see it. If they're sent back to People's China, there's the question of whether to accept them or not. If Peking takes them, it's as good as admitting it's been up to some hanky-panky here. Of course this is purely a local movement . . . spontaneous.'

'Yes,' Montague temporised, 'I can see the embarrassment. Any other reason?'

'Again, I'm not wholly sure. But suppose, just suppose one or two – or all – decided they'd rather go to Taiwan . . . to the Nationalists. Big slap in the face for Peking, that.'

'Sounds logical.' Montague suppressed his suspicion that the argument was specious. 'And what am I meant to do?'

'Review the case, man. Review the case – and make your own decision. The order was issued hastily by the so called Government of Singapore. You can override it.'

'I suppose I could,' Montague mused. 'But why should . . .'

'Mind you, Montague,' Pritchard interjected, 'I'm not asking you to fly against your own judgement or your own conscience. Just to review the case – and make your own decision.'

'I could do that.'

'Look at the political issue: Overreaction by the Chief

Minister and so on. There are also legal questions. Headmaster The Sam-lok and one other are Straits-born, not China-born. Theoretically, they're entitled to British citizenship, though that's a tangled web, as you know. Can you really deport them legally?'

'I assume that's been gone into.'

'Hasn't, you know.' Pritchard smiled. 'You'd know if it had. The papers would've come across your desk.'

'Perhaps it hasn't,' Montague conceded.

'Well, then, just look into the matter. My clients don't presume to dictate to you. But you now know how they feel.'

'I suppose I could re-examine it. Actually, I should have done so weeks ago.'

'Well, there you are,' Pritchard said expansively. 'No problem at all. A simple matter, as I said.'

Montague rose and stretched. He felt as if heavy manacles had just been unlocked from his wrists. His relief was nearly unbearable. Almost gaily, he slopped whisky and ice into their glasses.

'I can certainly look into the matter again.' He raised his glass in salute. 'But I can't promise any certain conclusion.'

'No need to, old man, no need to,' Pritchard assured him. 'Just look into it. And, if my clients are happy, Bob's your uncle. The scroll's yours . . . and so is the note. *If* they're happy, it's all finished, all tidied up.'

'A receipted bill would be necessary,' Montague said forcefully, glowing with triumph at taking command of the conversation. At last, he had Pritchard where he wanted him.

'No problem, old man, no problem at all. I told you they don't want the bloody thing back.'

Montague regarded the red-faced cockerel benevolently.

He could almost feel affection for the little lawyer, who was, when you came down to it, just doing his professional job – representing his client's interests as instructed. If only he hadn't made such a fuss in the first place. It was, as he had pointed out, all quite regular and proper.

Montague's disciplined bureaucratic mind was already planning his actions. He would openly call for the file tomorrow morning. If a revision were justified, he'd put his recommendation to the High Commissioner forcefully – and it would be accepted. Above all else, the High Commissioner, like himself, wanted to keep the peace in Singapore. The surest way to avert disastrous riots would be to release the five men who were under sentence of deportation. A timely compromise, a show of understanding, would cool tempers and restore orderly government.

The more Montague considered the prospects, the more favourable they appeared. He would, of course, examine the file carefully before reaching any decision. He certainly would *not* automatically give Pritchard's clients what they wanted – regardless of the consequences to himself.

'Your health, sir!' He lifted his glass in salute. 'Your very good health, sir!'

'Cheers!' The vulgar little man chuckled. 'Cheers, old boy!'

XVIII

When he emerged from the cool dimness of Town and Country, damp heat enfolded Miles, and the sun seared his eyeballs. Momentarily dazzled, he stumbled against a tall student wearing the inevitable white shorts and shirt.

'Sorry,' he said. 'Thought I was falling.'

The youth contemplated him without expression before speaking in slurred South Seas Mandarin.

'*Wang-ba-dan! Yang-gwei-dz!*' he said slowly. 'Turtle's egg bastard! Foreign devil!'

'*Sieh-sieh ni! Ni shr jung-guo-ren ma?*' Miles answered. 'Thank you! You're Chinese, are you?'

The startled student nodded.

'I appreciate your traditional Chinese courtesy,' Miles continued in Mandarin. 'I am delighted by the courteous behaviour you have learned as the heir to Chinese culture.'

The boy gaped, shaken out of the contemptuous composure bestowed by his political and racial superiority.

Miles laughed aloud as he jack-knifed himself into the Porsche. Though the gesture was childish, he had deflated the student's arrogance. It was a small triumph. But even a small triumph could help armour him for the trials ahead.

He edged the ostentatious red sports car into the traffic, pleased this once that it was so conspicuous. While he pondered his next move, he would blaze a false trail across the island.

He had to assume that he was under surveillance by the opposition. (Miles fell automatically into the terminology of the half-world of espionage, which he thought he had escaped.) He had no knowledge of the opposition's assets but he had evidently been under surveillance since he first crossed Humphrey Enwright's trail. Tired of waiting passively for them to come to him, he would now force the pace. If rattled, the opposition might tip its hand.

The Porsche idled past the white tower of the Cathay Building, that many-terraced, slightly decrepit monument to the pre-Pearl Harbour British conviction of absolute security. The 'Singapore mind,' it was later called, that complacent assumption of invincible supremacy. The inflexible Singapore mind still directed the actions of most senior British civil servants on the island. Its mirror image directed many junior British officials. Miles called their psychology the '*New Statesman* mind' after the political journal they studied as devoutly – and as credulously – as fundamentalists view the Bible.

Senior officials *knew* the sun would never set on the British Empire, which was disintegrating around them. Their earnest young deputies knew they could not hasten the sun's movement, but strove to hasten the disintegration of the Empire.

They ritually detested the Chinese Nationalists and compulsively glorified the Communist People's Republic of China, just as they denounced Franco's Spain and defended the even harsher Soviet Union that was Stalin's legacy. It did not matter to them what regimes actually *did*, but only what they *said* they did. If leaders called themselves 'progressives' and declared that they were working for the good of mankind, they automatically won approbation – whatever the reality.

Such tolerance for inhumanity in the name of humanity extended to the depredations of the Malayan Liberation Army. That Chinese guerrilla force, dedicated to imposing Chinese rule on the Malay majority, still fought its cruel battle on the mainland north of Singapore. But the terrorists *said* they fought for independence and democracy.

Gunning the Porsche into Orchard Road, Miles pondered the death wish behind the *New Statesman* mind. Above all, the junior officials wished to atone for the injustices inflicted by British colonialism. But Miles was free of that guilt – free, as well, of any death wish. He was concerned with Miles Corrigan, not with suffering humanity in the abstract.

His immediate business was to find the elusive painting called *The Everlasting Sorrow*. It belonged in truth to neither Y.N. nor Cecil Montague – and Peking had forfeited its rights by the criminal conspiracy. It might just end up belonging to Miles de Sola Corrigan.

All along the Bukit Timah Road defiant signs still hung before shuttered factories. The slogans demanded release of the martyred deportees and pressed the workers' just demands. The demands *were* just, for Singapore's entrepreneurs, Chinese or British, had long given employees as little as they possibly could. Repression was still authority's automatic answer to labour's grievances – although the workers of Singapore were better off than any other workers in Southeast Asia.

The strike continued, but daily life was resuming. Police Land Rovers moved purposefully among heavy-laden trucks, among the rainbow colours of private cars, and among black midget taxis, which glittered like water-beetles. One of those taxis was probably following Miles, but all looked alike in the sun glaring through the fringed palm trees.

He turned abruptly into the narrow service road that ran parallel to the two-lane highway. General C. T. Chan had pressed him to examine his collection. He did not like the avaricious former Nationalist official who was conducting a complex flirtation with the Communists, but Chan had stolen some good pieces in the course of his official duties.

As promised, his servants admitted the American dealer, although the general himself was not at home. Miles dallied, turning over porcelains that held little interest for him, commercially. Nonetheless, some were spectacularly beautiful. After an hour, he emerged, jauntily puffing a Havana cigar extracted from his absent host's humidor. If his visit made for an unpleasant couple of hours for the general with the general's new Communist friends, that was just too bad.

Miles strolled leisurely towards the Porsche. Sliding in, he gave his pursuers plenty of time before he swung the sloping nose towards town. Three taxis left their rank behind the Porsche.

He took a circuitous route through the back-streets. A taxi, registration number S-1065, followed him through Dalvey Road to Nassim Road where he rejoined the main stream of traffic on Orchard Road. He lost S-1065 for a time, but it had reappeared when he parked near the First National City Bank.

He needed cash and a telephone. Laughton Pomeroy, the tall, sad-faced New Englander who ran the branch, was happy to oblige. He had in the past handled transactions for Miles that ran into tens of thousands.

At the desk in the small office the bank kept for favoured clients, Corrigan dialled the number Tanya had given him for Maggie Wong. For an infuriating twenty minutes, while he smoked three cigarettes, the line was busy. He doggedly dialled again and again.

'*Been-gwah? Been-gwah?*' A stertorous female voice finally saluted him with the forthright Cantonese hello: 'Who's that? Who's that?'

Miles winced. He would have to try his pidgin Cantonese.

'*Wong-siu jieh hai-doe ma?*' he stumbled. 'Is Miss Wong there?'

'*Chut-gai la!*' the voice told him triumphantly. 'Gone out!'

'*Tan siu-jieh hai-doe ma?* . . . And Miss Tan?'

'*Chut-gai la!*' The same answer in the same gleeful tone.

'You can speak English?' he asked hopefully.

To his delighted surprise, the answer came back: 'Little bit can do.'

'Missee Tan go out with Missee Wong?' he asked.

'No!' The amah's tone was uncompromising. 'Missee Wong Kuala Lumpur yesterday.'

'But Missee Tan come see you today?'

'*Hai-ya!*'

His heart lifted at the flat affirmative, and he asked: 'Can I speak to Missee Tan?'

'No can! I already say she go out.'

'When go out?' he demanded.

'Maybe ten . . . fifteen minutes before.'

'Where Missee Tan go?' He felt trapped in an imbecilic round of Twenty Questions. 'You savee what place?'

'*No-ah!*' The amah racked up a point for her team. 'Me no savee!'

Miles pondered, but the amah broke in: 'You all finshee? Me go now. Got plentee work.'

'Just a minute,' he pleaded. 'Missee Tan go out alone?'

'Aronee? Aronee?' the amah replied suspiciously. 'Me no savee aronee. Me hang up now.'

'Just one minute more.' He spaced his words clearly. 'Missee Tan go out one piecee man? Somebody go with Missee Tan?'

Why for you no askee before? Missee Tan go out with other mans.' The harsh voice was logical and infuriating. 'All finshee now?'

'One more minute, please!' Miles knew he sounded like a cracked record.

'What b'long man go with Missee Tan? *Been-gwah?*'

'No more talkee,' the amah replied peremptorily. 'Got plentee work.'

'I must know,' he begged. 'What man go with Missee Tan?'

'Missee Tan put on new dress b'long Missee Wong . . . *New dress!* And she go out besides young master and two flends.'

'Where go? *Been-doe?*'

'Dunno! Me no savee! Got plentee work. Me go now! Finshee!'

The clatter of the handset cut off the last word and left Miles fuming impotently. He smoothed down his hair and lit another cigarette. He was smoking too much. He always did under pressure.

The full impact of the amah's chopped words did not strike him for almost half a minute. Tanya had in effect disappeared, voluntarily or otherwise. His first instinct was to rush after her. But where? A hair-trigger response would not regain the initiative lost by Tanya's rashness.

Surprised by the effort he required to think coolly in

the face of her disappearance, Miles enjoined himself not to panic and drew up a quick balance sheet.

First, he alone knew where Montague's promissory note was hidden: two points in his favour. Second, he did *not* know how the opposition had planned to use the note: one point against him. Third, he did *not* know what had become of Tanya: another two points to the bad. Fourth, she might have shifted to a new hidey-hole or she might have been taken by the opposition: no points either way till he knew. Fifth, if she had been taken, the opposition, playing on his affection for her, would make the promissory note the price of her safety: two big points against him.

Would he ever sacrifice Tanya? Perhaps, but he could not wholly predict his own reaction at the critical moment of decision. Perhaps he would not! Perhaps he could not sacrifice her! Morgan Tan would not allow his henchman to hurt his daughter; even Morgan Tan could not be that heartless.

All those imponderables yielded a balance slightly in Miles's favour. Above all, the opposition had begun to surface.

Miles had been drilled to put aside all concerns except the mission at hand. Failure, perhaps death, was the penalty for distraction. All other concerns, all other individuals *must* be sacrificed for the mission. Yet Miles asked himself again: 'Are you really prepared to sacrifice Tanya? Is the scroll worth risking her life?'

Tanya had touched him deeply, he told himself, but she had no claim on him. He had to *act* as if she did not matter to him. Otherwise, he would be surrendering his tenuous advantage. He must think of Tanya as a pawn he could sacrifice to make the opposition reveal its plans. But could he?

His dilemma unresolved, Miles lifted the handset and dialled the Ocean Park.

'No, Mr Corrigan,' Michael Tong told him. 'I'm sorry. No answer from your room. I'll send a boy to see, but I'm certain no one's there.'

Miles waited without hope, drumming his fingers on the teak desktop.

'No, Mr Corrigan, no one's there. I'll keep watch and . . .'

'If the lady returns,' Miles interrupted, 'please tell her to wait for my call. In your office, *not* the room. I'll ring again in an hour.'

He replaced the handset. Since Tanya had neither called nor returned, he had to assume that she had been taken by the opposition. The next move was his, but he would have to play the pawn blind.

He lifted the telephone directory and settled down for a long spell of dialling. Alex Cutler of the BBC was never easy to find. He had not become the best-informed man in Southeast Asia by lolling among the decaying splendours of his haunted mansion. On the sixth try, Miles thought he had finally run Cutler to earth, but the head waiter said the correspondent had just left the Cockpit, more formally the Hotel de l'Europe. Three calls later, an American voice reedy with age spoke from the Coconut Grove. Bill Bailey promised to put Cutler on the line.

'Hullo, Miles,' the sonorous voice boomed. 'I was wondering when you'd surface.'

'I've been busy, Alex. Your town is a hell of a place for a peaceable art dealer intent on his lawful occasions.'

'So it is,' Cutler agreed with vast good humour. 'Getting worse all the time.'

'What do you foresee?'

'A good question, a very good question!'

'Don't tell me you're glad I asked the question,' Miles interrupted. 'And don't tell me the situation is fluid.'

'Well,' Cutler answered, 'I am glad . . . damned glad . . . you asked the question. I always like dazzling an appreciative audience. And the situation *is* fluid, practically in flux.'

'What do you expect next?'

'Ho-ho!' Cutler's forced laugh reverberated in the receiver. 'Ha-ha.'

'A little less ho-ho, Alex. And could you tone down the ha-ha while you're about it? I'm just a city boy from Manhattan lost in the mysterious East. How about it?'

'Don't be wet, Miles. But I give it forty-eight hours. If the government deport the five martyrs, Singapore will blow up: rioting, looting, burning, killing, the lot. If the government back down, they might as well go out of business . . . close up shop and hand the keys to the Masses Operation Party, who'll mop up for Peking. Nice little dilemma, isn't it?'

'Why are the five so important, Alex? Why the fuss?'

'I'm not certain, Miles. The five martyrs could be merely the pretext. If the villains win this one, they'll have got almost everything they want. If they lose, how much will they have really lost? Practically nothing! And they'll have gained invaluable experience for the next go around.'

'But isn't it risky for the bad guys? If the government stands firm, they're finished.'

'That's possible, but not likely,' Cutler replied. 'You've heard the word around town? One of the deportees may be Peking's key man for Southeast Asia. Lose him, and they have to build their organisation all over again. However, the spooks can't corroborate the rumour. Anyway, come by about eight, and we'll chew it over.'

'I'd like to but don't know if I can. Expect me when you see me.'

'Fine!'

'Just one more question, Alex, before you trot back to the bar. Where would you go if you wanted to get in touch with the opposition? The men at the centre, not the fringes.'

'I'm not sure I follow, Miles.'

'Well!' Miles reframed his question cautiously. 'Suppose they wanted to talk to me. Where should I make myself available to the people from the head office, not just the local types?'

'You're up to something nasty, my boy. Tell me about it.'

'It's just a feeling, Alex. But where would I go?'

'I'll winkle it out when I see you . . . I suppose the Chengtu Restaurant. I suspect it's a message-centre, the hot-line to Peking. Patronised by sailors off ships from Hong Kong, Tientsin, and Shanghai. Everyone has a good reason for visiting a restaurant.'

'I feel a sudden urge for Szechwan food,' Miles said. 'I'm off to the hot-pots.'

XIX

The ancient GE air-conditioner wheezed with the incurable emphysema contracted over the years. Nonetheless, it contended heroically with the heat that seeped into the Chengtu Restaurant from the steamy streets. The air-conditioner contended heroically, but largely in vain.

Perhaps the still air inside was a shade less humid than the pressure-cooker atmosphere outside. But not much. Although not as brutal as summer on the broad plateau of Szechwan, from whose capital the restaurant took its name, the tropical heat lay heavy on the black Formica tables, on the hanging red lanterns with their limp scarlet tassels, and heaviest on the men who packed the Chengtu for late lunch.

They were not lethargic, for they were acclimatised to the deep tropics. Neither were they animated. Their movements were economical, almost lackadaisical. No Singaporean wasted an erg of energy in the heat of high afternoon.

Nonetheless, brass pots crowned with tall cylindrical chimneys for charcoal fires bubbled on all tables. Tropical heat or not, Overseas Chinese, homesick for a China most had never seen, clung to customs they believed to be profoundly Chinese. And what was more Chinese than eating the food of the Motherland?

They made two concessions to the climate. They called the boiling pots 'steamboats', rather than 'fire-pots', as in North China. And their wooden chopsticks dipped into the broth prawns, scallops, and fish, rather than the thin pink slices patrons cooked for themselves in restaurants celebrated for 'rinsed mutton', such as the Dung Lai Hsün in Peking.

Miles wiped his face with the damp washcloth the waiter brought, careful not to touch his eyes, which already smarted from the charcoal fumes. Perhaps it was unnecessary in reasonably hygienic Singapore, to take the precaution he had learned in China, where trachoma was widespread. Yet Singapore in 1955 was not necessarily that much more hygienic than Nanking less than a decade earlier.

He listlessly nibbled dried melon seeds from the small dish on his table and sipped from a glass carpeted with tea leaves like marine plants. Hearing the unmistakable broad accent of Shantung Province in North China from the adjoining table, he tuned in. The conversation was not illuminating. It was, however, uninhibited owing to the unshakable conviction of most Chinese that no foreigner can possibly understand their unique language.

The three men attacking an enormous platter of diced bean curd with minced pork and chili peppers were sailors off a ship in the harbour. They bitterly denounced their captain between complaining of the exorbitant price of Singapore's waterfront whores. From another table, the equally unmistakable sizzling tones of Shanghai fell on Miles's ears, but he could at best make out only a few words of that language.

It was worse than clutching at straws to hope that the

opposition would, somehow, reveal itself to an eavesdropper. A very long shot indeed.

Perhaps Alex Cutler had misdirected him. The opposition must have spotted him by this time if the Chengtu were in truth their haunt. He was wildly conspicuous, the only non-Chinese in the room, and the red Porsche parked outside was like a beacon.

Perhaps he should have taken Cutler into his confidence instead of trying to play a lone hand. The BBC Correspondent could command resources in Singapore to which he himself never could even aspire.

But was too late to backtrack. Time was running out, and he had to play the dangerous game on his own. If widespread rioting began, its momentum would be irreversible – and he would have lost his gamble. Peking would, he believed, no longer be interested in whatever deal it was now seeking with Montague. Peking would be too busy pressing the revolution in Singapore.

Miles signalled the harried waiter and ordered in Mandarin, thus making himself even more conspicuous. Waiting for his *dza jiang mien*, strips of spiced pork and raw cucumber over noodles in broth, he picked up the telephone on the counter after the cashier nodded permission.

'No, Mr Corrigan, I'm very sorry.' Michael Tong reported from the Ocean Park. 'The lady's not rung or appeared. There was a call for you half an hour ago, though. A man. He sounded like a Chinese . . . from China. Wouldn't leave a message. Said he'd call again.'

'If he does, tell him I'm at the Chengtu. The number is . . . let's see. Yes, 927645. Thanks, Mike.'

No harm in throwing out a little more bait. The unknown call might be a straw in the wind. Tanya was most likely in the hands of the opposition, who might now be nibbling at the bait he had already strewn. Of course the caller could have been just another eager vendor of *objets d'art*, another refugee anxious to unload whatever treasures he had brought from China. But why not be hopeful?

Miles's heart lifted as he returned to his table, and his pulse beat faster. A middle-aged Chinese wearing rimless spectacles was seated at his table, contemplating the steaming bowl of noodles. The man's grey hair was combed over a balding forehead; a striped tie bestowed middle-class respectability on his white shirt; from his breast-pocket protruded a rank of ball-point pens. The resemblance to a senior bank clerk snatching a quick lunch was completed by the black attaché case balanced on his lap.

'You permit me?' The interloper spoke the Mandarin of the Yangtze Valley, rather than the slurred South Seas Mandarin of Singapore. 'No other seat was free.'

Miles's pulse quickened further, though he nodded an apparently indifferent assent. Addressing him in Chinese was virtually a declaration. A Singaporean clerk would normally use English to an unknown Westerner.

'Where do you come from?' he asked.

Just as between Americans, that question was the normal courtesy between Chinese meeting for the first time. But it could convey a special meaning now – if the stranger chose to so interpret it.

'From the north,' replied the man who looked like a bank clerk. 'And the gentleman?'

'From the west,' Miles answered just as casually. 'But, may I ask, where in the north? Kuala Lumpur? Alor Star?'

'Much farther north!' The rimless spectacles twinkled. 'Even farther north than Bangkok.'

'I see.' Miles twined noodles around his chopsticks. 'That *is* interesting.'

'Not really. I'm just a poor merchant . . . not at all interesting. You must have spent many years in China to speak my language so well.'

'*Guo jiang! Guo jiang!*' Miles replied in old-fashioned self-abnegation. 'Beyond my merit! Beyond my merit! I'm sure your life *is* interesting. And I am always interested in learning something new.'

'Perhaps I can oblige you.' The bland tone did not change. 'I happen to have with me an interesting example of Chinese handicraft.'

The stranger opened his attaché case and extended a black-velvet evening purse embroidered with a small white crane. Tanya had carried that bag when she came into his room last night. Miles exulted. They had taken his bait. The next instant full awareness struck him like physical pain: the purse proved that Tanya was a captive.

Regardless, the opposition was nibbling at his hook, while thinking it was luring him. Only by taking its bait could he help Tanya.

'Very interesting handiwork.' He opened the gold dragon clasp. 'Is it for sale?'

'Perhaps! Under the proper circumstances. Do examine the workmanship inside. It's very interesting.'

Miles extracted a note printed in pencil on cheap paper.

You have seen the evidence [it read in English] *and you should draw your own conclusion. We have a thing you value, and you have a thing we value. An exchange can be possible if the proper precaution and the mutual sincerity is observed. You must get in hand the thing we value. We will call you this evening to give further instructions.*

'Interesting,' Miles observed drily. 'Very interesting!'

'You do understand?' the emissary asked anxiously. 'Completely?'

'It seems clear.'

'And you are agreed?'

'I'm not sure I can raise the price,' Miles stalled. 'Perhaps, though I don't have it at the moment.'

'But you *can* get it?'

The dark eyes behind the rimless spectacles were clouded with anxiety.

'I just might. Naturally I'd need a guarantee of quality on your part. Your merchandise must be undamaged. And I must see it before paying.'

'I can make no commitment,' the apparent bank-clerk replied. 'I am only the messenger. But my principals will be in touch with you.'

'Fine!' Miles grunted through a mouthful of noodles. 'Have them do so. But I'm not promising anything. My mind is not made up. I may decide not to meet their price, even if I can.'

'You *are* interested?' the stranger pressed.

'Interested, yes. Eager, no. Your merchandise is not overwhelmingly interesting to me. Others, one in particular, are much more interested. That one would be very disturbed if the merchandise were damaged in any way. After all, it is *his* merchandise . . . has belonged to him from the beginning.'

'Still, he has many similar things. I don't think he's so concerned about this one.'

'Not any so fine,' Miles riposted. 'He would be infuriated if the merchandise were damaged.'

'*Aye-yah!*' The stranger looked at his wrist-watch. 'I must go immediately.'

He threw down a red Straits five-dollar note, snatched

the purse back, closed the attaché case, and disappeared through the front door within the space of twenty seconds.

Miles sat quite still until the door slammed shut. He then moved even more swiftly than had the messenger. He dropped a bank note on the table, swirled through the kitchen doors, and brushed past two sweating cooks who wore only baggy underpants and wooden clogs. In less than thirty seconds, he was through the open back door into an alley strewn with shrimp shells, chicken heads, and pig guts.

Sprinting around the alley's sharp bend, he saw with satisfaction the messenger emerge from its shadowed mouth. The man was hurrying down the street, impeded by the boxes and bales heaped high by unloading trucks. His quarry swung right at the Cable and Wireless Building and darted into the throngs in the open air People's Market. The messenger's goal was evidently the waterfront.

Shadowing a Chinese in Singapore unseen was all but impossible for a red-headed foreigner who topped the crowds by five inches. But the disorderly welter of the streets provided temporary cover if he stooped. Besides, the red Porsche still standing blatantly before the restaurant, was a useful decoy.

A roll of newsprint six feet across rolled down an inclined platform and almost knocked Miles over. He dodged clumsily, seeing the workmen grinning from the corner of his eye. He took refuge behind an enormous refrigerator truck that was unloading steer carcasses. His quarry's white shirt blended into the throng. Nonetheless readily identifiable by the distinctive black attaché case, the messenger slithered into the narrow aisle between rows of stalls selling vegetables and chickens.

Two sweating bare-torsoed coolies bearing a heavy box

of machine parts from West Germany entered the aisle, uttering their usual high-pitched warning: 'Hoo-hoo! Hoo-hoo!' Miles fell in behind, and they screened him like a moving duck-blind. Accustomed to foreigners' mad antics, the stall keepers ignored his stealthy, stooped progress.

Miles watched for the flash of rimless spectacles, but his quarry did not look back. The man was intent on his errand, presumably confident that his henchmen would keep Corrigan engaged. But those henchman were still complacently watching the Porsche.

A narrow passageway led from the stalls to the docks. The doors to disused warehouse space opened onto that passage at irregular intervals. The messenger quickened his pace in the gloom of the passageway. Abandoning stealth, Miles broke into a run. His quarry whirled at the sound, just too late.

Miles threw himself across the intervening space to tackle the Chinese and bring him crashing to the filthy cobblestones. Before the man could recover, Miles whipped his right arm behind his back and forced him into a deep doorway.

The training in unarmed combat he had resented at the time was a blessing. He need not carry an incriminating weapon, and he need not necessarily harm his adversary. Besides, hard bruising body contact could be even more intimidating than the threat of a firearm. He jerked the messenger's arm upwards three inches, eliciting a shrill cry of pain and fear.

'Try to break away and you'll break your arm,' Miles whispered. 'Stand very still.'

'What do you want?' the man gasped. 'Let me go.'

'Where is she held? Where's your boss?'

'I can't tell you!'

Ignoring the pain his own bruised shoulder, Miles probed the vulnerable spot an inch below his captive's ear with his thumb. He knew the pain was excruciating – and just a little more pressure could kill. The messenger's eyes bulged in agony.

'Where are they?' Miles repeated. 'Quickly or I'll finish the job. Five centimetres deeper will kill you . . . very painfully.'

Miles increased the pressure, knowing the man was in torment. He disliked terror, but he would use that instrument implacably. He did not wish to kill the man, though another body in a gutter of riot-wracked Singapore would not attract great notice. But the man could not speak if he were unconscious or dead.

It was a delicate exercise, applying sufficient pressure, but not too much. Shifting his grip, Miles forced the man's right arm upward, until he could all but hear tendons fraying and the elbow-joint parting.

'*Gou-la! Gou-la!*' The messenger screamed. 'Enough! Enough! I'll tell you.'

Miles relaxed his hold on the man's arm. But he twisted his thumb in the hollow where the skull ended and the nerve fibres came together.

'Quickly!' he commanded. 'Now!'

'Let up on my neck,' the messenger pleaded. 'I can't talk . . . Can't think.'

Miles's thumb just touched the bruised nerves under the reddened skin. His own bruised shoulder was aching. Tormentor and victim were joined by the invisible link of common pain.

'Now!' he commanded. 'No more stalling.'

'They're at . . . but you won't know unless I show you.'

'Tell me first!'

He twisted his victim's arm an inch upward, and the

man screamed again. He would not be able to use his right arm for a week; he might never use it freely again. Miles felt a twinge of sympathy, but he had no choice.

'They're at . . .'

Behind him, Miles heard running feet. Clapping his left hand over his captive's mouth, he swivelled in the deep doorway to face towards the narrow passageway. A thrill of pain ran up to his shoulder as teeth closed on his palm.

'*Jiu-ming! Wai-guo-ren sha jung-guo tung-jr!*' the messenger screamed. 'Help! A foreigner's killing a Chinese comrade!'

Running students pelted into the doorway. A club glanced off Miles's shoulder, and a wave of pain broke over him. Releasing his captive, he crouched in a defensive posture. But a salvo of blows struck him, and he fell to the gritty cobblestones.

XX

The room rocked slowly and a rough fabric rasped against Miles's face as he slid unresisting back and forth. The claws clamping his temples tightened each time he was pitched sideways. His shoulder and ribs throbbing painfully, he sank into blackness to emerge an instant later to half-consciousness. Like a stricken porpoise, he just broached the surface, sank below it, and broached again. During one moment of awareness he heard water slapping iron, and he gagged at the pervading smell of mould and decay.

Miles forced his eyes open with a profound effort and saw that his shirt was covered with vomit and slime. His head reeled with the fumes of the cheap whisky that drenched his hair and his clothing. Groping automatically for a cigarette and finding none, he gingerly assessed his predicament.

He was lying on a narrow bunk covered with a coarse grey blanket. Twisting his head despite protesting neck muscles, he looked around. A small, scratched wash basin fouled by coal dust and tendrils of black hair projected near a steel door. A highly coloured portrait of Chairman Mao Tse-tung beamed compassion upon his misery. Or were the plump bland features smirking in satisfaction above the bold face Chinese characters: SERVE THE PEOPLE? A small porthole beside the portrait admitted a blinding shaft of sunlight.

He had failed, Miles realised, his self-disgust heightened by his pain. He was out of the chase, the hunter himself struck down. They had Shanghaied him, sent him out to sea on a tramp steamer to get rid of him. But the regular motion was gentle, and he felt no pulsing of engines. He forced himself to his feet and, leaning against the bulkhead, hobbled to the porthole.

He saw a tourist postcard of the sun going down over Singapore. Far to the right reared the tawdry ziggurat of the Cathay Building. At the centre junks crammed the mouth of the Singapore River below the colonial solidity of the grey Fullerton Building. Green-roofed Clifford Pier, surrounded by swarms of small craft, was no more than a mile distant. The ship was not moving – not yet, at least.

Miles slumped on the bunk, his head in his hands in near despair. Nonetheless, finding the filth that covered him unbearable, he stripped off his torn shirt and stumbled to the wash basin. The midget tap yielded a trickle of rusty sea-water. Wincing each time he touched another sore spot, he rinsed his face and torso. At the end, he was barely cleaner, but his thinking was a little less muddled. He moved his head from side to side to loosen his neck muscles, which again protested with needles of pain.

The metal door creaked open to allow an immensely fat Chinese to squeeze into the cabin. He stood at least six foot four, and his head looked as big as a water melon. He wore paint-stained sailor's dungarees with a sweat-soiled T-shirt. A Russian Tokarev pistol was a child's toy in his enormous hand.

'Mr Corrigan, you've given me a lot of trouble,' he said in high-pitched but unaccented English. 'I am not pleased with you.'

'And I could do without your hospitality,' Miles replied.

'You really should not have attacked my messenger. Surprising how little notice another drunken foreign sailor attracts on a Singapore dock.'

'Miss Tan's father won't be overjoyed at your seizing her.'

'Mr Corrigan, you're a dangerous man – most dangerous to yourself. Do let *me* worry about Mr Tan.'

'What do you want?'

'Surely you know. I must have Mr Montague's promissory note.'

'I told your man. I don't have it.'

The genial curve of the heavy lips did not alter. Nor did the smiling eyes grow cold. But the hand holding the pistol flicked out to cuff Miles and hurl him into a corner.

'Mr Corrigan, you must not lie to me,' the Chinese said mildly. 'I know you have the promissory note – and I mean to have it.'

Miles sat silent, gathering the shreds of his strength.

'And if I don't have the note?' he finally asked. 'Or can't get it?'

'Mr Corrigan, I've read your dossier . . . studied it. We know you are almost as stubborn as you are greedy. We also know you are not a complete fool.'

'*Sieh-sieh, ju-jen!*' Miles muttered the guest's traditional courtesy. 'Thank you, my host!'

'Speak English. I can't bear your bastardised Chinese. You are not a complete fool – and only a fool would sacrifice his life for a painting. What aesthetic pleasure or financial reward will you gain if we slip you overboard with a hundredweight of chain around your ankles?'

(213)

'If I had it . . . I'm not saying I do, since I don't. But, if I could find the note, where would I be then? How would you guarantee my safety?'

'Finally, you're thinking reasonably,' his captor said. 'Your liberty for the note. Then it would be up to you. You could seek whatever protection you chose or, better, get out of Singapore.'

'To have your people follow me?'

'Your vanity is enormous. Once the note is in my hands, I'll no longer have the slightest interest in you.'

The big man threw open the cabin-door and stepped outside. A bedraggled figure in a violet cheongsam took his place.

'Half an hour, Mr Corrigan!' The steel door clanged shut on the warning. 'Half an hour to choose!'

Miles dragged himself to his feet, and Tanya came to him. She was hardly a weight in his arms.

'Miles!' She spoke evenly, but her voice was husky. 'What now for us?'

'Let me look.' He kissed her cheek. 'What have they done to you?'

Still clutching his hands, she stepped back, and he saw a purple bruise on her cheek. The torn cheongsam with the high side-slits was far too big for her.

Tanya turned her back and slipped the dress from her shoulders. He gazed in helpless anger at the scarlet welts that criss-crossed the delicate skin.

'I got you into this,' he said. 'It's all my . . .'

'It's my own fault. I brought you the promissory note. I got you involved. And, now, I've betrayed you.'

'What happened?'

'They beat me, as you can see. I could hardly believe it was happening to me . . . to Morgan Tan's spoiled daughter. Then, Miles, I told them you had the note.'

'What else could you do?' He comforted her. 'We had a rule in the old days. Don't try to hold out, we were ordered, tell them what they want before they kill you. At least then, you've got a chance of surviving.'

'Well, I told them,' she confessed bitterly. 'I told them everything . . . I thought you'd just give them the blasted note . . . and they'd let me go. I can't believe my father *wants* me to be hurt.'

'Nor can I. Not really.'

'It's all my stupidity,' she insisted, 'my stupid trusting nature. Maggie'd gone to Kuala Lumpur with her father. But her younger brother was home. He's fifteen, a student at the Motherland Middle School. I begged him not to tell *anyone* where I was, and he promised. With his background – his father's wealth and his father's fierce anti-Communism – I never dreamed . . .'

'Yes?'

'He came back with two schoolmates, boys of eighteen or nineteen. They lectured me on loyalty to the Chinese Motherland . . . said I was a traitor. Maggie's brother boasted that he's deputy chief of Killer Squad 13. Then they forced me to go with them.'

'If anyone's to blame it's me,' he said. 'I should've warned you against *everyone*.'

'Miles, I acted like a spoiled child. I struck at my father, but I still believed deep in my heart that he'd protect me.'

'Illusions die hard, Tanya Tan.' He was deliberately harsh to shock her out of her self-absorption and her self-pity. 'But we all have to grow up someday.'

Turning away to give her a moment to recover Miles squeezed his head out of the porthole. It was clearly too small for him to get through, though Tanya might just manage. But she could never swim to shore, and few sampans plied the harbour after dark. A shout startled him, and a chain slapped the rusty hull two feet from his ear. He hastily withdrew his head.

'Do you know,' he asked, 'what ship this is?'

'The *Hai Wong*,' she answered dully. 'Under the red flag.'

The *Hai Wong*, Miles realised, was a perfect base for the opposition. He had seen the battered old steamer anchored in the roads, flaunting the yellow-starred crimson flag of the People's Republic of China. Already six months at anchor, the *Hai Wong* was no longer a tourist attraction, despite her bizarre history.

Rust streaks weeping down her sides, the tramp had steamed into Singapore with a mutinous crew. The captain was loyal to the white-sun flag of the Chinese Nationalists, which then still floated above the *Hai Wong*'s grimy fantail. But the crew, led by the second officer, declared their allegiance to Peking. The captain and the first mate had been disembarked to return to Nationalist-held Taiwan.

The Singapore courts were reluctant to offend Peking and lose trade for Britain by cutting decisively through the intricate issues of not only admiralty law but Chinese politics raised by the case. The judges had issued an injunction forbidding the ship to sail, but had taken no further action. Accordingly, the *Hai Wong* still swung at anchor, legally a ship without a country, though she now flew Peking's red flag. Singapore wits joked that she would soon find it impossible to sail because she was firmly aground on the thousands of soya sauce and rice wine bottles thrown overboard by the crew.

'At least she's not going to sea for a while,' Miles laughed. 'If ever!'

'We might as well be in Peking, even though we're just

a mile from Clifford Pier. No one is allowed aboard. Miles, what can we do?'

'We'll give them the note. Nothing else we can do.'

'Will they let us go then?'

'Who knows?' He shrugged. 'But we can still bargain.'

The steel door clanged open. The trim young Chinese who entered wore the two gold stripes of a second-officer on the epaulettes of his short-sleeved white shirt. He smiled and reached into his breast pocket for a gold-and-red packet of Gate of Heavenly Peace cigarettes. Gratefully, Miles extracted two, one for Tanya and another for himself. Taking a light from the second mate's gold lighter, he drew the sweet Virginia tobacco smoke deep into his lungs.

'Please don't do anything foolish,' the mate advised in Mandarin. 'You've met Comrade Yang, our political commissar. He is sometimes not too gentle.'

Miles ruefully rubbed his chin where the big man's back handed swipe had left a painful bruise.

The mate asked: 'Have you made up your minds?'

'What exactly,' Miles riposted, 'do you want of us?'

'Come now, Mr Corrigan,' the officer said mildly. 'You know what we want . . . and probably why.'

'I also know that you're bluffing, whatever Commissar Yang threatens. You can't just dispose of me. If you kill me before getting the note, your operation will collapse. And you can't threaten Miss Tan. When your boss finds out, you'll catch hell for mistreating her.'

'Mr Corrigan, you're confused.' The jaunty second-officer lit a cigarette for himself. 'Mr Morgan Tan is an esteemed co-worker, but hardly my superior.'

'You're still bluffing.'

'No, Mr Corrigan. You misunderstand my position and you overrate your own importance. You would not be missed if you disappeared. Months from now some clerk in the Immigration Department might discover you had entered Singapore and not left.'

The mate flicked a shred of tobacco from his front teeth with his fingernail.

'But I have no desire to kill either Miss Tan or yourself, though Comrade Yang may disagree. When you return the promissory note you stole, we can release you – and send Miss Tan back to her father to be disciplined at home.'

'How could you possibly release us?'

'Frankly, there's nothing you could do. Even if you told the authorities your melodramatic tale, you'd have no evidence. Mr Montague would just deny all, tuck his scroll away safely – and do as we require.'

Miles cursed his own stupidity. Long after the puzzle should have been clear to him, the pieces had at last fallen into place. Alex Cutler had reported the rumour that one of the deportees was the linchpin of Peking's activities in Southeast Asia. Montague was obviously under pressure to revoke the deportation order. Miles finally knew the purpose of Peking's operation – but too late to use the knowledge.

'You're stymied without the note,' he stalled. 'You can kill us or hold onto us. It comes to the same thing. Unless you have the note in your hands, your game is finished.'

Sighing in an ostentatious display of patience sorely tried, the second officer seated himself on the bunk. He said through a cloud of tobacco smoke: 'I'll explain further, though my tolerance is not unlimited. Comrade Yang, as you know, is very impatient.'

'Go ahead!' Miles said.

'Only my dislike of unnecessary killing has kept you alive. Consider the objective conditions. You must have realised by this time that it's neither here nor there, my possessing the note that you affect to believe is essential to my plans.'

'Of course it is,' Miles broke in. 'No note of hand means no pressure on Montague. And your operation fails.'

'Mr Corrigan, have I overestimated your intelligence? It doesn't matter whether I hold the note or not. Not while Mr Montague believes I have it – and knows to his sorrow that he does *not*.'

'You've got to produce it eventually.'

'Not really. Given Mr Montague's craven nature, the threat suffices. Fortunately for you, I am still hampered by bourgeois conventions. I dislike lying to Mr Montague, and I'd prefer not to harm you. I am, therefore, prepared to go to some lengths to get hold of the note. But not to any length. And I am not prepared to wait much longer.'

The reasoning was plausible, Miles reflected, plausible but not quite convincing. Montague was certainly greedy and was perhaps craven. But he was not stupid. He would not act before the note was in his hands – with an iron-bound guarantee of future immunity. The note was still the key, and Miles Corrigan held the note.

'You win,' he nonetheless said. 'I *can* lay my hands on the note, but . . .'

'Now, that is sensible,' the mate smiled. 'Go on.'

'But Miss Tan must set free *before* I turn it over to you.'

'Nonsense,' the mate snapped. 'We'll have Comrade Yang in again if you don't talk sense. You'll *both* remain here till I get hold of the note.'

'That's impossible, I'm afraid,' Miles said. 'Only I can get the note. The bank won't release it to a messenger.'

'Then Miss Tan remains here as surety for your good behaviour.'

'And my surety for your good behaviour?'

'None, I'm afraid, except the fact that I've chosen not to kill you. Also, any scandal would slightly hamper my operation.'

'I'll be in your hands. No one would even get a writ of habeas corpus.'

'Quite right,' the mate answered. 'The *Hai Wong* is effectively Chinese soil. But we want action, not publicity. Once I've given Mr Montague the receipt, he can face down any wild charges. Still, publicity about Miss Tan's disappearance could be annoying. That's your surety for her release.'

'He's right, Miles,' Tanya interjected. 'They won't hurt me. My father's too important to them, and they know his violent temper. It all makes sense. From their point of view, I must *not* be found aboard the *Hai Wong*.'

'Do as the lady says, Mr Corrigan,' the mate advised. 'I'll put you ashore early tomorrow morning with one of my men. As soon as he delivers the note, Miss Tan will be freed.'

'You leave me no choice,' Miles agreed reluctantly. 'But, if anything happens to her, you're vulnerable. And I'll destroy you.'

'Let us worry about that if it happens.' The mate smiled. 'Here is your wallet, intact. It did not contain what we hoped, but we are not thieves.'

'Thieves you may not be,' Miles rejoined. 'Murderers you certainly are.'

'It was not I who brought in the Green Lotus Lodge.'

Deliberately provocative, Miles asked: 'And the death of Dr Turner Lee, a great Chinese scholar?'

'We only wanted him removed from the scene. Mr Morgan Tan's agents were overzealous.'

'As were the hijackers?'

'The People's Government regrets the three children who died subsequently. Getting the right concentration of gas was tricky.'

Miles, who had not known of those deaths, declared hotly: 'But the children died, and others were injured.'

'A revolution cannot be sweet and gentle!' the mate declaimed. 'As Chairman Mao points out, a revolution is not an invitation to a tea-party.'

XXI

Hardpaw Woo had distinguished himself early among the runny-nosed infants scrabbling in the muddy lanes of his impoverished fishing village on the coast of Fukien Province. At fifteen months, he already displayed the insatiable greed that was to win him his nickname. Whenever his mother turned to crouch over her charcoal brazier, he snatched a gristle-studded sausage or a duck's gizzard from his three-year-old sister's bowl. When his mother turned at the girl's screams, all evidence of his gluttony had disappeared down his gullet. His sister was cuffed, and he was consoled with his mother's breast.

He was the male who would carry on the family name. She was just a female who had to be fed until she was sold at seven to a properous family as a prospective daughter-in-law – and a household drudge.

By the time he was four, Hardpaw had earned his nickname. His bony fists threw fear into all the small boys in trousers with seats cut out so they would not foul themselves. By five, he was their unchallengable leader in robbing lobster pots and snatching barbecued pork from foodstalls. His doting mother was convinced that his greed and arrogance demonstrated character and intelligence.

To Hardpaw's disgust, his father therefore sacrificed scarce coppers to the aged village schoolmaster.

Graduate Lee had barely failed to pass the first rung of the ladder of Civil Service Examinations that qualified men for appointment as officials of the Manchu Empire. He had barely failed thirteen times since his first attempt at seventeen.

Forty-three when he failed for the last time in 1903, he was seventy-two when Hardpaw first came under his bleary eyes and stinging bamboo rod in the disused temple that was the village school. Thirty years of trying to beat the rudiments of Chinese writing into rows of cropped heads like small round boulders had not sweetened a temper soured by perpetual failure. The world had stopped for Graduate Lee when the Civil Service Examinations were abolished in 1905. He knew in his bones that he would have qualified that year – given just that one extra chance.

The iron-willed little rascal Hardpaw Woo and the evil-tempered dotard Graduate Lee detested each other. Hardpaw's muscular buttocks and calloused palms often stung from the blows of the bamboo switch in Graduate Lee's soft hand. Hardpaw set his mind against learning more than a few hundred characters and against parsing even the simplest aphorisms of the elementary *Three Character Classic*. He was fully occupied in nurturing his natural talents for larceny and extortion amid the welter of petty and grand rackets that thrived in wartime China.

By the age of ten Hardpaw Woo was an accomplished hooligan, the master of the entire county's juvenile gangs. He was also an eager apprentice to the adult gangsters of the Pure Lotus Secret Society, who worked indiscriminately for the Communist guerrillas or the Japanese invaders, whoever offered greater gain.

Even his doting mother finally despaired. In 1940, when he was thirteen, she shipped him off to her brother in Singapore. Childless Second Elder Uncle, a moderately successful grocer in Chinatown, was delighted to adopt the boy. His sister did not tell him that she had sent him her son because she had heard that *all* the children of the South Seas were little devils. Her own little devil, she felt, would thrive in barbarous Singapore.

Her judgement was brilliantly vindicated. Hardpaw had been an industrious minor malefactor in his home village. His talent for bigger crime flourished on the opportunities of the populous port.

A Singapore secret society welcomed the recruit. An adolescent could go where a grown man would arouse suspicion – and risk a bullet from an irritable Japanese sentry.

Hardpaw took the hair-raising blood-oath at fifteen, swearing to die rather than reveal the secrets of the blood brotherhood that was dedicated impartially to crime and to patriotism. The sacred butterfly was tattooed on his wrist, and the Incense Master of the Green Lotus Lodge killed the ceremonial white cock. When Hardpaw drank from the bowl of wine mixed with his brother members' blood, he became a Five Tiger General, an Avenging-Fist Warrior. His métier was intimidating longshoremen and looting warehouses.

The Green Lotus Lodge moved with the times. On his lodge master's orders, Hardpaw attended school intermittently. Although he never attempted to learn spoken Mandarin, content with his own Hokkien dialect, he finally attained a reasonable knowledge of written Chinese. Shortly after the war, he proudly received a certificate attesting to proficiency in English at the eighth grade level. He had since forgotten almost every word of written English he ever knew, but he kept that deficiency secret.

Hardpaw Woo met Miles Corrigan on the rust-caked deck of the *Hai Wong* as Singapore harbour began to stir with the new day. Hardpaw wore the white shirt and white trousers of a clerk, rather than his normal voluminous black Chinese trousers and soiled T-shirt. Miles, too, had been provided with a clean though skimpy shirt.

The pair descended a swaying rope-ladder to a sampan bobbing on the morning swell. A stringy-muscled boatman propelled them towards the shore, sculling at the stern with a single long oar. They scrambled up slime-covered steps to Clifford Pier, where touts for enterprising merchants charmed tourists off oceanliners and tattooed sailors eyed hard-eyed prostitutes at nine in the morning.

'We go bank now,' Hardpaw demanded in his own variety of English. 'Chop-chop!'

'Not just yet, Mr Woo,' Miles replied. 'If I walked into the bank looking like this, they'd call the police instead of giving me the envelope. I must shave and dress properly.'

'Can do,' Hardpaw replied laconically. He prided himself upon being an intelligent businessman, not just an iron-handed, thick-skulled Avenging Fist.

The red Porsche had miraculously survived the night undamaged except for the slogan scratched on its hood in Chinese characters: 'Topple the imperialists!' The long drive from Chinatown to the Ocean Park Hotel on the opposite coast passed in silence. Like a small boy in a toyshop, Hardpaw's eyes roved greedily over the dials on the dashboard. His hands caressed the soft leather upholstery, and he grinned broadly when the Porsche accelerated, the surge of power thrusting him deep into his seat. He spoke only twice, when impromptu road-blocks manned by students, workers, and their secret society allies waved down the expensive toy.

'The cock crows,' he said – and the barriers parted.

Hardpaw had made up his mind that the sports car would be his before the week ended. He had repeatedly been promised that the good things of the world would come into the hands of the oppressed when the revolution triumphed. He could imagine nothing that would please him better than the Porsche.

Miles observed Hardpaw's patent greed with an amusement that was tempered by fear. It would, he sensed, be less dangerous to transport a time-bomb than this simple child of avarice. But he assured the Indian guard at the hotel entrance that Mr Woo was his guest. Mike Tong, harried and nervous as ever, raised his eyebrows till they almost disappeared into his busy hairline, but he was resigned to Miles's eccentricities.

Hardpaw Woo strode unerringly through the maze of corridors to Miles's suite, virtually confirming Miles's suspicion that the thug had led the attack on him two days earlier.

'You seem to know the way, Mr Woo,' he said.

Hardpaw grinned again, the grimace transforming his round face into the image of a jolly Buddha. He settled himself proprietorially into the most comfortable armchair and tuned the radio to a Hokkien-dialect soap opera.

'Do make yourself at home, Mr Woo,' Miles urged. 'Would you like something to eat while I dress? Perhaps an omelette?'

'No funny eats,' Hardpaw replied. 'Eggs and beer OK.'

Sighing in resignation, Miles phoned room service and reached the kitchen after no more than a five-minute delay. He stepped into the bathroom for a long shower, which he followed with a close shave and another shower.

(226)

Today time was on the side of the slowest battalions, and the Ocean Park's dilatory service was his best ally.

They lunched in silence that waxed companionable as Hardpaw poured four bottles of beer down his throat and consented to eke out the eight-egg omelette with two hamburgers. Miles's gold Rolex indicated 2.56.

'Now we go!' Hardpaw remembered his duty. 'But one more bottle beer first.'

'My pleasure, Mr Woo,' Miles answered. 'Though I don't want to be late.'

'Plenty time,' Hardpaw said expansively. 'No can see *low-ban* before seven, maybe eight o'clock.'

Miles registered the indiscretion. He had even more time than he had hoped to gain by his delaying tactics. Another indiscretion might give him the identity of Hardpaw's *low-ban*, which meant literally – the old chief, meaning the boss.

'Maybe it's better if we go together to see Mr Tan, the *low-ban*,' Miles suggested.

'You so very clever, friend.' Hardpaw blinked with owlish cunning. 'I go myself . . . one piece man. *Low-ban* not Mr Tan. Mr Tan fighter, big fighter same me, but not *low-ban*. You no catchee me.'

Miles only nodded, fearful of straining the tenuous camaraderie he had established with the amiable thug. After two bottles of beer for Hardpaw and a small whisky for himself, his watch showed 4.30.

'I'm sorry, Mr Woo,' he said. 'But we'll have to be going. There'll be no one at the bank after half past five.'

'OK, we go now. Car can go very damn quick.'

Laughton Pomeroy's puritan features twisted in surprise when he saw Miles Corrigan's companion. His mouth pursed, and his eyes popped like a startled goldfish, but he rapidly resumed the archepiscopal gravity he considered fitting for a banker. He had dealt with even odder characters than Hardpaw Woo. Little old coolies in baggy trousers and rusty black tunics had produced hundreds of thousands in small notes from the recesses of their underclothing before his eyes.

'Your envelope, Miles,' Pomeroy acknowledged. 'Of course. If you'll just sign here.'

Miles waited until Hardpaw and he were again seated in the Porsche before handing over the brown envelope with the flap secured by red sealing-wax.

'Now,' he asked, 'where would you like to go?'

'You too damn quick one more time. Too quick and too clever,' Hardpaw grinned. 'But good fellow all same. First, I look see.'

Breaking the seal, Hardpaw examined the promissory note. He held it up to the fading light and squinted at it from several angles before laboriously spelling out the signatures and the date.

'Okay now,' he announced. 'I go now, myself one piece man. *Low-ban* look see this chit. If all OK, missy come longshore very damn quick.'

'As you say, Mr Woo.' Miles smiled thinly. 'Tell your *low-ban* if Miss Tan is not safe on Clifford Pier tomorrow morning at eight, I'll tear him *and* the *Hai Wong* apart.'

'No worry!' Hardpaw said. 'All thing OK now. You no try fool *low-ban*, he no fool you. He very honourable man.'

Miles ostentatiously swung the red Porsche in a wide U-turn, pointing the sloping hood in the opposite direction from that Hardpaw had taken. Ten that evening was the absolute deadline. He had no more than four hours to move decisively. If he failed again, chances were that neither Tanya nor he would ever stand on Clifford Pier again.

XXII

Miles believed that he had been exposed to every possible variety of vile smell during his years in Asia, but the nauseating stench in the canvas-covered cabin of the scavenger-boat was foul beyond all his experience. Darkness, descending like an indigo curtain, kept him from examining too closely the heaped debris on which he perched. He could feel water-logged driftwood, a worn automobile tyre, and old kerosene tins with unimaginable contents. But what smelled like two-week-dead rats frying in crankcase drippings?

Scavenger-boats were the pariahs among Singapore harbour craft. They waited hopefully beneath the garbage chutes of ocean going ships or scoured the oily water for flotsam only the impoverished could value. Other small craft disdainfully avoided scavenger-boats, and sailors on the big ships turned in disgust from the scabrous sampans, which they called stink-boats.

The stink-boat edged circuitously towards the darkened *Hai Wong*, which was showing only a dim anchor light and three yellow portholes. The silent oarsman in the stern halted twice to fish floating objects from the oil-stained water – once a child's chamberpot, next a dead fish half as long as his arm.

Miles shuddered, but was reassured by that demonstration of his hireling's desperation. The Straits 50 dollar note, worth about 17 US dollars, now tucked into the boatman's filthy trouser-band was more than he could make in a month of scouring the harbour. A promise of greater fortune lay beside that note, half a Straits 100 dollar bill. Miles had kept the other half to ensure that the boatman would not scull away at the first sign of trouble. Miles was expecting trouble.

He smiled ruefully into the darkness. He had sworn that he would no longer pander to his own romantic streak by indulging in heroics. The image of himself as a gallant knight errant might titivate his imagination, but he was at the core a realist. His days of derring-do he had believed gone forever. Yet he was preparing to storm not a mere castle, but, far worse, an isolated tramp steamer already alert against such an assault.

Yet what choice did he have? What course could he have taken other than this one?

He had not come aboard the ship voluntarily the first time. Yet only by following the messenger who looked like a bank clerk and, thus, being Shanghaied, which was not in his plans, could he have discovered where Tanya was being held. And he had no choice now. He had to free Tanya.

Had to free her? Why?

Whatever strategy he chose to get hold of the scroll and thwart Peking's conspiracy, he could carry out just as well without her. In fact, better, if he were not encumbered by her.

Why, then, did he feel obliged to free her? Because, he supposed, he had manoeuvred her into her present predicament. Yet even that was not the true reason. He was compelled to free Tanya because he could not live with his cowardice if he did not make the effort.

Was there no other reason? Of course there was: Tanya herself. But he would think about his feelings for Tanya later.

Meanwhile, just the thought of seeing her again made his spirits rise. He was extraordinarily cheerful just before mounting an assault that must to any objective eye appear foredoomed.

While the stink-boat drifted on the current towards the prow of the *Hai Wong*, Miles reviewed his preparations. His face and hair, which he had blackened with oil from the water, were further concealed by a boatman's mushroom-shaped straw hat. Black sneakers encased his feet; black gloves covered his hands; his tunic and trousers were black. A scalpel-sharp knife hung in its sheath at the small of his back, and a tear-gas grenade bulged in one pocket, a heavy screwdriver in another. He had reluctantly decided against a pistol. If it came to shooting, he would already have failed.

He reached out to fend off the anchor-chain. Noise was a more immediate danger than being sighted in the gloom. The current was so weak that the chain inclined at only a slight angle. Almost vertical, it was virtually hidden from any watcher on the deck by the flare of the *Hai Wong*'s bows.

Miles sprang silently onto the chain, and barnacles sliced through the thin cloth of his tunic to scrape the skin of his arms. Slowly, but irresistibly, he began to slip down the grease-slick links towards the dark water. Pain clawed at his left shoulder and knifed his ribs. He tightened his grip, and the barnacles cut into his arms like razor blades. But still he slid downwards.

If he tumbled, fell into the water with a splash, all would be finished before it had fairly begun. Once alerted, the *Hai Wong*'s crew would shoot or send down swimmers to deal with him. And his boatman would flee. Days later, another stink-boat might come upon his gas-bloated body drifting sightless in the tropical sun.

Miles frantically clamped his legs around the last three-foot link. The barnacles cut into the heavy trousers over his clenched thighs and slowed his descent minutely. But he was still slithering downwards. Near despair, he clutched at the link. Finally, his fingers, scrabbling in the dark, caught a strand of seaweed.

His heart pounding with the adrenalin of fear, he was still slipping inexorably downwards. With the recklessness of near terror, he lifted his right leg free. Searching blindly for almost half a minute, he finally wedged the tip of his rubber-soled shoe into the middle opening of the long chain-link.

Cold sweat dripped down his chest in the evening heat as he waited for his heart to slow its wild drumming. He had not climbed an anchor-chain since leaving the Navy. But up he must go, for he could not go back. The stink-boat had drawn away as instructed.

His own fate, as well as Tanya's, was entirely in his own hands. He waited for the strength to return to his cramped limbs. Although time pressed desperately, he could not hurry.

Perhaps he should have played straight with the opposition. But it was now far too late to change tactics now. He would not give up the scroll! Tanya would have to take her chances alongside him. Cupidity, thy name is Miles Corrigan, he whispered to himself as he began to clamber upwards again.

No more than fifty feet of chain linked him to the deck

of the *Hai Wong*, but every foot was a separate protracted agony. Each time he eased his foot out of a link and pulled himself up with his arms and legs, to find a foothold on the next, was a torment. Then the blessed moment when his rubber sole was again planted firmly. But the agonising effort had to be repeated in the next instant. He could not hurry, yet he had so little time.

Miles froze when a passing launch idly swung its searchlight towards the *Hai Wong*; but his black shape was apparently invisible against the dark hull.

A head peered over the *Hai Wong*'s prow, and he froze again. If sighted, he would be helpless. A swinging chain could knock him from his perch. For two interminable minutes, the dark head peered directly at him. Then a light glowed.

Abruptly, the flame died and was replaced by the red firefly of a cigarette. The head withdrew.

Someone was watching above, apparently unaware of his approach, though on guard. Yet he could only continue upwards. Retreat was impossible, and he could not cling unmoving to the chain for long. His exhausted muscles could not bear the strain of inaction – and he would fall.

The last three links were the easiest. Constant chafing had scoured them almost free of grease. He stood on top of the final link where the anchor chain disappeared into the hawse pipe five feet below the prow. His head even with an opening in the gunwale surrounding the foredeck, he paused to recoup his strength.

He had forgotten his bruised shoulder in the agony of the climb, but pain now tore at his arm – and cleared his head. He peered cautiously through the opening in the rusty gunwale.

A pair of Chinese cloth shoes was striding towards the

bridge, away from the dim yellow disc cast on the deck by the anchor light. Miles sighed in relief. Then the feet wheeled and paced toward his hiding place. Inching higher, he saw that the dark figure was burly and that the cigarette glowed six feet above the deck. Political Commissar Yang was on guard.

Miles tensed his exhausted body for the long climb downwards. The taste of defeat was bitter – and the peril in retreat almost as acute as the peril in going forward. But retreat was preferable to certain death. He was no match for the giant Commissar – probably no match even if he were fresh and unhurt.

Braced for blind retreat, Miles realised that the feet paced out a regular pattern. Commissar Yang was taking his evening constitutional. As the massive figure withdrew again, Miles slithered through the opening in the gunwale. It was a tight fit, an impossible fit if he had not been so well greased, and his arm was torn by a jagged edge. After a last convulsive effort, he lay concealed behind the anchor capstan.

Again the feet padded towards him, and his heart stopped beating for measurable seconds. Yang did not turn at the anchor capstan as he had earlier, but leaned over the bows. The cigarette tumbled glowing towards the water to die with a hiss in silent night.

In that instant Miles struck. Not his brain, but spinal cord reflexes commanded his movements. He would have only one chance – and he could neither retreat nor fail.

The knife slipped into his right hand and in the same fluid motion sliced upwards into the Commissar's soft belly, angled towards his heart. The tormented giant grunted, drew his arms in, and clutched at the steel blade that impaled him. An instant later, he slumped forward. Miles wrenched the blade from the belly and drew it hard across the Commissar's windpipe. Arterial blood gushed, but the massive figure still twitched, shrieking soundlessly through writhing lips.

Miles allowed himself to feel neither remorse nor revulsion. Suppressing his fear, he saw with cold satisfaction that the dead man appeared from the rear to be gazing meditatively into the sea. Sliding the knife back into its sheath, he slipped into the shadow of the bulwarks.

The Chinese passion for concealment had doused all illumination on deck except the anchor light and the three open portholes amidships he had already seen from the stink-boat. The long months of routine security measures never challenged had evidently bred complacency. Seeing no sentries, he was reasonably safe from discovery as long as he did not move. But move he must – and fast.

A door opened. A figure in a soiled apron was visible in the glow through the doorway. He carried a garbage can, which he lightly tipped over the side. Miles reflected irrelevantly that his stink-boatman might find additional pickings. Seeing the dark figure of the Political Commissar leaning over the prow, the cook paused.

'Wei, jeng-wei, dze-mo yang? Wo siang Ching-dao geng-hao,' he called. 'Hey, Commissar, how goes it? I'd rather be in Tsingtao.'

The cook stood irresolute when the Commissar neither moved nor replied. He shook his head in disgust and went back through the door, muttering under his breath: 'You stuck up son of a bitch!'

Political Commissar Yang evidently inspired no great affection among his shipmates. Miles was, however, grateful that the Commissar evidently inspired so much fear that the cook dared not disturb his apparent meditation.

Miles padded aft in the shadows, passing the silent darkened bridge. The three open portholes in the midships deckhouse lit the deck like miniature klieg lights. He dropped to his belly to crawl beneath those yellow shafts. Inching along the rough steel plates, he propelled himself forward with his elbows in order to keep his body low.

Rhythmic chanting echoed through the portholes. The crew, evidently gathered for an indoctrination meeting, were shouting political slogans. Unlike the officers planted on board the *Hai Wong* to stage-manage the mutiny, the sailors were apparently recent converts to the Maoist creed. They would, therefore, require intensive political training. Although Commissar Yang had left that task to a subordinate, Miles reflected gratefully, that indoctrination was clearly assigned a higher priority than standing guard over a ship safely anchored out of reach of land.

The door of the aft deckhouse, standing ajar, was outlined by faint yellow light. Miles crawled across and lifted his head to peer quickly over the raised threshold. A single guard stood before the cabin where he had left Tanya that morning. A pistol was tucked into the guard's waistband, but his head was buried in a Chinese comicbook. He was, Miles saw with relief, small and slight.

Miles groped for the screwdriver and the tear-gas grenade in his pockets, made awkward by the need to make no preliminary sound whatsoever. Lifting his arm, he tossed the screwdriver to the far end of the passageway.

When the guard's head swivelled towards the metallic clatter, Miles covered the intervening six feet in one rush. The tear-gas grenade crunched on the back of the guard's head. Miles caught the limp body and lowered it to the deck.

Regaining the screwdriver, he worked the rusty doorbolt loose and inched the door open. Tanya sat staring on the edge of the bunk.

'Miles?' She whispered in disbelief. 'You've come back?'

He kissed her fleetingly, threw his arm around her shoulders, and pulled her towards the door. The most dangerous part still lay ahead, guiding the frightened Tanya silently to the deck and inducing her to jump over the stern, where the scavenger-boat should be waiting. She clung to him, and, for an instant, he forgot their danger.

'A touching scene!' The remark in Mandarin was heavily ironic. 'Journeys end in lovers' meeting!'

The dapper second-mate stood in the doorway. The Tokarev pistol in his hand swung back and forth like the head of an aroused cobra.

Miles thrust Tanya away and she tumbled onto the bunk. He stepped towards the menacing figure.

'I wouldn't, Mr Corrigan. Miss Tan goes first, then you. The Tokarev's an efficient little killer.'

A nauseating awareness of failure churned Miles's gut. He stood stockstill, though he felt like retching.

'Mr Corrigan, this is foolish,' the mate grieved. 'You really shouldn't have come back so melodramatically.'

'Did you expect me to trust you?'

'As I told you, it was for you to prove your good faith – not me.'

'Your man has the promissory note!'

'So I needn't burden my bourgeois conscience by deceiving Mr Montague. But, I fear, it's too late for you. You're much too impetuous to let free. You've viciously attacked a Chinese sailor on a Chinese ship. My superiors will decide your punishment – after Mr Woo has confirmed delivering the receipt.'

'The police will be here in fifteen minutes.'

Miles tried a last, desperate cast. The mate obviously still did not know of Political Commissar Yang's death.

'*If* they come. *If* we choose to admit them to Chinese

territory, they'll find I've captured a burglar . . . a murderer if my sailor dies.'

'I'm very sorry, Tanya.' Miles's shoulders slumped in an image of abject defeat. 'I really thought it was for the best.'

He turned, interposing his body between her and the pistol.

'Step aside, Mr Corrigan!' The mate dropped back to cover them both. 'The game's over for you. Accept defeat with good grace!'

The mate did not turn when he heard calloused feet running down the corridor. Hardpaw Woo erupted into the room, brushing the officer aside. His face was flushed, and his fists were clenched in anger.

'He lied!' Hardpaw shouted. 'The son of a turtle bitch lied. It wasn't the note. Just a copy.'

Outwardly unperturbed, the mate did not react. But a rush of blood stained his high cheekbones, drawing crimson half-moons against his suddenly pallid cheeks.

'Mr Corrigan, that was very foolish.' His voice was still controlled. 'We are not children playing games.'

Miles drew Tanya close, but did not speak.

'Mr Corrigan,' the mate said softly, 'I'll give you one more chance before calling Commissar Yang. *Where* is that damned promissory note?'

'Who knows?' Miles shrugged demonstratively. 'I never said I had it. You told me I did.'

He was still playing for time, if only a few more minutes. He knew they were trapped, but he was still looking for a way out. Even in the peak of condition, he would have hesitated before challenging these two, one armed with a pistol, the other a hardened brawler. Yet if he could manoeuvre one out of the cabin, he might be able to deal with the other. His hand moved towards the tear-gas grenade in his pocket.

'Stand still!' the mate commanded. 'Move again – and I shoot.'

Miles froze, but he could not accept defeat.

'I *must* know where the note is hidden.' The mate's soft tones were more menacing than his earlier threats. 'I'll give you thirty seconds.'

'The note's at the hotel,' Miles finally said. 'A concealed pocket behind the accordion file in my attaché case.'

The mate glanced at Hardpaw, who shook his head decisively and spoke rapidly in the Hokkien dialect, which was unintelligible to Miles.

'It won't do, Mr Corrigan. Hardpaw and his men ripped that room apart again. They tore up your luggage and found the hidden pocket. Nothing there but your telegrams.'

'Then someone else got it.' Miles shrugged. 'I'm afraid I can't help you.'

'Hardpaw, break him!' the mate snapped. 'Make him tell us where he hid the note.'

The thug's heavy hands clamped Miles's arm and neck – and swung him from side to side like a terrier with a mouse. Though lanced by pain, Miles thrust his free hand into his pocket and pulled out the tear-gas grenade. His fingers fumbled with the release pin.

A whip cracked, and the cordite fumes of an exploding cartridge filled the cabin. Hardpaw's grip relaxed, and he looked in disbelief at the blood welling from his upper arm.

The image of his dead father, Y. N. Lee stood in the doorway behind the mate. Smoke drifted from the silencer screwed to the Smith and Wesson revolver in his hand. Dishevelled and weary in a baggy blue Mao-suit, he had aged years in the thirty-six hours since Turner was stabbed. Y.N. plucked the pistol from the mate's hand and waved him to a corner.

'Let's get out of here,' Miles urged. 'We can make it.'

'A minute, Corrigan!' Y.N. commanded. 'The hoodlum killed my father. The other ordered his death. I must deal with them.'

'For God's sake, hurry!' Miles demanded. 'And thank you! Thank you very much!'

'Leave off the thanks, and do as I say. Tie their hands behind their backs with the sheets – just their hands, not their legs, then seat them on the deck.'

Miles obeyed. Still clutching the pistol, Y. N. Lee fished a hand grenade out of his pocket and handed it to Miles. A second grenade lay in the palm of his free hand.

'Extract the pins,' he ordered.

Cowed by Y. N. Lee's fury, Miles obeyed again. The grenades were the US Army, pineapple model. A pin attached to a ring locked the long firing lever. Even after the ring was pulled and the pin was removed, the grenade would not explode as long as the lever was held fast. Once the lever sprang free, the eight second fuse would be armed.

'Now,' Y.N. commanded. 'A grenade between the thighs, one for each. Wedge the lever so they're holding it closed with their thighs. Carefully!'

As Miles bent to that macabre task, Y. N. Lee spat out his fury: 'Mr Second Mate and you Hardpaw, you scum, you'll be perfectly safe now . . . perfectly safe as long as you don't move. If you try to free your hands or you relax your thigh muscles, the safety-lever opens . . . and the grenade goes off. All quite clear?'

Y.N. peremptorily waved Tanya and Miles out of the

door. Before shooting the outside bolt home, he spoke again to the terrified prisoners: 'You're getting the same chance you gave my father.'

As Miles and Tanya started towards the door to the fantail, Y.N. said: 'I was leading the crew in a study session . . . on serving the people, God help me . . . Then this thug appeared and demanded to see the mate. I was already suspicious . . . a lot of little signs. I had almost concluded that they killed my . . . my father. When I recognised the thug, it was all clear – too damned clear. His dagger killed my father.'

'For God's sake, let's go,' Miles urged. 'There's a sampan waiting. Let's go before the crew find us . . . or the grenades go off.'

'Just a minute more, Corrigan. They're still roaring out "Arise!" I'll rouse them, too. You're holding a tear gas bomb, aren't you?'

Miles saw that he was still clutching the grenade he had in desperation tried to trigger. It seemed hours since he had felled the guard, though less than twelve minutes had passed.

'Tanya, wait here,' Y. N. Lee commanded. 'Corrigan, come with me.'

As they approached the midships deckhouse, Miles heard the rousing chorus: 'Arise all you who refuse to be bond-slaves!'

Y. N. Lee threw the door open and hurled the gas grenade at the astonished sailors. As the corrosive, nauseating fumes rose, he slammed the door shut and dogged the butterfly bolts on the outside.

'Now!' Miles demanded. 'Over the stern! Quick!'

Y. N. Lee passed an uncertain hand across his forehead. He appeared dazed after his decisive burst of action.

'I hadn't thought about getting away,' he confessed. 'I'm afraid I lost my head.'

'You can lose your head like that any time.' Miles could smile again. 'But move now! Move, damn it!'

Calling on the last of his strength, Miles lifted Tanya before she could protest and dropped her over the side feet first. Y.N. followed, and Miles jumped last, just missing the faithful stink-boat. The boatman was waiting patiently for the other half of his hundred-dollar note.

Rough hands pulled him over the low side, where the dead fish had slid an hour earlier. Tanya, Y. N. Lee, and he lay exhausted on the heap of driftwood, tyres, and tins as if they were a silk mattress.

'Row!' Miles gasped. 'For God's sake, row!'

Lights flicked on board the *Hai Wong*. Either not all the crewmen had been trapped or they had found a way out of the saloon. A pistol cracked, and a rattle of sub-machine gun fire split the night. The bullets were swallowed by the darkness.

A muffled explosion sounded from the ship. Y. N. Lee gloated: 'One!'

Miles was automatically counting seconds. When he reached four, a second muffled explosion sounded.

A searchlight flared blue-white on the bridge of the *Hai Wong*. The brilliant shaft stabbed the dark harbour, searching for the sampan. Y. N. Lee sat unmoving, his lean features expressionless in the faint light reflected from the water. He was tensely awaiting a consummation only he could foresee. The probing shaft of light moved closer to the stink-boat.

'Come on, Y.N.!' Miles spoke harshly. He had to shock the younger man out of that half-catatonic state. 'Get ready to jump. They'll catch us with the light in a moment. Tanya, you'll have to . . .'

'Not yet, Corrigan!' Y.N. whispered. 'Wait a moment!'

A third explosion roared aboard the *Hai Wong*, far louder than its precursors. An instant later, the ship appeared to quiver along her entire length.

'Wait!' Y.N. commanded imperiously. 'Another moment!'

A gout of yellow-and-blue flame shot from the squat funnel, and rivulets of fire snaked around the decks. Within seconds, the *Hai Wong* was blazing like a Fourth of July bonfire. Smaller explosions popped like firecrackers, and tracers arched like flaming tennis-balls over the oil-slick water.

'I told you I was already suspicious,' Y.N. explained placidly. 'I'd already made preparations. Then I only had to finish the job.'

'For God's sake!' Miles demanded. 'What more did you do?'

'A long fuse . . . two long fuses, one to their ammunition store. They had a small arsenal aboard. The second to the case of dynamite I hid near the fuel tanks. Sorry, I was late in coming for Tanya, but I had to light the fuses. I didn't expect you, Corrigan.'

Miles and Tanya stared at the slim Chinese in awe.

'And how did you expect to get away?' Tanya asked.

'You know,' Y.N. answered softly, 'I hadn't really thought.'

XXIII

A pillar of fire rose from the stricken ship, and there opened above the *Hai Wong* a canopy of blue-and-yellow flame shot with black smoke. The *Hai Wong* was brilliantly lit, as if she lay on an immense funeral pyre. Little tongues of flame licked greedily at the crimson flag with the five golden stars that hung at her stern.

Sirens shrieking, two police boats skittered like big black water beetles towards the blazing hulk. Three men hurtled from the deck towards the water, whirling through the air like acrobats, their arms extended. The flames devouring their oil-soaked clothing transformed them into fiery crosses. As she sank, the *Hai Wong* was ringed by the oil blazing on the water.

Keeping to the rim of darkness, the scavenger-boat drew towards the shore well to the west of the docks. The boatmen used such discreet landing places when secret cargoes were put their way by the big operators. They smuggled liquor, cigarettes, pornography, and, occasionally, heroin that was lucrative contraband despite Singapore's legal tolerance of licensed opium addicts.

From Clifford Pier, Raffles Place, and the government offices around the grassy padang well to the east, Miles heard the irregular booming of riot-guns interspersed with the sullen thud of concussion grenades. The militants had anticipated Alex Cutler's forecast of the start of full-scale rioting by just twenty-four hours. It was so well coordinated, a celestial conductor might have pointed his baton to signal the opening of this macabre symphony with the explosion of the *Hai Wong* on the water. The percussion instruments of death were now playing their violent melodies on shore.

'What now, Miles?' Tanya's hand gripped his. 'Do we go straight for the scroll like piglets to the trough? Or do we try to stop the killing? It's your choice.'

'How's that?' Miles was startled by her initiative, since his immediate plans included neither Tanya nor Y.N. 'I haven't had time to think. Anyway, first, the note and then the scroll. They're the keys. I must get hold of the scroll, before I can act to . . .'

Tanya Tan counted five seconds before speaking. She told herself she must be reasonable, even placating. She now knew she wanted Miles Corrigan – for tonight or for all her life, as fate might decree. She would not win him by playing the shrew.

But his tunnel vision infuriated her. Could he think of nothing but the blasted scroll, nothing but his own profit, while the city erupted around them?

She cautioned herself to speak softly, but her mixed heritage overrode the counsel of prudence. Her mother's Slavic fire ignited the volatile Chinese temper inherited from her father.

'We've got to do something about the rioting! . . . Right now!' she told the two men. 'Tomorrow'll be too late. We've got to find the ring leaders and warn them we'll reveal their plots . . . their double-dealing with the men they call imperialist aggressors. And then . . .'

'I'm sorry, Tanya!' Y. N. Lee spoke authoritatively. 'There is nothing, absolutely nothing, we can do tonight – except, perhaps, die in the riots.'

She turned on this new antagonist in anger, ready to beat down his objections. But the apathy that gripped Y.N. after the *Hai Wong* exploded had been transmuted into the steel of determination while he watched the ship blaze. He put his hand on her forearm and spoke with authority.

'Corrigan, you get hold of the note, wherever you stashed it. Then the scroll. When both're in our hands, we'll know what to do next . . . I'll look after Tanya. You can risk it, Miles, with your white skin, but neither Tanya nor I can be seen tonight. The Green Lotus'll be mad for revenge.'

'Makes sense, Y.N.,' Miles agreed. 'But who'll hide you two on a night like . . .'

Tanya stared at the two men in astonishment. Why were they both so craven? Of course, neither was a native of Singapore, not even to the extent she was. Neither cared deeply about the city as she did. They were, therefore, presumably thinking more coolly, perhaps even more logically than she.

But male logic was too often self-serving, as she had learned from her father's behaviour. And female logic? It was, perhaps, as men snickered, sometimes highly emotional. Yet the higher logic was on her side: the imperative need to save as many lives as they could.

'You both say it's too late to do anything tonight? Are you sure? Absolutely sure?' She kept her voice low and reasonable. 'Either the scroll is now irrelevant or it's still vital. I know it's a slim chance. But it's our only hope of disillusioning the rioters . . . by showing them how cynically they're being used, that Peking is conspiring with the imperialists.'

'Maybe that would work! Maybe not.' Miles rejoined. 'But *not* tonight. Things're too tense. Also, I'm working on another angle . . . Do you really know a safe place, Y.N.?'

'A small boarding-house in Chinatown. The owner's a class-mate of my father. And he hates Peking. To the staff, we'll be visitors from Kuala Lumpur.'

'Good, Y.N.,' Miles began. 'That sounds . . .'

'What about me?' Tanya asked icily. 'You two are disposing of me like a trussed hen. Don't I have any say?'

'What do you want to do?' Miles asked.

'I want to try to stop the rioting. Otherwise, I want to be with you, Miles, whatever happens.'

'I'd like nothing better, but you're in much greater danger than I am. Y.N.'s right. You'll be safer with him.'

'Miles, you don't care, do you? Not really?'

'Of course, Tanya, of course I care!' he reassured her. 'It's just that Y.N.'s way makes best sense.'

'So I'm to be bundled off. You brave men will arrange everything.' She knew she sounded unreasonable, even a little hysterical, but in her grief she knew that she was right. 'Miles, I *know* you don't care.'

'How can you say I don't care?' He was on the edge of exasperation. 'Didn't I act like a damned fool for you? Who else climbed aboard that damned boat like a crazy comic-strip character?'

'For my sake entirely? Or for your sake, your own greed?' Tanya demanded. 'You had to cover your back before you grabbed the scroll!'

'I can't argue with you now. There's too much to do if all Singapore isn't to explode like the *Hai Wong*.'

'Now it's your cause, your duty, is it?' Tanya rejoined. 'All right, go get the blasted scroll. I'll go with Y.N.!'

'That's the best way!' Miles leaned over to kiss her, but her lips were stiff and unresponsive.

'I love you, Tanya!' His blurted declaration surprised them both. 'And I'll know where to find you.'

'If you want to . . .' Shocked by her own vehemence, Tanya added: 'I'll be waiting, Miles. Despite everything . . . I love you, too.'

She put her arms around his neck and kissed him fiercely. Releasing Miles, she grasped Y.N.'s arm, and the two faded into the darkness.

Miles stood irresolute and regretful for an instant. But what else could he do? She would be all right with Y.N., he reassured himself. And he would find her just as soon as he could without bringing more danger to her. But a chilly presentiment, a faint unease, gnawed like a maggot at his assurance.

Resolutely dismissing that apprehension, Miles handed the other half of the torn hundred-dollar note to the boatman. The scavenger poled into the darkness without a word of thanks. It had been a profitable night's work. Now he wanted to put as much distance as possible between himself and the mad foreigners who had just destroyed a vessel ten thousand times bigger than his sampan.

The docks were quiet as Miles slipped through the shadows towards Alex Cutler's cubbyhole office in the Cable and Wireless Building. He was challenged once by a police patrol, but his white face beneath the oil streaks was the best passport that night in Singapore. The constables had no time to worry about foreigners who told improbable tales of falling into the harbour. Their radio net was alive with calls for reinforcements as Chinese rioters, burned, slashed, and killed – blazing a trail of blood and flame across the city.

The Malay night watchman in the Cable and Wireless Building was equally unconcerned. Older even than his creaking, wooden-slatted lift, he had over many years seen too many newspapermen in moods of mad elation or violent depression to be put out by Miles's wild appearance.

'Tuan Cutler's out with the police,' he said in remarkable precise English, opening the door to the cluttered BBC office. 'But he'll certainly come back later to file.'

Miles spent almost half an hour in the tiny washroom, while repeated applications of hot water assisted by pumice soap, a rough washcloth, and a nail-brush, removed the worst stains of the night. A minute's work with comb and brush smoothed his unruly coppery hair. He tossed his filthy black garments into a waste-paper bin and gratefully re-dressed in the clothing he had left in the office earlier. But he kept the knife sheathed at the small of his back.

> Alex,
> I've taken you up on your offer. [He scrawled a
> short note.] Don't worry about Mary's car. I'm not
> planning any more heroics. You'll have it back safe
> before morning.
> Many thanks, M.

He knew the riots had moved. Shrieking sirens, booming riot-guns, and thudding concussion grenades now resounded from the maze of Chinatown and the adjoining industrial district. Chinese champions of the proletariat were killing workers and destroying Chinese property.

Not only their own property. When Miles stepped out of the building, he saw the red Porsche blazing festively.

Perhaps it was simply wanton destruction by the rioters, yet other cars parked nearby were undamaged. He suspected that a charge had been triggered when the ignition was switched on. Perhaps Hardpaw Woo's gang had yielded to the temptation to steal the glittering toy, unaware either than their leader was dead or that his masters had already wired it for destruction.

Regardless, the sports car had already served its purpose. It would have been far too conspicuous now. The rental agency could try to claim for the loss of the Porsche, which would hardly be the only car immolated that evening. Lawyers for claimants and insurers could look forward to an orgy of litigation focused on defining the terms 'act of God' and 'civil insurrection.'

Miles lifted the bonnet and checked the engine of Mary Cutler's small black Morris Minor. Then he looked into the boot and tried the fuel-cap. Finally, he scrutinised the underside with a torch. Satisfied at last, he slid into the driver's seat and inserted the ignition key. But a sudden rush of caution made him slip out again.

A length of stiff wire lay among the odds and ends in the trunk. Miles put the ignition key into its slot and looped the wire through the hole in its head. Standing ten feet away, he twisted the wire to turn on the ignition. All was silent.

Returning to the car, he set the gear-lever in neutral and pulled out the manual choke. Fortunately, the starter of the venerable Morris pulled out just as did the choke. He looped a second length of wire around the head of the starter-knob and paced off twenty feet before stepping behind the shelter of a parked van.

There was no response to his first tug on the starter-knob. The engine spluttered on the second – and died.

The third time, the engine coughed and took up its normal tinny clatter.

Jamming Alex's battered jungle-hat over his telltale copper hair, Miles turned the Morris Minor towards the General Post Office two blocks away. Though the city was convulsed by rioters, British phlegm and colonial bureaucracy still reigned. The small side-door was open. The night duty clerk, his face seamed by half a century of ill paid service, sat unperturbed behind the counter.

'Corrigan? M. Corrigan?'

The clerk spoke the English of Chinese families resident for centuries in the Straits Settlements, lilting but clipped. Priding themselves on being more British than the British, more royalist than the House of Lords, they called themselves 'Queen's Chinese'.

The old man riffled through the letters filed under C and finally acknowleded: 'Yes, Mr M. Corrigan, General Delivery, GPO. Please show me your Identity Card.'

'Sorry!' Miles glanced at the name-plate on the counter. 'I'm sorry, Mr The. I'm a visitor. So no Singapore Identity Card.'

'Mr Corrigan, regulations require you to produce a Singapore Identity Card or other satisfactory official document. You need an affidavit attesting to your identity.'

'What about a passport?'

'A passport will do perfectly. It is an official document,'

The smile on the ancient face faded when Miles pushed his American passport across the counter. The aged clerk regarded the green booklet as if it were a harmless, but unpleasant cockroach. He did not pick it up from the counter.

'An *American* passport!' he finally said with polite disdain. 'I'm sorry, sir. I can only accept a British passport as a *proper* official document.'

'Mr The, this is an emergency.' Miles searched his wallet. 'Here's an international driving licence – and an invitation to a reception at Government House.'

'An *international* licence? Not British? But an invitation to Government House? Perhaps, I could . . .'

Miles's hopes rose. He might yet find a way around the old man's rigid devotion to regulations.

'Mr Corrigan, I'm afraid it won't do.' Mr The rendered his verdict after pondering for almost a minute. 'It *must* be a *British* document. Please return in the morning with the affidavit.'

The old man's smile showed that he meant no ill will. But his eyes conveyed the message he was too courteous to utter: 'An *American* passport . . . an *international* driving licence . . . *not* British . . . What nonsense!'

Mr The Oei-soon's unyielding devotion to duty would have been amusing under other circumstances, even admirable. Tonight it was catastrophic. Miles was tempted to climb across the counter and simply take the envelope. But he was repelled by the thought of further violence directed towards such a decent old fellow.

He turned towards the door. Half-way there, he whirled with sudden inspiration.

'Mr The,' he asked, 'you do want to help, don't you?'

'Of course, Mr Corrigan. I'm here to serve the public. But my hands are tied. I must record an official British document. What would happen if we all disregarded regulations?'

Miles bit back the obvious retort. Half Singapore was not merely disregarding regulations tonight, but was tearing all law to shreds.

'Mr The, I do possess an official British document which'll identify me.' Miles opened his green American passport and pointed. 'You'll note the official stamp and the signature.'

> *Mr M. de S. Corrigan is permitted to land and remain in Singapore for 14 days. Thereafter, application for an extension of stay and an Identity Card must be made at Police Headquarters.* An indecipherable signature was scrawled above the rubber-stamped *R. C. Koo, Insp., Immig. Dept.*

'That is a different matter.' The old clerk smiled happily. 'It's certainly an official British document. As soon as I take the particulars, I shall let you have your letter. Good show, this!'

The Edwardian slang rang in Miles's ears like a Haydn chorale. Mr The Oei-soon took up a steel-nibbed pen almost as old as himself and painstakingly recorded the number of the visa and the number of the green passport that had been hallowed by the signature of one of Her Majesty's servants.

'Thank you, Mr The!' Miles accepted the envelope formally. 'Thank you so much.'

As he turned towards the door, the old man called his name – and his heart sank. What new difficulty had appeared?

'I'm always pleased to be of service,' the clerk called. 'It is rather a noisy night, isn't it?'

That unexpected humour cheered Miles. If all Her Majesty's servants were as punctilious as Mr The Oei-soon, Singapore would not be tormented by violence. He now had to deal with quite another kind of civil servant.

The circuitous drive to Cecil Montague's villa took almost an hour. Miles could not drive fast for fear of provoking the nervous police to shoot, and he had to skirt the main roads to avoid the rioters. He swung far to the east through the network of back roads, before turning northwest towards Tanglin, the White Highlands of Imperialist Privilege, as the leftists called the almost exclusively British district. He heard sirens wailing in the distance and the occasional booming of riot-guns a few blocks away.

Miles was halted just once by a police road-block. A young British sub-inspector approached the dilapidated Morris, revolver in hand. Behind him, four Malay constables held their riot-guns at the ready. The sub-inspector lowered his revolver when his torch revealed Miles's white face and the *Press* sign on the windshield.

'You're out late, tonight,' he said sternly. 'Don't you know there's a curfew on?'

'Had to file, Inspector,' Miles mumbled. 'Had to get the news out.'

'Just remember, you pressmen aren't fireproof either. It's open season on white faces. Get back home!'

'OK, Inspector.' Miles let in the clutch. 'I'm on my way.'

Half a mile down the tunnel-black street a projectile crashed against the windshield. The safety glass did not shatter, but crumbled into opacity between its protective layers. Driving blind, Miles floored the accelerator-pedal – and the little Morris surged forward. In the rear-view mirror appeared four white-clad students flinging bricks. Six others trotted behind them, bearing a burden above their heads. In the instant the image vanished from the mirror, Miles thought he saw dangling arms streaked with blood.

Craning out of the side window, he drove on. The wind pummelled his cheeks and squeezed tears from his eyes. After half a mile, he stopped to knock out the starred windshield with the hilt of his knife. Another two hundred or three hundred yards later, the barred gates of Montague's villa appeared in the opening where the windshield had been.

Her Majesty rewarded her servants differently – and not necessarily according to their deserts. Old Mr The Oei-soon, the faithful postal-clerk, sat alone and unprotected in the General Post Office; he would make his perilous way alone through the riot-torn city to his crowded flat when his shift was over. Cecil Montague, who was in part responsible for the riots, slept secure behind four police guards in his proconsular mansion.

'I must see Mr Montague,' Miles demanded. 'An urgent matter!'

'*Tuan*, Mr Montague sleeps.' The Malay sergeant was courteous but unbending. 'I cannot disturb him.'

'An emergency,' Miles insisted. 'Official business. Tell him the password is Everlasting Sorrow.'

Forty-five seconds after the sergeant picked up the external phone, the gate swung open. Two minutes later, Miles was received by Montague in a green-silk dressing-gown.

'I expected Pritchard!' Montague snapped. 'Who the devil are you?'

'An emissary, Mr Montague. You might call Pritchard the Spirit of Christmas Past. I'm the Spirit of Christmas to Come.'

'Damn your Yankee cheek. What the devil do you want?'

'Mr Montague, you may be grateful for my Yankee cheek. Just hear me out.'

'State your business quickly.' Montague flushed scarlet in irritation. 'I haven't got all night!'

'All right, you asked for it. I want the scroll and . . .'

'What scroll?' Montague interjected. 'I know nothing of a scroll.'

'. . . and, I was about to say, I have a note of hand for you. You may know about that.'

'Don't know what you're talking about. Show me!'

Miles tore open the envelope from the General Post Office, and Montague stretched out a shaking hand.

'Mr Montague, there's also a photostat tucked away securely,' Miles said. 'Even the photostat's good enough to fire up a scandal.'

'Come and have a drink,' Montague commanded. 'Whether you're the devil or not, have a drink.'

The Political Adviser smoothed the receipt under the goose-neck lamp on his desk. He then raised it closer to his eyes. Miles felt he would have kissed the creased paper if he had been alone.

'All right!' Montague tossed down his whisky. 'Damned if I know how you come into this. Damned Yank renegade, no doubt . . . I've got the receipt . . . and your people've got what they wanted. The deportation order'll be rescinded tomorrow morning. I understood I was also to receive a receipted bill of sale for the scroll.'

'Mr Montague, I'm afraid the arrangements have been altered slightly. I'll take the scroll, and you can have the note in return. That's fine. But there is one more thing.'

'I was promised there'd be no more. What now?'

'The deportation,' Miles directed, 'is to proceed as originally ordered.'

'My good man, you're quite mad. It was the hell of a fight to get the order rescinded. I can't just . . .'

'In that case, the photostat'll do it,' Miles retorted. 'Maybe they won't break you. Maybe they'll let you retire for administrative reasons. But Peking will still kick up very nasty given the chance . . . If you hold onto the scroll, I'll release the photostat to the press.'

'You're worse than the others,' Montague complained. 'What side are you on?'

'Don't worry about that. Just think of me as your guardian angel. If the scroll vanishes . . . your promissory note, too . . . the game's over. And you're clean!'

'Makes sense,' Montague conceded. 'I'll do it.'

'As if you had a choice. I'd advise you to be damned careful in the future. But the five *must* be deported tomorrow.'

'And then?'

'And then the matter's closed! Singapore settles down after the government gets tough. You're also, of course, to press to have all Chinese-language schools cleared of the illegal occupation by students. Then Peking swallows a defeat. And you're the hero of the hour. You'll probably get another gong, maybe the knighthood you want. Just think of the fat directorships when you retire.'

'And the photostat?' Montague demanded. 'What happens to the photostat?'

'You'll get it when things've settled down. For now, it's my insurance. That's all.'

'I suppose I have no choice.'

'For God's sake, Montague,' Miles exploded. 'I'm saving your career, saving your name . . . And you're bargaining with me. You *cannot* keep the scroll!'

'All right,' Montague yielded. 'Have it your way.'

Leaving the villa, the long box containing the silk-wrapped scroll under his arm, Miles laughed in delight. Unlike the stereotypical Englishman, Cecil Frederick Edward Montague knew when he was beaten. Once convinced, he had produced the scroll with alacrity and had then burned the promissory note before Miles's eyes. He would never receive the photostat, never know that it did not exist. It would do him no harm to worry.

Miles had already examined the scroll cursorily. The two Chinese characters of the signature Wang Lung, Dragon King, were rusty-brown and flecked; and the pigments were faded as they would be after almost ten centuries. Only chemical luminescence tests could authenticate the scroll. Nonetheless, it could from external evidence be the original, the painting that had disappeared seven hundred years ago during the Mongol conquest of China.

If it were, Alex Cutler's information must be right. No purpose less vital than keeping in place an agent of overwhelming importance like the director of espionage and subversion for all Southeast Asia could have moved Peking to hazard such an invaluable part of the Chinese heritage.

With no perceptible transition from exhilaration, Miles suddenly felt exhausted. He was totally drained of both energy and emotion. His triumph left him leaden-footed and heavy-eyed, barely capable of sliding behind the wheel of the old Morris. The long day and the longer night had sapped his reserves, leaving him jaded and vulnerable.

Yet triumph raised new problems. The scroll itself, was he absolutely determined to keep it? Tanya had said it belonged to Y. N. Lee morally, perhaps legally as well. Even more vital, Tanya herself was a problem. When they had parted, she had been furious with him, although he was acting in her best interests. But, he assured himself, Tanya would come around – and there was always tomorrow.

Tomorrow, Miles groped for the thought through a

stupor of fatigue, tomorrow was the test. If the government cracked down, rioting might cease on the orders of the thwarted opposition, which would wish to conserve its resources. Yet the city could explode into total violence, near anarchy, if the opposition allowed its rage to prevail over its long-term interests. Whatever was to occur, he himself could do no more for Singapore.

But Tanya was *his* problem, an immediate pressing personal problem. Momentarily Miles regretted sending her off with Y. N. Lee, who claimed to know a safe hideaway. But he told himself, that had been the only sensible course. With him, she would have been in grave danger. He could easily have been assaulted, perhaps killed, by the rioters. He had come close enough to that fate. What chance would there have been for a Eurasian girl in company with a hated foreigner?

And tomorrow? Amid his exhaustion, a rush of sheer pleasure welled over him. The prospect for tomorrow was radiant, for he would see Tanya tomorrow. As for the other problems, they could wait. Tomorrow he would worry about tomorrow.

Miles pulled the starter-knob. He drove slowly through the gates, nodding in reply to the Malay sergeant's salute. The black nose of the old Morris pointed towards Alex's haunted mansion. At last the venerable vehicle was going home.

XXIV

The crimson-leather benches flanking the central aisle of
the chamber were stiff and shiny, virtually unused. Previous deliberations of the Legislative Assembly of Singapore had been few and brief. The red-and-gold chamber
was extraordinarily gorgeous for a government with lim-
ited powers that could neither abdicate responsibility nor
exert effective authority over its diverse and restless
citizens. The miniature legislature of the small city that
was not yet a wholly independent state numbered thirty-
nine representatives. Twenty-five had been elected by the
people, but the powerful minority that held the balance of
votes had been appointed by the British Governor. Not
remarkably, the people of Singapore did not think of the
Legislative Assembly as wholly their own, but largely as a
freak foisted upon them by British bureaucrats and oppor-
tunistic local politicians.

The Right Honourable Speaker ensconced on his throne
at the end of the chamber wore the full-bottomed white
wig and the black robes of the Speaker of the Mother of
Parliaments in Westminster. But his complexion was dark
with tropical blood and tropical sun. He spoke in the

diffident lilt taught by the Raffles Institution, rather than the confident accents of Eton or Harrow.

Sitting beside Alex Cutler in the press gallery, Miles marvelled at the elaborate stage-setting. The Assembly Chamber had until this morning been hardly more than a theatre pretentiously decked out to flatter the puppets who performed there – and divert the people's attention from the continuing exercise of real power by the British Governor. Today the puppets were required to act on their own initiative. After a week of violence, the puppet-masters had lost both their nerve and their purpose. Their relief barely concealed, the British were now thrusting responsibility on unprepared Singaporeans, many terror-ised by the brutal rioting.

'They've got what they've been screaming for: *Merdeka!*' Alex whispered through his beard. 'They've got virtual independence because the British are in a blue funk. But what the hell to do with *Merdeka?*'

'When does the show get on the road?' Miles demanded. 'They've been fooling around for hours now. When does the Assembly go into formal session?'

'Patience, Yank!' Alex advised. 'Would *you* hurry in their position? I'll just slip out and see what's happening.'

Miles fidgeted on the hard wooden bench apparently designed to make the press as uncomfortable as possible. He wanted a cigarette, but he was loath to leave. The session had been called for 10.30. It was now close to noon, and nothing whatsoever had happened.

Besides, he was present by courtesy of Alex Cutler. His press pass read: Special Correspondent, British Broad-casting Corporation. Even the patient Alex would be annoyed if something should happen in his absence – and his temporary assistant was sneaking a smoke in the corridor. Resentfully, Miles twirled an unlit cigarette between his thumb and forefinger while he watched the self-important clerks come and go bearing thick files.

'You can have that cigarette now,' Alex boomed behind him. 'There'll be nothing doing for at least half an hour. They're still hammering out the terms of the betrayal.'

Brown, golden, and pink faces turned inquiringly towards the bearded Englishman who spoke so forthrightly. The BBC Correspondent was a licensed eccentric in the eyes of both the timorous local press and the foreign wire-services.

Alex led Miles to a corner of the corridor near the men's room. Only the chamber itself had been hastily redone. The corridor was shabby, its peeling paint flecked with black mould and its woodwork scarred.

'Looks as if your friend lost his nerve at the last minute,' Alex said softly. 'My compatriot the Chief Secretary is mediating the sell-out. He's not called Colonial Secretary any more. We're expected to believe Singapore is a self-governing state with only foreign affairs and internal security still British responsibilities.'

'What's really happening, Alex?' Miles asked. 'Get down to cases.'

'If you want the whole sordid story. First, workers and students're rioting all along the Bukit Timah Road. Also in Chinatown and the dock areas. And the Masses Operation Party – the good old MOP – has threatened a march of a hundred thousand enraged Chinese if Government dare to touch their precious children or their sacred Chinese-language academies of learning and subversion. The fix is in!'

'How?'

'It's a fine piece of chicanery. Our esteemed Chief Minister Patrick Wee is to form a government of national union. *National*, I ask you? In this piss-pot island? It's hardly a city, much less a nation. Any event, he'll take some MOP men into a coalition government . . . give them five of the eleven ministries. The deportation order is cancelled. And the martyrs are to be released.'

'My God! It's a *total* sell-out.'

'There's worse to come. The rationale: Any further use of force will alienate the population completely – and bring at least two . . . perhaps three . . . hundred thousand enraged Chinese into the streets. Then Singapore, the argument runs, would be ungovernable. You see . . .'

'That's crap, as you know,' Miles interposed. 'Most of the Chinese don't give a damn about politics. They're only terrified.'

'Quite true! Nonetheless, the scenario gets worse. In six weeks, there'll be new elections. *All* members of the Legislative Assembly to be elected. After this total surrender, the MOP will come to power with an overwhelming majority. How do you like them onions?'

'I guess that's it,' Miles said dully. 'One small consolation. I sent the scroll out on the early Pan Am flight to Hong Kong . . . That bastard Montague, I'll get him. He'll regret this.'

'I wouldn't be so sure, my boy. He's the hero of the hour, the great compromiser. My compatriots, all the Brits, are closing ranks behind Mr Montague.'

The corridors stirred as the spectators began eddying back to their seats in the gallery. They knew somehow that proceedings were about to start. Miles and Alex slipped into their seats as the Right Honourable Speaker entered behind the six-foot ceremonial mace and seated himself on his throne. The dark eyes shining in his intelligent brown face were fixed on Paul da Silva, leader of the opposition, secretary-general of the Masses Operation Party, general-counsel to the Universal Workers' Union. Machiavelli or dupe?

'The chair,' the Speaker intoned, 'recognises the Leader of the Opposition, the Honourable Member from Katong.'

Paul da Silva rose slowly and surveyed the bandbox chamber dramatically. His swarthy face glowed with excitement, and his eyes sparkled. The beige safari-jacket that was his trademark, was tightly belted over his paunch. A red ascot was tucked into its open neck in token recognition of the portentous character of the session.

'Mr Speaker, Honourable Members, Ladies and Gentlemen,' da Silva began. 'I am honoured by the opportunity to speak to you at this grave moment in the history of our infant state.'

The Honourable Members, the press, and the few members of the general public present leaned forward to catch the soft spoken words. Then da Silva's voice soared.

'This is the gravest moment we have ever faced. Also the greatest opportunity. Today will decide whether the State of Singapore shall perish amid rioting and disorder . . . or whether we shall make our fair city a model for Asia and the world. The choice is yours, Honourable Members, yours alone.'

Miles felt the hairs on the back of his neck bristle. Da Silva was very good. A natural orator, he had made his resonant voice a trumpet to stir all hearts.

'Before us lie two choices,' da Silva went on. 'We can scourge our children, scourge the students and workers who are fighting for freedom . . . for democracy . . . for social justice. We can lash them. We can break their heads and their hearts. We can imprison them and destroy their spirits. We can kill even more than their proud spirit. We can kill the spirit of Singapore itself, the glorious dream of a multiracial society with equal opportunity for all.

That is one choice. I defy my colleague, the Honourable Chief Minister, I defy him to make that choice . . . to choose that utter, criminal foolishness.'

The majority of the Legislative Assembly sat silent, but three MOP members cried: 'Hear! Hear!' Four of the five elected independents took up the chant. Hesitant at first, they were soon in full cry.

'Order! Order!' The Speaker's gavel hammered down the tumult. 'Order, I say!'

'Or we can make the other choice.' Da Silva's voice sank low for effect. 'We can *dare* to choose the glorious road that lies open to us. We can defy the power of the bloated moneybags. We can say unto our British rulers: "You have gone too far, gentlemen, much too far! The people's voice will be heard!"

'We can demand, nay, we can *force* the bloodsucking capitalists to grant the workers' just demands. And the innocent five, the five martyrs as they are so rightly called? We can insist that they be released and allowed to return to their peaceful, productive tasks in our community. That, Honourable Members, is the other choice, the choice demanded by prudence. Demanded, above all, by honour, and by justice.

'Otherwise, I fear, we shall know violence such as this fair city has never before seen. Blood will run in the streets and incarnadine our tropical streams . . .'

Chief Minister Patrick Wee, round-faced and heavy-bodied in a white sharkskin suit, rose from the Government front-bench.

'A point of order, Mr Speaker,' he called. 'On a matter of privilege and urgent necessity.'

'I yield!' da Silva conceded without hesitation. 'I yield to the Right Honourable Chief Minister.'

'This is it,' Alex whispered in Miles's ear. 'He's going to announce the deal.'

'Mr Speaker, Honourable Members, Ladies and Gentlemen,' Patrick Wee's voice possessed neither his opponent's fire nor his opponent's suppleness. 'I submit that we have had enough violence . . . and enough talk of violence. I do not criticise the Right Honourable Leader of the Opposition. Indeed, I understand his indignation. And I sympathise fully.'

A murmur of surprise at that concession rippled across the Government benches. Voices rose in surprise as legislators questioned each other.

'Order, Gentlemen, order!' the Speaker admonished. 'The proceedings of this body must not be marred. Chief Minister, your rose to a point of order. An urgent communication, you said. But it appears that you are making a speech, rather than addressing a Parliamentary question.'

'I beg your pardon, Mr Speaker.' Patrick Wee was not ruffled. 'I hoped a few introductory words might soothe tempers. I am coming to my announcement, if you will allow me. I believe that violence has gone much too far . . . that any further violence would be disastrous, whether instigated by indignant citizens or by the police ostensibly seeking to suppress violence. I therefore propose certain measures that will allay the concern and the fears of the Right Honourable Leader of the Opposition. Those measures are . . .'

The Chief Minister turned irritably. His private secretary was tugging insistently at his sleeve. He waved the secretary away, but the persistent young man pressed a note into his hand.

'If you will excuse me for a moment, Mr Speaker. I am told that an extraordinarily urgent matter has arisen.'

The Chief Minister seated himself and opened the note.

'Mr da Silva, would you care to resume?' the Speaker asked. 'You have the floor.'

'That would be discourteous to the Chief Minister,' da Silva answered suavely. 'I am content to wait for his announcement.'

Patrick Wee was on his feet again, his heavy features twisted by anxiety.

'Mr Speaker, I request a fifteen-minute recess,' he said. 'The Government urgently requires time to complete its formulation.'

'Shame! Shame!' cried four opposition members, but their leader nodded benign assent.

'Confident bastard!' Alex whispered. 'Let's get another cigarette. Damned if I know what's up now.'

All the spectators returned to their seats in the gallery after ten minutes, and the crimson-leather benches bore their full complement of Honourable Members. But Patrick Wee did not reappear even though the chamber muttered ominously. When he did return after some thirty minutes, his face was set and pale. He carried a yellow foolscap pad covered with jotted notes.

'Mr Speaker, may I continue on my point of privilege?' he asked. 'I have important new information to impart to the House.'

'Pray continue, Chief Minister,' the Speaker answered. 'Unless the Right Honourable Leader of the Opposition . . .'

'No objection!' da Silva said negligently. 'None at all!'

'Honourable Members,' Patrick Wee said sombrely. 'I have first to report that the understanding between Government and Opposition has been breached. The rioting has grown worse, rather than ameliorating. More than thirty citizens have been injured. Moreover, six persons have died while we sat here.'

Paul da Silva was on his feet, waving a file in protest. 'I object to this diversion, Mr Speaker!' he shouted. 'I yielded on a point of privilege. The Chief Minister has now descended to irresponsible charges. He has accused me of breaking some imaginary agreement of which I have no knowledge, an agreement I never made. He is attempting to inflame the House with atrocity stories and . . .'

'The Right Honourable Leader of the Opposition is out of order,' the Speaker ruled. 'The Chief Minister has the floor on a matter of urgent privilege. I shall, however, not permit him to misuse that privilege for partisan political purposes.'

Paul da Silva sank sulkily onto the crimson-leather bench, and Patrick Wee continued.

'Six persons, Honourable Members, have died while this House sat in hope and the Government entertained the full intention of satisfying all grievances. Among the dead are two police constables, one stoned to death, the other doused in petrol and set alight.'

Legislators and audience gasped aloud.

'Also dead are an unidentified Chinese of middle-age, from his dress a labourer, as well as a schoolboy, Lim Teck-see. It is, further, my sad duty to report to this House that two others have been beaten to death by mobs of schoolboys. Miss Tanya Tan, daughter of the illustrious Mr Morgan Tan, was killed an hour ago in company with a young visitor from Hong Kong, one Mr Y. N. Lee. I ask the House to rise in tribute to all the victims and to demonstrate our profound sympathy for their families. If I may so request, to Mr Morgan Tan in particular.'

Legislators and spectators rose slowly to their feet, Paul

da Silva shouting over their shocked babble: 'Mr Speaker, this news is very sad indeed. But it is, however unfortunate, a red herring. I do not see . . .'

Miles sat stunned, his head sunk in his hands. He heard neither the demagogue's protests nor the murmurs of the gathering. He should have gone to find Tanya this morning. He should have found her and seen that she was safe. Now he would never find her.

'I'll know where to find you,' he had said, and she had answered: 'If you want to . . .' The black bird, Hyacinth Lee had said in Hong Kong, the black bird of sorrow that perched on others' shoulders, but never his own. He might be unharmed, but his sorrow, he knew, was only beginning.

'Under the circumstances I have no choice but to . . .'

Through the roaring in his ears Miles heard the flat voice of Patrick Wee.

'I am determined to crush this violence before our city becomes a charnel house. With the consent of the Governor, British troops are moving out of their barracks. Their orders are to shoot to kill if they are not obeyed. Helicopters are bringing additional troops across the straits from Malaya.

'I now proclaim a State of Emergency. In conjunction with the Governor, I am assuming personal rule until the Emergency is ended. The Chinese-language schools are suspended indefinitely. Police emergency units are moving onto all their campuses to expel all students. Any unauthorised gathering of more than four persons is declared illegal.'

Alex stage-whispered: 'Good God! I never thought the man had it in him. Somebody's put backbone into him. But Tanya, my God, Tanya, that beautiful girl. Pity you never really knew her, Miles.'

Miles did not reply. Even if he were not intent on the Chief Minister's words, he could not have spoken.

'I would further inform you,' Patrick Wee continued, 'that the five so-called martyrs have been conclusively proved to have conspired to destroy the peace of our city and to stage a *coup d'état*. They have conspired with certain labour leaders and, I regret to say, with certain members of this House. Under my emergency powers, I am ordering the detention of sixty persons, including certain members of this House.'

'He's really getting tough.' Cutler gasped. 'Who would've thought . . .'

'The five so called martyrs, really agents of a foreign power, are at this moment being placed aboard a special aircraft for deportation. I shall report further to the public this evening on the wireless. In the meantime, I declare this House prorogued. We shall resume our sessions when the Emergency has been broken. I hope within a week or so.'

'What a break, Miles, what a break!' Alex exulted. 'You've won the toss after all. Only Montague and the High Commissioner could have forced him . . . could have given him support for this show. Congratulations, Miles. We've beaten the bastards . . . for the moment, at least.'

'For the moment, perhaps!'

Miles felt no triumph, but only the hollow ache of grief. Tanya was gone, and he had sacrificed her. Silent, his head sunk in his hands, he gazed down an endless black tunnel of guilt.

EPILOGUE

The too familiar features grinned fatuously from the glossy page. By posing nonchalantly before a Shang Dynasty bronze ewer and a Hokusai print, the photographer had promised Miles he would look 'suave and just a little reckless'. Those words set the tone for the profile in *Time* magazine that called him 'the laughing buccaneer of the art world'.

The news peg was his most recent coup, a hitherto unknown statuette of a Tang warrior arrogantly bestriding his war horse that Miles had sold for 150,000 dollars. The profile hinted archly at Miles's political and intelligence coups, but offered no details. Even the inevitable gibe was almost laudatory: 'No one but Miles de Sola Corrigan knows exactly where some of his best pieces come from – and Corrigan isn't telling.'

Otherwise, the profile was almost too kind, though he squirmed at the sentence: 'Mystery man of the arcane trade in Oriental *objets d'art*, bachelor Corrigan's great and good friends range from Japanese starlets to Italian contessas.' It was, of course, invaluable publicity for the gallery, as well as muted recognition of his achievements beyond the world of art. But such glamorisation would complicate his personal life as well as his professional life. Besides, the half-grin on his face still looked slightly moronic, though the photographer had assured him that it would flutter female hearts.

Fed up with the fulsome article and with his own eager pursuit of essential publicity, Miles dropped the magazine. The coloured pages fluttered upon the blue carpet of Suite 2016 of the Mandarin Hotel, which had become Hong Kong's most civilised hostelry, overtaking the old Peninsula. Almost reluctantly, he slipped the scroll called *The Everlasting Sorrow* from its silken sheath, unrolled it, and hung it on the hook that had supported a flower painting.

Not only the soft colours of the scroll were faded by time, but also his memory of its violent acquisition. Yet not faded enough. Like the story depicted by the centuries-old painting, those events of two decades earlier were still strong in his mind, almost too strong to bear. Frozen forever in despair, the weeping concubine stepped forward to meet death while the helpless Emperor sat on a rock, his head sunk in his hands. Miles felt something of that despair.

He wanted to cover his eyes or at least look away, but the painting commanded his attention. He had been unable to part with the scroll, though he had not looked at it for more than a year. The parallels were too close. The Emperor Hsüan Tsung had sacrificed his best loved concubine Yang Kwei-fei in order to keep his throne – and had thereafter suffered unending remorse for the woman who was, as he realised too late, more to him than the throne. Miles had sacrificed Tanya to obtain the scroll – and remorse had thereafter marred not only his greatest coup, but all his days.

'The laughing buccaneer . . . the mystery man . . .

(272)

lover of some of the world's most beautiful women.' The glib journalese was revolting. Much better the bitter Spanish proverb: 'Take what you want – and pay for it!'

He had taken what he wanted, and he had paid, though not in dollars or in reputation. He had, however, paid heavily in his heart. His renewed preoccupation with the scroll now reawakened the poignant, painful emotions he had thought long dead. It was time for *The Everlasting Sorrow* to return to Peking. It was past time for him to be rid of the scroll – if he could ever be rid of it. Its beauty was a knife in his side, as sharp as the blade that had transfixed Political Commissar Yang. That memory, all the other memories, would they pass when the scroll left his hands?

The prophecy had been fulfilled. It was apparently true that *The Everlasting Sorrow* brought disaster and good fortune to successive owners. Turner had died violently in Singapore, and Miles had 'gone from coup to coup like a gambler who cannot lose', as *Time* put it. Only serenity and happiness had evaded him. Perhaps Turner and he were both victims.

Miles irritably poured himself a marc. Slumping on the couch, he contemplated the painting with his eyes while his mind looked beyond it. Behind the façade of *The Everlasting Sorrow* lay the haunting past.

How much, he wondered, had the political triumph been real and how much illusion?

Although the Democratic Alliance Party of Chief Minister Patrick Wee had established public order by quashing the riots, it had splintered two years later. In the following election Paul da Silva's Masses Operation Party had swept into power on the twin bandwagons of Chinese chauvinism and anti-colonialism.

Da Silva had proved a brilliant leader. The Social

Democrat had broken with his Maoist allies, interned them without trial, and, ironically enough, deported the most dangerous. Under da Silva's ruthless leadership, Singapore had become a bastion of anti-Communism and a model of highly successful free enterprise. Anti-Communism and free enterprise, unfashionable in the West, were the wave of the future in Asia.

Paul da Silva's rule was too authoritarian for Miles's taste. Da Silva was too quick to suppress honest dissent; he imposed intellectual uniformity as a 'defence' against external and internal perils. Yet da Silva had made Singapore a far more pleasant place for the mass of the people. Moreover, his regime staunchly supported international efforts to stem subversion and conquest from the north.

Had the external menace Miles saw in those days been an illusion too? He thought not, but he could not be absolutely sure. If the MOP had ridden to power on a wave of violence, the end result *might* have been entirely different.

That was the old conundrum, the 'fork of history question' that no honest scholar could answer. Events might have proceeded otherwise if the 'five martyrs' had not been deported or the riots had not been broken. Yet events might have led to the same conclusion. Although it *might* have happened otherwise, it *had*, nonetheless, happened thus – in part because of his own intervention.

For China, the colossus that bestrides Asia, the same turbulent events had helped shape the present and the future. Diverted from its imperial ambitions by rebuffs like those in Singapore and Malaya, Chinese policy had altered radically during the intervening years. After surviving an agonising internal upheaval that had almost destroyed her as a nation, China had moved towards friendship, rather than enmity, with her neighbours.

Asia was now precariously balanced, but it was, nonetheless, in equilibrium – and the future looked very bright. It would, Miles believed, have been very different if Mao Tse-tung's 'people's war' had conquered Singapore, Malaya, or Indonesia. Yet it *might* not have been different. Once again the enigma of the 'fork of history'. And, once again, that was how it *had* happened – with his own small contribution to history.

As for himself? Well, he preferred not to think too much about himself. It would be pleasant if he could accept the idealised portrait in *Time*, but he could not.

He dreamed of Tanya occasionally. He dreamed of holding her and parrying her gentle mockery. He would awaken overjoyed at having regained her who had appeared irretrievably lost.

Then the futility, the sense of overwhelming loss would again descend upon him. In Po Chü-yi's poem the lamenting Tang Emperor searched for the spirit of Yang Kwei-fei through the many Chinese heavens. But Miles was a realist, and he could not even lament aloud.

He looked out at the harbour, which was bright with the reflection of enormous neon signs. Only a few years earlier dozens of junks would have sailed like enchanted craft into the dusk. This evening a single junk spread its moth-wing sails against the darkening sky. Probably a poor fisherman from China. Almost all Hong Kong junks were now driven by smoke-belching diesel engines, and the Colonial buildings along the waterfront with their tracery of balconies and cornices had yielded to steel, glass, and concrete blocks.

Progress was inexorable, but the Asia Miles loved was disappearing. Asia's people were undoubtedly happier and healthier than they had been when the Far East was still a realm of wild romance – at least for outsiders. He was, he supposed, pleased that the people were so much better off, but that abstract consolation did not touch his heart.

Miles was awaiting a visitor. The time fixed was 6 p.m., and Peking's emissary would be on time. Nonetheless, he started when he heard a gentle knock.

Comrade Wong himself stood in the carpeted corridor, out of place away from his cheap desk in his cramped office in Canton. After two weeks of preliminary discussions, Peking had sent its foremost authority, 'the senior responsible comrade' concerned with *objets d'art*.

'I am honoured by your presence, Comrade Wong,' Miles said.

'And I,' Mr Wong replied in his precise Mandarin, 'am delighted to see you again, Mr Corrigan.'

Tea waited on the low table, six thimble-cups surrounding the blue-and-white porcelain teapot like sentries guarding a castle. Miles had found the finest Iron Goddess tea for his guest. That, too, was a gesture to the past.

They chatted for ten minutes, exchanging compliments and regretting the changes in Hong Kong. They agreed that progress was sometimes deplorable, but was always necessary. Comrade Wong was outwardly so relaxed he allowed himself to question the benefit of some progress. Sipping his third cup of tea, he finally glanced at the scroll on the wall.

'Ah,' he said almost negligently. 'It is, of course, *The Everlasting Sorrow*. It *is* beautiful, is it not?' He rose to examine the painting closely. 'Extraordinarily beautiful!'

'Beautiful!' Corrigan replied. 'But very sad . . . tragic!'

'You will regret parting with it?'

'Perhaps. I'm not sure.'

'So, let us complete our discussions. My colleagues have

assured me that this is the original of *The Everlasting Sorrow*. I concur – and I have come to take it home. My superiors are reasonably satisfied with your explanation of how you came into possession. But one point bothers them.'

'What's that?' Miles asked defensively.

'We accept your account. Professor Turner Lee was my friend, too, and I know his character. We recognise his bequest . . . We accept his death-bed legacy as valid. We do not question your rights, although, of course, technically the scroll was the nation's and, therefore, not his to give. But we shall not insist on legalities.'

Miles's smile masked his relief. He had been convinced that Peking, now outwardly far more reasonable, would not wish to explain in a British court of law why it had sent a priceless national treasure to Singapore in the turbulent 1950s. It would have been highly embarrassing for Peking when his defence against the charge of misappropriation revealed the conspiracy to seize Singapore. Nonetheless, Miles had feared that Peking would be awkward – exquisitely polite and implacably obdurate.

He had told Comrade Wong's representative of Turner Lee making him responsible for the scroll. He had not mentioned his assault on the *Hai Wong* or his confrontation with Montague, now retired with honour to Kent as Sir Cecil. The men in Peking naturally knew the full story, if not every minute detail, but Peking, too, evidently wished to ignore the distasteful episode in Singapore. And Peking wanted *The Everlasting Sorrow* very badly.

'What point,' Miles asked again, 'still bothers you?'

'Miss Lee . . . Hyacinth, I believe she calls herself. Miss Lee's claim on the scroll may be as valid as your own. Though you, of course, possess it.'

Strict legality was the line. There must be no suggestion that the People's Government had attempted to use *The Everlasting Sorrow* for political blackmail. Comrade Wong therefore subscribed to the fiction that the painting had actually been the property of Turner Lee – to dispose of as he wished. That fiction was buttressed by his concern for Hyacinth Lee's rights.

'Miss Lee has no claim whatsoever . . .' Miles began.

'Ah, is that so?' Comrade Wong stiffened.

'Not in law. But I, too, believe she has a moral claim. Professor Lee mentioned her in the same sentence in which he bequeathed me the scroll.'

'I see.'

'You may, as you please, think I was a fool or a clever businessman. Shortly after acquiring the scroll, I paid Hyacinth Lee twenty-five thousand American dollars for her interest. That sum was then worth two to three times what it is today.'

'Yes?'

'This is her receipt assigning all her rights to me.'

Comrade Wong waved the document aside.

'Your word is good enough, Mr Corrigan. No need for documents. Speaking personally, may I express my gratification at your action? Miss Lee has chosen to remove herself from the People's Republic. I am told she is married to an American named Jackson and living in Palo Alto, California. Incidentally, her . . . ah . . . maidservant Ah Soo still serves her. But the People's Government is pleased that you have dealt fairly with her.'

Miles was mildly surprised, not for the first time or the last time in dealing with the Chinese. They had checked out every last detail.

'*Guo-jiang! Guo-jiang!*' He uttered the old formula of self-deprecation. 'Beyond my merit! Beyond my merit!'

'Then it's all settled,' Comrade Wong said briskly. 'I have a certified cheque drawn to you for five hundred thousand dollars.'

'Certification wasn't necessary, Comrade Wong.'

'We prefer to act correctly. Now only the scroll remains.'

'Here are the cover and the box, Comrade Wong. I'll pack it for you.'

'Would you rather I did, Mr Corrigan? I imagine parting is difficult. There may be some unpleasant memories as well.'

Miles was no longer surprised by the extent of Comrade Wong's knowledge. He was only faintly surprised by Comrade Wong's consideration.

'If you'd prefer . . .'

Comrade Wong rolled up the scroll with practised skill, drew on its silk cover, and reverently placed it in its long wooden box.

'Goodbye for the moment, Mr Corrigan,' he said. 'I am sure I shall have the pleasure of seeing you again. Perhaps, next time, you will be a buyer rather than a seller.'

'I hope so, Comrade Wong,' Miles grinned. 'In the meantime, I also hope you won't sell the scroll to the Japanese for twice as much.'

Comrade Wong winced at the gibe, but replied evenly: 'I am quite sure that will not happen.'

Miles accompanied the senior responsible cadre to the lift amid a flurry of formal farewells. After the metal door slid shut, he walked slowly back to his suite. His step was lighter, for he felt that a weight had been lifted from his back. It was truly high time for *The Everlasting Sorrow* to return home.

Yet when he re-entered the suite, the bare wall drew and held his eyes. So many memories remained, so many memories that could never be banished. Ironically, his greatest coup would never be known to *Time* magazine. He refilled his balloon glass with marc and opened Po Chü-yi's poem. The immortal words still belonged to him – and to the entire world – the words written almost 1,200 years ago. He slowly read the last verse aloud:

'The Earth endures and the Heavens endure, though, someday, both shall perish. But this everlasting sorrow is eternal, beyond the grasp of time.'

Miles raised his glass in salute and drank half the burning spirits in a single draught.

'It's good for whatever ails you,' he had told Tanya. But it was no good whatsoever for what ailed him.

He walked slowly to the big window. The harbour was dark, but the lights were going on in Kowloon.

A Selected List of Fiction Available from Mandarin

While every effort is made to keep prices low, it is sometimes necessary to increase prices at short notice. Mandarin Paperbacks reserves the right to show new retail prices on covers which may differ from those previously advertised in the text or elsewhere.

The prices shown below were correct at the time of going to press.

☐	7493 1352 8	**The Queen and I**	Sue Townsend	£4.99
☐	7493 0540 1	**The Liar**	Stephen Fry	£4.99
☐	7493 1132 0	**Arrivals and Departures**	Lesley Thomas	£4.99
☐	7493 0381 6	**Loves and Journeys of Revolving Jones**	Leslie Thomas	£4.99
☐	7493 0942 3	**Silence of the Lambs**	Thomas Harris	£4.99
☐	7493 0946 6	**The Godfather**	Mario Puzo	£4.99
☐	7493 1561 X	**Fear of Flying**	Erica Jong	£4.99
☐	7493 1221 1	**The Power of One**	Bryce Courtney	£4.99
☐	7493 0576 2	**Tandia**	Bryce Courtney	£5.99
☐	7493 0563 0	**Kill the Lights**	Simon Williams	£4.99
☐	7493 1319 6	**Air and Angels**	Susan Hill	£4.99
☐	7493 1477 X	**The Name of the Rose**	Umberto Eco	£4.99
☐	7493 0896 6	**The Stand-in**	Deborah Moggach	£4.99
☐	7493 0581 9	**Daddy's Girls**	Zoe Fairbairns	£4.99

All these books are available at your bookshop or newsagent, or can be ordered direct from the address below. Just tick the titles you want and fill in the form below.

Cash Sales Department, PO Box 5, Rushden, Northants NN10 6YX.
Fax: 0933 410321 : Phone 0933 410511.

Please send cheque, payable to 'Reed Book Services Ltd.', or postal order for purchase price quoted and allow the following for postage and packing:

£1.00 for the first book, 50p for the second; **FREE POSTAGE AND PACKING FOR THREE BOOKS OR MORE PER ORDER.**

NAME (Block letters) ....

ADDRESS ....

....

☐ I enclose my remittance for ....

☐ I wish to pay by Access/Visa Card Number ☐☐☐☐☐☐☐☐☐☐☐☐☐☐☐☐

Expiry Date ☐☐☐☐

Signature ....

Please quote our reference: MAND